THE WARRIOR PRINCE OF BERUSH

by

Amber Gabriel

Book One in The Edge of the Sword series

The Warrior Prince of Berush

To all those with hidden scars, this book is respectfully dedicated.

CONTENTS

ACKNOWLEDGMENTS

Wayne J. Gabriel, I appreciate your expertise as a soil scientist, your patience as I spent lots of my spare time on the computer, and all the documentaries you watch that had lots of interesting facts to help me with my research. Most of all, I am honored to receive your unceasing love and devotion. You are the ideal all my heroes aspire to.

Mom and dad, thanks for inspiring me with a love of books and allowing me the freedom to read incessantly.

Tyson, thanks for always thinking I can do anything.

Dr. Nikita D. Tate-Casanova, PhD, your insight and approval of my handling of issues related to post-traumatic stress helped give me the courage to move forward with preparing my story for publication. You were the first one I let read it, and your enthusiasm was very heartening!

Yvonne Kay Hauge, MD, you are such a good sport for letting me bounce ideas off of you and for finding them intriguing.

Mrs. Oleson, my seventh grade English teacher, I never forgot that you told me I would write a book one day.

April Luce, thank you for telling me that it's ok for teachers to have a life outside of school.

Michael Grinnan, thank you for reviewing my chapters on sailing . I really, really appreciate it.

Every person I have ever met, every book I have ever read, every movie or television show I ever watched, every country, landmark or natural wonder I have visited, every family member, every pet, every co-worker or boss, every pastor and teacher, every student, every shoe I have worn, every piece of chocolate I have ever eaten, every song I have heard or sung, every emotion I have felt has helped to make me who I am, and I have written this novel. Any errors are entirely my fault.

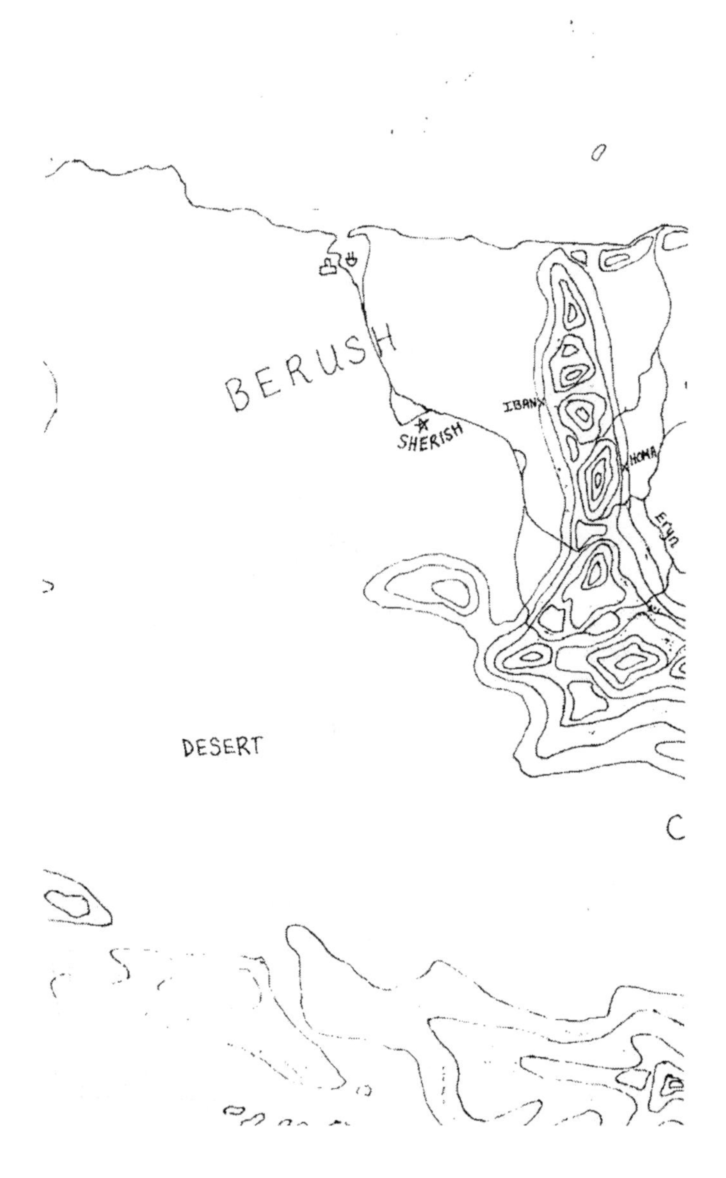
BERUSH
SHERISH
IBAN
HOMA
Eryn
DESERT

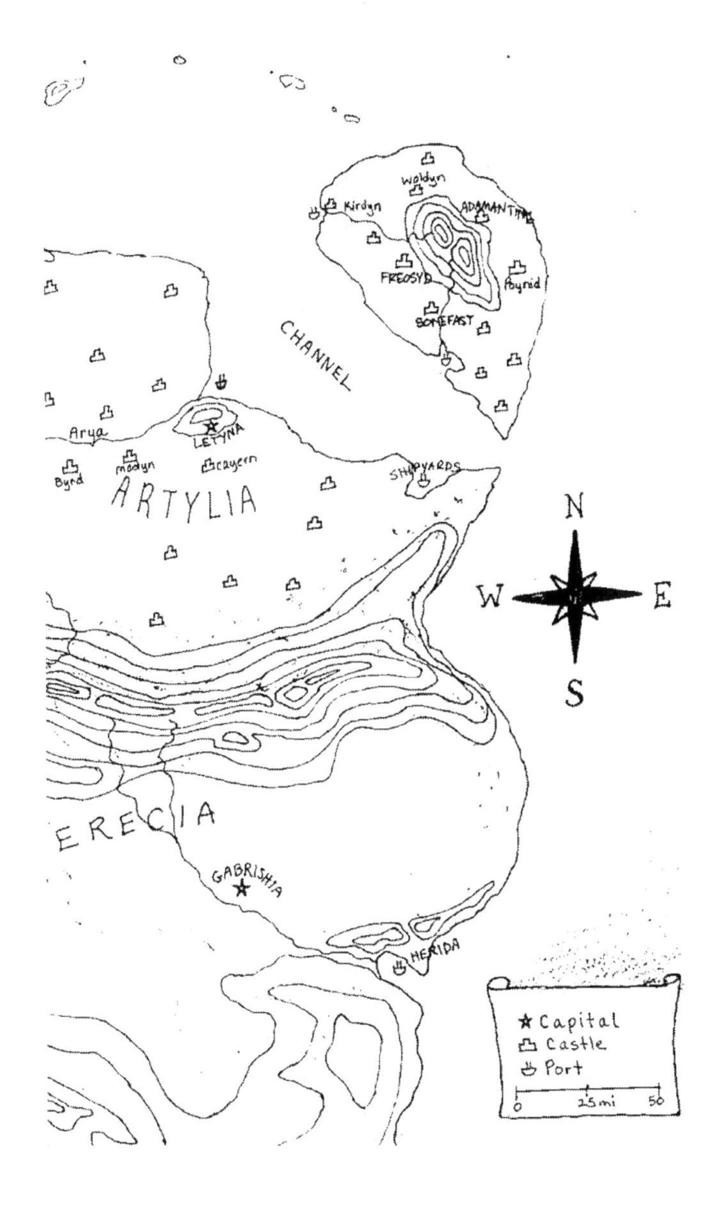
Woldyn
Kirdyn
FREOSYD
Poynid
CHANNEL
Arya
LETYNA
Byrd
modyn
cayern
ARTYLIA
SHIPYARDS
N
W
E
S
ERECIA
GABRISHIA
MERIDA
Capital
Castle
Port
0
25mi
50

CHAPTER ONE

The boy's head was crushed. At first Darius thought it might have been an accident, that he had fallen and hit his head, perhaps while trying to fight off the raiders. It was easy to lose your footing on this rocky terrain. Then he turned him over and saw that the skull had been bashed on more than one side.

"Here, my lord, look at this," called Effan, Darius' captain. He was pointing to a rock lying on the ground nearby. Darius straightened and walked over. The rock had blood on it, and a few pieces of black hair. Anger started welling up inside of him. How dare they kill a defenseless boy? No matter which side of the border he was on. He had to fight off the red haze as it threatened to take over.

Effan squeezed his shoulder. He and the prince had fought together long enough for him to know what his lord was thinking. Darius shook his head to clear it. His dark, straggly beard and shaggy mane of hair gave the action an almost canine quality.

The rest of the men continued to examine the area for signs. Of the boy's herd, only three goats could be found scattered along the narrow pass. A nanny goat bleated forlornly, looking for her kid and not finding it. She was not the only mother who would be bereft today. Darius took a blanket from his saddle bag and wrapped the boy in it. Another one of his men picked up the boy's staff and handed it to Effan. The bells on the end of it gave a light, merry tinkle that sounded out of place in the grim scene.

A solemn procession of dusty, weary men trailed back down the mountain to the boy's village. They had been patrolling these mountains for months and memorized every path, every cave, and every ravine along the entire range. For centuries, the border between Berush and Artylia had been constantly shifting. Every rainy season, mudslides and flash floods changed the landscape and gave the local tribes reason to dispute their territories. Landmarks were occasionally covered by rock slides, and sometimes they were deliberately moved. Circling buzzards had led them to explore this pass today. The Artylians were becoming bolder.

The boy's village was located at the foot of the mountain in a small, green hollow where a cool spring bubbled out of a narrow cave. These hardy folk lived off of their goat herds. Rich milk and cheese and occasional roasted meat, with the herbs, roots and berries they gathered provided everything they needed. The clothing they made for themselves out of goat-hair was coarse and durable, but they produced tents, rugs, and rope to trade for finer goods and other necessities. Darius and his men had been invited to a feast there only two weeks ago. There had been several pretty, young girls there who had been very accommodating. Today would be very different. There would be mourning instead of indulgence.

When they arrived at the village, the residents were lined up to meet them. Always alert, they had heard and seen them coming. Darius had laid the boy on his own horse and led it down the mountain. Walking down had taken a good two hours, and it was nearly dusk. Other boys had already arrived home with their herds. Scores of goats drank thirstily from troughs inside the fold made of stacked stone walls.

The boy's father recognized the staff in Effan's hand and cried out. Darius lifted the boy's body off of the horse and handed it to the man gravely. A woman ran over wailing. They unwrapped the blanket to see his face, and the woman cried louder once there was no doubt the boy was hers. He had been young, maybe only ten years old. The couple sank to the ground, and the woman held the boy's head to her chest, rocking back and forth as she sobbed.

The village headman walked over to Darius. He was stately and grey-haired. To live to his age in this harsh setting was quite an achievement. Darius recalled the headman's name was Iban. "What happened, my lord?"

The prince told him.

Iban's expression was stony. "We have lived with this threat for so long, my lord, but tensions are growing. Something must be done."

The boy's father looked up at Darius with stricken eyes. "He was my only son. My joy," he choked. "The light is gone from my eyes."

"If this act is not avenged, their aggression will only continue," stated Iban.

Darius knew this was true, but he also knew a foray across the border for vengeance would escalate matters further. His brother, King Cyrus, had hoped that increasing patrols would discourage the Artylian raiders from crossing the mountains. Cyrus had not specifically forbidden him from crossing the border, but he would not be pleased if he did. However, their father had taught them that sometimes an attack is the best defense. This boy's blood cried out to him. Cyrus would understand.

"He will be avenged." The conviction in his voice was unmistakable. Darius had never lost a battle. If he decided something, it was going to happen.

"Take me with you!" The boy's father stood and pleaded. Darius was reluctant to take along anyone other than his own soldiers. This man was not a warrior, and Darius knew emotions could get in the way, but he could not deny this father a chance to see his son's killers punished. Darius nodded, and the man ran off to fetch his donkey. They were more sure-footed than horses. The man would know this mountain even better than he would and possibly help them find a faster route to the nearest encampment on the other side.

The villagers quickly brought out a simple meal to fuel the men on their mission. They ate silently and efficiently, and were ready to go by the time the sun had sunk behind the horizon. The women had quietly taken the boy into one of the huts to prepare him for his funeral pyre. The ceremony would take place as soon as the men returned.

Darius' men knew what they were doing without being told. They did not have to be convinced that it was the right thing to do. His men would follow him anywhere. Darius' bold battlefield tactics were legendary. This mission wouldn't call for much in the way of strategy, however. If the raiders had known how close his patrol was, they would not have dared an assault right under his nose. If they struck quickly, the renegade Artylians would not be expecting any retaliation.

The men rode out under cover of darkness. They kept their horses' noses pointed in the right direction and trusted them to find their footing up the mountainside. In silence, they rode the steep path back to the pass where they had found the boy. Once there, Darius divided his men into two groups. They had not had to be very concerned about noise so far, but once they began to descend the other side, they would have to be careful not to alert the raiders to their presence. The two groups, about twelve men in each, would carefully circle the Artylian camp and approach it from opposite sides.

Picking their way quietly, Darius' group stealthily followed the man on the donkey down the other side of the pass. Effan led the other group around by another path. After some time, the man signaled that they were close, and they skirted around the camp on the northern side. When they were in position, Darius gave a pre-arranged signal. An owl hooted from a position on the opposite side of the camp. The bleating of goats could be heard, and it smelled like meat had been roasted recently. Darius gave a yell, and the horsemen surrounded the circle of tents.

"Get everybody up!" At his command, his men dismounted, drew their swords and started dragging people out of their tents and into the space in the center of the circle. The Berushese horses were trained to stand when their reins trailed and would stay put. A herd of goats was penned inside a rickety wooden corral. They shifted around nervously. There were no horses or donkeys visible. The raiders would have driven the goats here on foot.

Darius turned to his guide. "Are these your goats?" The man walked over to the herd to inspect them.

"Yes, these with the notch in the left ear are mine."

He looked over the animals quickly. "Over half of them are mine."

Darius turned back to the people huddled in the circle. "Where is your headman?" he said in Artylian. Fear showed on the faces of everyone in the encampment at the harsh edge in his authoritative voice. Darius dismounted and asked again, "Where is your headman?"

A short, stocky man wearing nothing but a long shirt stepped defiantly forward. Darius walked over to him. "You will have one chance to live. One of your men killed a Berushese goat herder during your raid yesterday. Give me that man, and you will live. If you do not," he growled, "every man in this camp will die."

The man glared at him and spit in his face. Darius drew his sword and cut clean through the man's neck in one swift stroke, separating his head from his body. He did not make empty threats. He tipped his head at the other members of the camp, and in the time it took him to get a sack from his saddlebag, every man in the camp was dead. "Burn the tents," he instructed. Effan took a smoldering stick from the fire pit and made a torch.

While the men burned the tents, Darius picked up the leader's head and put it in the sack. He handed it to the father of the dead boy. "Take this to show his mother." The man nodded and took the bag, shocked by the violence he had thought he wanted to see. Darius leaned in and spoke to him in an apologetic tone, "We cannot take the goats. By dawn, we must be back across the border in Berush."

The man nodded. "This is enough," he gestured to the bag. "I can breed more goats."

Darius put his hand on the man's shoulder in sympathy and then walked to the goat pen, signaling some of his men to follow. No goats would be left alive for the Artylians to make use of. Then they threw the bodies of the dead men onto the smoldering tents and burned them. When they had finished with the camp, the smell of smoke mixed with blood and burning flesh was sickening.

With some amount of pity, he turned his attention to the group of shivering, crying women and children. "Get out of here. Head to the nearest village and tell them what will happen if they venture across our borders." The mothers did not wait for him to change his mind, but rushed their children along a path away from the camp and further down the mountain.

Darius' soldiers held back a couple of the young women for themselves, but Darius made his men release them. Berush's strict laws against kidnapping or slavery of any kind did not normally extend protection to the enemy during wartime, but this was an unsanctioned attack, and they were returning immediately to Berush. He knew Cyrus would not approve, and the ride back was too long to listen to a bunch of screaming, anyway.

They reached the crest of the trail just as the sun rose at their backs. By the time they returned to the village, they had been on the move for over twenty-four hours, and the men were tired. He reported the success of the raid to Iban, and asked if he could quarter the men for a day or so. Iban agreed, and thanked him.

"What we did today may end up causing you more problems," Darius warned.

Iban nodded. "Sometimes, you have to say enough is enough. To lose your life is one thing, to live in fear is another. We know there may be consequences."

Darius arranged with Effan for the men to stay in the area for two days, sending out scouts to watch for activity on the other side of the mountains. If there was no unusual movement, then they were to resume their regular patrols and he would meet them at a village farther up the mountain range. He would take a couple of men and ride back to the capital to make a report to Cyrus before he heard about their retaliatory mission from anyone else.

Stopping no more than was absolutely necessary, Darius rode hard all day. He struggled against exhaustion to stay in the saddle. At night, he and his two men took shelter with a nomad he knew well. They slept for a few hours and then continued their journey with fresh horses. Though it was not yet the beginning of summer, the sun was hot. Fortunately the road now followed a river and was lined with trees that drank water through long, deep roots. Most of the day they rode in shade until the river flowed into a lake forming a large oasis in a wide, fertile valley. This was Sherish, the capital of Berush, a country of primarily nomadic people who herded cattle and goats.

Darius rode up to the palace, a large, ornate dwelling built with stone brought down from the mountain. He could not remember how many generations of his family had lived there, but now it belonged to his brother. When he rode through the gate, with trumpets announcing his return, he felt glad to be home. His men took the horses, and Darius went to find his brother.

Cyrus had heard the trumpets and met him in the outer court. "Brother," He put his hands on Darius' shoulders and surveyed him with contentment. "It is good to see you. Come in and refresh yourself, then you can tell me all your news. Come and meet your newest nephew!" Cyrus laughed. Slightly taller than Darius, Cyrus kept his black hair and beard trimmed and neat. It was just starting to turn gray at the temples. He wore an informal, loose-fitting, embroidered shirt with loose trousers, and his hazel eyes matched his brother's, with just a few more crinkles around them.

"I would rather give you my news first, and in private."

Cyrus' face turned serious. Whenever Darius took that tone, it was something important. Instead of into the salon where his family was relaxing, the king led his brother into one of the libraries. The room also served as an office and had numerous maps and charts on the wall in addition to shelves of scrolls and books. The collection even included copies of works by ancient wise men, or magi. Cyrus enjoyed reading that sort of thing.

Cyrus motioned Darius into one of the wooden chairs, softened with tanned leather hides thrown over them, and he sank into another. The king put his fingertips together and looked at Darius through half-closed eyes. "Tell me."

Darius gave him the entire story from the beginning, leaving nothing out, and making no excuses. Cyrus listened without interrupting, and sat silently for some time after Darius had finished. "Well, we had better not let them make a liar out of you," he finally responded. Cyrus stood and shuffled the maps on his desk until he found a detailed chart of the mountainous border area. "This happened two days ago?" He looked at Darius for confirmation.

"Yes."

"If they are going to do anything, it will be in the next couple of days."

"My men are keeping an eye on things and will send a report of any movement on the other side."

"Good." Cyrus studied the map. "We will need to

post men at every one of these passes," he pointed at several places on the map. "Not one raider must get through. How much cover is there in these areas?"

"Enough. There are low trees and plenty of brush. Many boulders to hide behind as well. You want to call up the entire army?"

"We should continue as you have begun, do you not agree? All or nothing. What alternatives do we have? We will turn it into an opportunity to stop this dispute once and for all."

Darius stared at the map and considered his brother's words. Even though he knew Cyrus would support him in almost anything, he was still grateful he did. He had not considered going this far with it, but now he agreed it was necessary. In a way, he was sorry. It was going to cause a lot of trouble for a lot of people. Every village along the border could be affected. "Do you really think the Artylians are likely to attack in force? King Uriya has not kept good control of his subjects, and his army is not very organized."

"I do not think Uriya's army will attack, no. However, it is possible that his mountain tribes may organize a limited invasion on their own in response to your little massacre." Cyrus' slight sarcastic tone was the only hint he gave of any displeasure in Darius' actions. "You yourself have been telling me that one of their leaders, Homa, is it not, has been gaining strength and uniting some of the smaller tribes under his banner. He may decide to spread his wings a little."

"That is possible. So what exactly are you authorizing me to do? Continue as we have been doing and protect the border?"

"I expect you to protect the border. I authorize you to do whatever you think expedient as the opportunity arises," said Cyrus with one eyebrow raised.

"Including, if they do attack, pursuing the raiders into Artylia?"

"If need be. Uriya has not responded to any of my complaints. Yarin is there now, you know, trying to reason with him. He refuses to see these raids as a serious problem. Yarin writes, with the greatest diplomacy, of course, that Uriya is mentally deficient."

They fell silent for a moment. "What if," Darius thought aloud, "what if we could take the entire mountain range? Push the Artylians across the Eryn river? That would be a border much easier to delineate."

Cyrus looked at his brother thoughtfully. Darius began to warm to the idea and continued, "If we push back Homa and his men, there is no one between us and the river besides them. Uriya's communication systems are in disarray. He has not kept up his army, and his lords are discontent and fighting amongst themselves. With some good irrigation, the land on that side of the mountains could become fertile farmland. I really think we could take it."

"I will not say no," Cyrus said slowly. He thought for a moment. "Let us move as if that is the plan, but be prepared to adjust our goals depending on Homa's response. I will send out riders to collect every available man and spread the word for the army to amass at the Marusene Oasis. And now, you must rest."

Cyrus looked at his brother with concern. "You are tired, and tomorrow, by afternoon at the latest, you must be ready to ride from the city with its men. If it happens, this is going to happen fast, and we must be ready." Cyrus pulled Darius into a hug and pounded him in the back. Then he ruffled his hair. "Go get some sleep, little brother."

∞∞∞

A nightmare woke Darius early in the morning. He was in the middle of a battle, and heads were rolling all around him. The heads all wore faces of his family and close comrades. Frantic to escape the scene, he sat straight up in bed, his sheet drenched in sweat. He grabbed his sword and tried to shake the images from his mind. Even awake, the vision swam before his eyes, and it took great effort for him to tell himself that it wasn't real, that he was imagining it.

Unable to think further of sleep, he rose, dressed, and went up to walk on the rooftop garden. The sun was just peeking over the horizon, and the lake reflected the light in thousands of shimmering slivers. A cool breeze floated across the water, and Darius began to feel calm and at peace again. The city on the lakeshore began to wake up, and he could hear movement in the palace courtyard. Cyrus would be sending out his riders.

There were currently around three hundred seasoned warriors quartered in the city itself. He would be leading them towards the mountain later in the day. Many other men would join them as well. Berush did not have a system of knights and lords, as such. The nomadic lifestyle did not lend itself to that. The people were organized by tribe and family. If a man prospered, and his flocks increased, his family and servants increased as well. The head of the tribe made sure that taxes were paid and order and discipline were maintained.

Any man could own a sword if he could wield it. In Berush, it was a privilege of a man's father to determine if he was worthy to carry a sword. It was a rite of passage. Competitions and tournaments were held in peaceful times to keep the men sharp. Therefore, the entire male population of the country could be called upon to serve in its defense. Fathers could even award daughters with a sword, especially if they had no sons. It was not common, but it happened.

The only woman Darius had ever really cared about had been a warrior in her tribe. Their affair had lasted a year or so, but she was ready to settle down, and he wasn't, so they had moved on. There had been other women since, but none of them could handle his night terrors. Occasionally he sought out female companionship for an hour or two, but for the most part he had found it was easier just to be alone.

The capital city was one of the few places in the country with permanent dwellings. On the other side of the lake, the river continued down to the sea. Workers in the capital sent goods down the river, and barges carried imports back. Inside the city was a vast array of merchants and traders. All the tribes replenished their supplies and bought, sold, and bartered here. The port at the mouth of the river was one other place with stone houses.

At the sound of footsteps behind him, Darius put his hand on the hilt of his sword and turned quickly. In the palace, of all places, he should feel safe, but it was an automatic response.

"Cyrus thought I might find you here." Cyrus' head wife, Sashia, approached holding a small bundle. "Marthi needed a break, and you have not met your new nephew yet." She smiled and held out the tiny baby for him to see.

Gingerly, Darius extended a finger to touch the soft fuzz on the top of the boy's head. A small hand escaped the tight wrappings and grabbed ahold of the extended digit. "He is perfect." A feeling of warmth washed over him as he looked at his brother's son. Cyrus was a good father and a good husband. He loved his family. He led them firmly, but fairly, the same way he led all his people. Most aspects of running the household, however, he left to Sashia.

"Do you want to hold him?"

Darius shook his head. He and his brother were very different. Cyrus was just as good a warrior as Darius, but it was not his calling. It was his job to lead the country and produce heirs. Darius, as his general, enabled Cyrus to be who he was. He did not have the finesse for politics and finance that a king needed. The delicate little fingers let go of his large, calloused one so they could be stuck into the tiny mouth. "What is his name?"

"Kalin, after his grandfather," said Sashia as proudly as if it was her own child.

Darius wondered, as he had several times before, how Sashia and Marthi got along so well. It was Sashia, after having three children in four years, who had encouraged Cyrus to take a second wife. Through some miracle of family planning, about which Darius had never wanted to know any details, they managed never to be pregnant at the same time. They took care of each other's children, and obviously took care of Cyrus. His brother was very happy, and the household was very harmonious. As far as he could tell, the two wives agreed on discipline methods, and you could hardly tell which child belonged to which mother.

A few tribal leaders still followed the tradition of having multiple wives, but it usually caused sibling rivalry and discontentment behind the scenes. Plus, in Berush a man had to have permission from his first wife to marry a second, and that rarely happened. In Artylia, it was actually against the law for the nobility to have multiple wives. They felt it caused too much bickering about the succession. What they did if there were no heirs, he didn't know.

Of course, Sashia's oldest were hardly children now. Tarin, the firstborn, ran the port. He had his father's gift for management and organization. Onia had just been married to the son of the leader of one of the largest tribes, and Varus was patrolling the eastern border.

The baby started to fuss, so Sashia took him back to his mother. Darius went in search of his brother and some breakfast.

CHAPTER TWO

Just after noon, two hundred horsemen and three hundred foot soldiers set out toward the eastern border. The majority of those on foot were untested in battle, yet each carried their own weapon, often handed down through generations. They had no standard uniform, but they were loyal Berushese, practiced in swordsmanship and obeying orders. The horsemen would arrive at the meeting place by the next evening, but it would take the foot soldiers at least another day to get there.

Every rider's saddlebags were packed with enough food for several days, and supply wagons would be traveling with the infantry. The message sent to Tarin had directed him to send the soldiers from the port to block the northern edge of the mountain range, and Varus would go straight to the southernmost pass. Darius would meet men from the central tribes and divide them up to plug the rest of the gaps.

After riding hard for several hours, a horseman

coming from the east galloped up to meet them. "Prince Darius!" The rider had to pause to catch his breath. "I have news from Captain Effan."

Darius signaled him to come alongside him. The messenger informed him that Homa was indeed amassing men near his stronghold at the base of Mount Barus. "The survivors from your incursion evidently went straight to him. He has called all the Artylian mountain tribes together."

"Most likely he sees this as an opportunity to strengthen his own position and gather all the tribal power to himself," Darius mused. "He just needs to execute a couple successful raids, and they will all line up behind him. He's a fool if he thinks Berush will just stand by and let him do it."

"They are not well armed, either, my lord. Most of his men are on foot with only knives and clubs."

"We just need to get there before they are ready to strike. It will come down to timing. Cyrus wants us to catch them on our side of the border." He urged his horse into a trot.

At dusk, the army watered its horses at the river and stole a few hours' sleep under the stars. They resumed their journey before dawn. By afternoon, they were at the meeting point. It was a place where the river widened and trees and grass formed a small oasis. His men set up a large tent to serve as a command center. Cyrus himself was to arrive in two days' time to assess the situation firsthand. Hopefully Darius would have good news to report.

Soon, men from the central tribes began to arrive. By evening, the number of horsemen had nearly doubled. Darius divided them into companies of one hundred and sent one group to each of the three passes Homa was most likely to use. Both Varus and the men Tarin would send from the port would take at least another day to get into position, but Homa would take just as long to get to either of those locations if he chose to use them. Darius suspected he would be satisfied with raiding a couple of quick, easy targets to build his people's confidence and then head home. Iban's village would probably be included, since that was where the whole thing had started.

The remaining hundred men he divided into smaller scouting groups, keeping some with him to use as messengers. More men joined them throughout the night. When Darius rose that morning, tents of several tribal leaders dotted the landscape, and a couple hundred more men awaited assignments. Darius summoned the leaders to his tent to confer.

The Artylians normally raided during the day, and the tribal leaders agreed Homa could strike as early as this afternoon, or tomorrow if he waited for greater numbers. Returning scouts reported between four and five hundred men had gathered at Homa's stronghold. It seemed they were preparing a feast, and Homa was making an appeal to the various tribes to unite under his leadership. This seemed to point that they would not be raiding today. That meant that Darius' foot soldiers would arrive before any fighting started, and the Berushese would be in full strength.

He sent Onia's husband, Tomus, with his men to take charge of the pass directly north of Mount Barus, and another group to the south of it. The pass near Iban's village, Darius would take himself. It was where he expected Homa to be.

In the evening another messenger arrived from Effan. Homa had sent out a couple of scouts, but Effan's men had been so well hidden that the scouts passed right by them without noticing them. They returned the same way joking that it would be an easy raid. They planned on razing Iban's entire village. He was glad they had not killed the scouts. He wanted Homa to remain overconfident.

Early on the morning of the sixth day, Darius rode with another two hundred men to join Effan. The foot soldiers had arrived the previous night, and Darius dispersed them into the foothills to catch any Artylians who broke through the lines. All the settlements along the border had been warned to keep their herds at home today, but many of their men joined the soldiers in the passes.

Upon arriving at the gap where they had found the boy, Darius signaled to Effan. His captain emerged from the brush.

"We have a hundred men hidden in the trees. We're ready for them."

"I brought you two hundred more." He motioned for his men to dismount, and they led their horses under the trees and melted into the landscape. A few horses shifted their weight back and forth, but there was no other noise to give them away. The latest scouting report showed Homa dividing his forces into only two groups, so most likely only he and Tomus would see any action today. Fortunately, they had more than enough men in both places to take on half of Homa's men, besides the fact that one of his men was worth ten Artylians.

They didn't have to wait long before they heard the sound of rocks shifting under many feet and voices echoing through the pass. Dozens of men began pouring through the gap, but not one of Darius' men moved. They waited for the signal that would come when the first man reached the end of the Berushese line. When the men at the end saw the first of the raiders, they surged forward with a roar. Then every one of Darius' men began boiling up out of their hiding places and attacked Homa's men with fury.

A few lucky men got cuts in here and there, but they stood no chance against Darius' experienced swordsmen. The Berushese surged forward, cutting down every invader in their path, with Darius in the lead. He was looking for Homa. Darius ducked to avoid a swinging club and then skewered its wielder through the heart. Pushing the corpse aside, he hacked his way up the mountainside.

The last of the invaders coming over the pass realized they were walking into an ambush and turned to run, but they had nowhere to go. They were surrounded. When he reached the top, Darius saw half a dozen men retreating madly downhill, and he sent some men after them. They returned quickly. Not a man escaped. Homa had not been there.

Darius gathered his men and began giving orders. "Take the wounded down the mountain immediately for attention. Effan, send messengers to every commander to cross the passes and take positions on the Artylian side. We are taking the mountains. "Topec," he called to a captain from the capital, "take a dozen men and begin organizing the foot soldiers to create supply lines. We need all our food stores carried through. Faban, choose a score of men and start piling up the bodies and burn them. The pass needs to be clear. Everyone else, follow me. We're going to press on to Homa's stronghold, hopefully meeting Tomus on the way."

About two hundred men mounted their horses and carefully began navigating down the eastern side of the range behind the prince. It would take several hours for them to reach the next pass, but it was faster to go around the eastern side. They met no one else on the descent. They passed the village Darius had burned and turned south, leaving fifty men behind to guard the pass.

An hour or so later, they discovered a small village next to a stream flowing out of the mountains. There were few men left in the village. Most of them were likely dead on the mountian. To those who remained, Darius gave an ultimatum, "Berush is now in control of this land. You may swear your allegiance and join us, or you can die." He was not going to leave anyone around who would become a burr under his saddle. By now all had heard the story of what had happened in the next village over, so the men swore allegiance to King Cyrus and joined Darius' troop. This was repeated in every village they passed with the same result.

The light began to dim and the sun dipped behind the mountaintops. When they reached the next pass, Darius instructed the men to make camp. He took twenty men with him and started up the pass. They had not gone more than half a mile before the sound of horses could be heard ahead. Darius waited for the riders to appear, and was soon rewarded by seeing the grinning face of his nephew-in-law.

"Good to see you, Tomus! How did you fare?"

"We got Homa!" was the first thing out of his mouth. His youthful enthusiasm for battle was obvious.

"Excellent! Congratulations! And the disposition of your men?"

"Two casualties, and a few minor wounds. We had to put down a horse who broke an ankle. Over three hundred dead invaders, including Homa." Tomus was excessively pleased with his success, and Darius gave him well-deserved praise. Darius had miscalculated Homa's lust for battle. The erstwhile leader had taken the easiest route for himself. Lazy imbecile. "We received your message to continue forward, so here we are," concluded Tomus.

Darius led the men back back down the mountainside. It was now fully dark, so they had to proceed with caution. When they met back up with the rest of Darius' men, they set a watch and gratefully took a few hours to rest.

In the middle of the night, Darius awoke with a yell. Someone was after him! He grabbed his sword and jumped up, slashing wildly at an unseen foe. Men scrambled to get out of his way.

"My lord, there is no danger!" That was Effan's voice. "It was a dream, my lord, no more. You had a dream." Effan kept repeating these words until Darius finally understood what he was saying and stood still. Effan approached and put a hand on Darius' shoulder, but Darius shrugged him off. The captain was not offended. They all had these dreams from time to time. They all understood, but it was something they tried not to talk about. Darius laid back down on his bedroll, but he would sleep no more that night.

∞∞∞

It took a week for Darius to move the entire army across to the Artylian side of the mountain range once he had taken over Homa's stronghold. Varus had met some resistance at the southern pass. One of the tribal leaders had not joined with Homa, and he had put up a fight rather than surrender. Cyrus had made sure that Varus' company was filled with experienced warriors, and they easily overcame the opposition. It was Varus' first experience in combat, and he still looked a little green when he arrived at the new command center in Homa's former residence. Darius exchanged a look with his nephew's seasoned captain, and the captain nodded, conveying assurance that the boy would be fine.

Once Darius had heard reports from each company, including the men from the port, he returned to the Marusene Oasis to confer with Cyrus. He took Tomus with him so that he could personally report his defeat of Homa to the king.

Cyrus clapped him on the back, "Well done, my son!" Then they began to discuss plans to establish and maintain control over the territory they had just taken. "Spoils of war are one thing, when you carry out a raid and return to your own country. Ruling your own citizens is something completely different," Cyrus admonished. "These people are now citizens of Berush, and must be treated as such. Make sure your men understand this," he held the eyes of Darius and Tomus in turn. They dipped their heads in acknowledgement.

"In every village, gather everyone together and read to them a copy of our laws, as well as our punishments, and explain their rights and our chain of authority." He had brought scrolls, written in Artylian, containing the laws with him for this very purpose. "Our laws may be harsher than some, but if everyone knows and understands them ahead of time, there will be less resistance. If we treat them fairly, they will accept our rule more easily." Cyrus paused to make sure his commanders understood.

"I have directed Tarin to place someone else in charge of the port temporarily so that he can run the capital in my absence. Darius," he turned to his brother, "you are the governor of this new territory, for now. When it is well in hand, send a messenger for me to come and inspect it. I will remain here, for the time being, in case I am needed. I will be curious to hear Uriya's response," he chuckled.

"I am using Homa's stronghold as a base and plan to strengthen and reinforce it," Darius explained. "It should be a fit place for a governor's manor when you are ready to appoint someone to it permanently." Cyrus agreed with this suggestion.

Before returning to the stronghold, Darius stopped in at the infirmary tent to check on the wounded men. Sashia had accompanied Cyrus to the camp, and she was in charge of the nursing. Marthi was left to care for the children, with the help of several nannies and tutors. The wounded were few, and the injuries were not serious. The men would be rejoining their companies before long.

Darius and Tomus rode back over the mountain. Darius was beginning to tire of this trip. Going up and down the steep trails used different muscles than riding over the flat land of the wide Berushese river valley.

That evening, he summoned all the captains and Berushese tribal leaders who had crossed the mountains for a council meeting. He conveyed to them Cyrus' directions about conferring citizenship on all the Artylians who remained in the territory they had just taken. They assigned men to take the message to every village west of the Eryn. The Artylian men they conscripted would return with them so they could care for their families. Darius arranged for extra food supplies to be sent with them as well. It would take some time for them to recover from the loss of so many men.

Troops would be constantly patrolling the river, which was their new border. Fortunately, the area at the mouth of the river was not heavily populated. The land ended in steep cliffs, and jagged rocks formed a barrier that made it virtually unnavigable. Artylia's primary port was further east at the end of one of the Eryn's distributaries. It was also where their capital was located, about four days' ride away. That meant they could expect to hear some sort of response from Uriya in a day or two more.

∞∞∞

It was, in fact, the very next morning when they first anything out of Artylia, but it was not from Uriya. A messenger rode into the base looking for Darius. "My lord, a delegation across the river wishes safe passage to speak with you."

Darius summoned Effan, Tomus and several more of his men to ride out and meet the visitors. The river flowed closer to the mountains here than in most places, but it was still two hours' ride away. By the time they arrived, the men on the opposite shore had been waiting at least four hours. "That is not Uriya's flag," observed Darius in surprise. The banner looked familiar. He had seen it on one of Cyrus' maps.

"No, that would appear to be the flag of Lord Byrd. He has a large tract of land east of the Eryn extending all the way to the border of Cerecia," replied Effan.

Darius was curious to discover what this meant. "Signal for them to cross," he said as he dismounted. The river was wide and deep at this point, but there was a ferry that looked like it could carry up to four horsemen at a time. The patrols had discovered it yesterday and kept an eye on it. Four men led their horses onto the ferry, and the ferryman slowly guided it across the river. Darius felt himself becoming impatient, but then he imagined the other men were even more on edge having waited on the bank for so long.

Finally, the ferry docked and the horsemen disembarked. The man in front had to be Lord Byrd himself. He was dressed in a very fine, black tunic, embroidered with gold, and brown pants and shirt. The three men with him wore tunics with their lord's coat of arms displayed on the front.

"Lord Byrd," stated Darius, as he held out his hand, "I am Darius, brother to King Cyrus and general of his army. You have safe conduct to speak with us. Would you like to accompany us back to camp, or would you speak here?"

Byrd clasped Darius' forearm in greeting. "We can speak here." The landing area for the ferry was well shaded from the sun by tall trees, and the temperature beneath their branches was quite comfortable for the early afternoon.

"You are not who I expected to see," ventured Darius.

"In truth, neither are you. I have feared we were ripe for invasion, but I expected it to come from the Cerecians." Darius raised an eyebrow indicating that he wanted more of an explanation. "We have been fortunate," Lord Byrd continued, "that the Cerecians have spent the last couple of decades fighting each other. However, my spies report that their new, young king has been able to unite them again."

"I have not heard this report. It is unwelcome news, but it has been nearly a century since they tried crossing the desert on our border."

"And yet it is Berush that now stands before me."

"As you see," replied Darius without elaborating. He waited to see what Byrd wanted from him.

"I take it tensions between the mountain tribes came to a head?"

"They did."

"I have been telling Uriya that letting the tribes remain virtually lordless was inviting trouble." Byrd decided to come to the point. "So is King Cyrus content to hold the mountains, or is he going to execute a complete invasion of Artylia?"

"At this time, he is satisfied with having a more defined border such as the river provides," said Darius cautiously. "You bear your own flag, not that of Uriya. Do you represent your own interests, or his?"

"Uriya has left me no choice but to represent my own interests. He has no control over his lords. Some lords prefer a weak leader so they can grab more power for themselves, but this makes us vulnerable to the same threat from outside, as anyone can now see. I prefer to live in peace." Byrd hesitated before continuing. "I would like to offer my allegiance to King Cyrus, if he will accept it."

"You wish to transfer your allegiance?" Darius' incredulity crept into his voice. This development was a complete surprise.

"Uriya's time is running out. If we are not invaded, one or other of his greedy subjects will try to overthrow him. If I were to have my pick of kings to be subject to, it would be Cyrus."

"Why is that?"

"Both he, and you, my lord," he inclined his head, "are reputed to be strong leaders and men of your word."

"I thank you, but you are one of the largest land holders in Artylia. You do not want to take the throne for yourself?"

"I am not that ambitious, my lord."

Darius considered Byrd's proposal. If Byrd switched his loyalty to Berush, Cyrus would control nearly one-third of the land area of Artylia. "How many other lords feel this way?"

"Every lord in Artylia is either discontent with Uriya's poor leadership, or taking advantage of it. I do not know how many of them would be willing to switch allegiances without persuasion."

"Have you heard nothing from him since we gained control of the mountains?"

Byrd sighed. "According to what I have heard, when Uriya received news of your invasion, he beat your emissary and imprisoned him, then continued on to the seashore for his daily bath. There has been no further news." Darius' hands balled into fists and he frowned angrily hearing of how Yarin had been treated. "If Cyrus wished to take the Artylian throne for himself, I can commit at least one thousand men to the enterprise," Byrd offered in hopes it would tip the balance his way. It did.

"I will relay your offer to my brother. It will take a few days before I can bring a decision back to you. Can I expect safe conduct for a messenger across your domain?"

"I will instruct my people that anyone you send is to be let through." They took leave of each other, and Byrd and his men took the ferry back across the river. Darius rode the two hours back to the stronghold and made preparations to return to see Cyrus. This was something he could not relay by messenger.

∞∞∞

Cyrus was as taken aback by Lord Byrd's proposal as Darius was, and that was saying something. Cyrus was rarely surprised. "This changes things." Cyrus pulled thoughtfully on his beard. "What is your opinion, brother?"

Darius had had a couple of days to think it over. "If

we keep the land we have, we will still face the continued problem of Uriya and an unstable Artylia. Uriya, from all reports, is an unreasonable, childish pleasure-seeker who has no idea how a kingdom should be run. It might be best to press our advantage now, rather than wait until we are forced into another fight and the advantage belongs to another."

"It would spread our resources pretty thin."

"With Lord Byrd on our side, I think we could handle it. The Artylian forces are completely unprepared to defend against an invasion."

"Uriya and the capital might be unprepared, but what about the rest of the lords?"

Darius had been considering this question as well. "I had an idea about this. If we take our men on barges down the Arya to the capital, and Byrd marches overland, we could take the capital before anyone else knew what we were about. Then you could send out messages to all the lords to give them a chance to offer you their allegiance before going to war against them. It may be that, in the face of overwhelming odds, they will choose to accept your rule rather than fight."

Cyrus weighed the risks of such a course against the good that might come out of it. He did not covet land for himself, but he wanted to do what was best for his people. In this case, it might be best to fight now rather than later. "Very well. I will return with you and speak to Lord Byrd myself. If he truly wishes to ally with us, then we will take the course you suggest. Had you an idea about the Artylian navy?"

The tall trees on the Artylian side of the mountains lent themselves to shipbuilding, and Artylia possessed a large fleet of ships. "If we act quickly, and they do not know we are coming, they will not be able to do anything to stop us. The navy reports directly to the king, and I doubt Uriya has made any special defense plans that include his warships. All they have been doing the last twenty or thirty years is patrolling the channel for Cerecian pirates. Our attack will be primarily overland and by river. We will only have to ensure that Uriya does not escape out to sea. If he has done anything to Yarin," Darius added, "he will pay for it dearly."

Cyrus grimaced in silent agreement. "And afterwards, we can just wait for the ships to return to port and resupply. Then we can offer them the same choice as everyone else."

∞∞∞

In just five days, all arrangements had been made, and the army was ready to move toward the Artylian capital. Berushese merchants often took the southern pass over the mountains, less often lately because of tension with the Artylian mountain tribes, and took their goods to Letyna, the Artylian capital, by river barge. Darius commandeered enough barges to hold one thousand infantry. These would float down river and attack the city from the water.

A thousand Berushese cavalry would ride with an equal number of Byrd's men overland. An additional thousand men would remain to guard the border under Varus' leadership. Tarin was ensconced in Sherish, and had everything well in hand at home. He also had soldiers at his disposal in case any issues arose elsewhere. Lord Byrd had made sure that no one had travelled through his lands spying on the Berushese forces.

The best news of all was that he had persuaded a neighboring lord, Modyn, to join their cause. This enabled the army to travel within a day of the capital without, they hoped, Uriya receiving warning of it. After spending most of the night camping in Lord Modyn's fields, they set out before dawn, under cover of darkness. Cyrus was riding with Lord Byrd, and Darius was leading the men down the river. They had timed their departure so they would both arrive at the same time.

Before Cyrus met Lord Byrd, he was inclined to be suspicious of his motives. Any man who would betray his king by bringing in an opposing army was a traitor in his mind. If he would betray one king, why not another? However, Lord Byrd soon convinced him of his sincerity. The man was truly at his wit's end trying to hold his land together. He constantly had to be on guard against his own neighbors. It was only because he had so many men at his disposal that he was able to hold them off.

Recently he had discovered that two of them were plotting together to take over his lands, and that had been the last straw. The king had actually sent him a message to the effect that he needed to take care of his own problems or he would give the lands to someone who could. Byrd was afraid if the Artylian lords went to war openly amongst themselves, the Cerecians would take to opportunity to invade. When Berush had invaded first, Byrd had seen it as a gift of fate. Cyrus had assured him that he would retain control of his holdings if he aided them, and Lord Byrd had pledged his fealty to Cyrus.

Most of Byrd's men were on foot, so they travelled at a march. When they were about ten miles from the capital, a small group of horsemen approached. "These are Lord Cayern's men. He is a pompous blowhard. He is all bluster and no action," Byrd informed Cyrus.

"Hai, hai, these lands belong to Lord Cayern. You cannot pass through here," waved the leader of the group.

Cyrus reined in his horse, but signaled Tomus, who rode with him, to continue leading the army forward. Lord Byrd remained next to Cyrus. "We have business with King Uriya, so we will be passing through here. If Lord Cayern has any complaints, he can bring them to me personally."

"And you are?" The man squinted at him. He noticed now that the man before him was dressed in very fine armor and sat on a very fine horse.

"Cyrus, king of Berush." At these words the man frowned. He looked around and saw the soldiers marching past, stretching behind Cyrus as far as he could see. It dawned on him that he was not in a position to be giving any orders.

"I will pass on your words to Lord Cayern," he replied, and turned his horse around and rode away.

Cyrus and Lord Byrd urged their horses to a canter to catch up with the front of the column. Cyrus reflected that Uriya, and most of his lords, must not have any sort of spy network in place. Such negligence was incomprehensible to him. As they rode, Cyrus explained his plans more fully to Tomus and Lord Byrd. He hoped to achieve their goals with little or no bloodshed. What he had seen and heard so far, made him think it was entirely possible.

Shortly after encountering Cayern's men, they approached a village. The residents looked at them through dark windows and partly closed doors. There was little activity, and the faces Cyrus saw were thin and careworn, much different than the people he had seen the days they spent on Byrd's holding. Much different from his own people, who, for the most part, were industrious and content.

By late afternoon, they could see the capital city of Letyna in the distance. The castle sat on a hill in the center, its white limestone walls bright with reflected sunlight. It really was a beautiful site, surrounded by emerald green fields against a backdrop of deep blue sea. Cyrus took a moment to drink it in.

When he had continued farther, evidence of mismanagement and neglect became apparent to mar the visual perfection. Some of the fields they passed, though green, had not been cultivated. They were a mixture of weeds and ratoon corn. It would be good for forage, but there was no evidence that Lord Cayern owned any cattle, or that any haying was in progress. It was too late to plant any spring crops. No good king would allow his subjects to waste resources this way, especially in sight of his own castle!

No one rode out to meet them as they approached the city gates. Cyrus instructed Tomas to position the men as they normally would for a siege, although Cyrus believed it would not be necessary. They would maintain a distance out of bow range, though Cyrus had been informed that the castle's defenses were in a very sorry state. He chose fifty horsemen, followed by fifty infantry to accompany him to the gate. With him went Lord Byrd and several of Cyrus' most experienced captains and advisors.

The career soldiers all had armor and shields, and they formed a guard around their king, but no heads appeared on the wall of the city. No one appeared to be guarding the gate at all. "Is this the normal state of affairs, Byrd?" asked Cyrus.

"Unfortunately, yes. Uriya cares nothing for his people. He does not bother guarding the city. The only soldiers in the city are the ones at the palace. He needs them around to do his bidding."

They rode through the gate unmolested. It appeared the portcullis was intact, though rusty, but the large, wooden doors were rotting off of their hinges, completely useless. Like Lord Byrd, he was surprised that the Cerecians had not yet taken advantage of this state of affairs. King Chysh must still be working to reestablish control. Berush had not had normal relations with Cerecia in two centuries, and since their countries were separated by a large desert, he had not spent much effort in spying on them. If he was going to rule over Artylia, that oversight would have to be remedied.

The horsemen clattered through the cobbled streets of the city, passing many startled citizens on the way. The people looked depressed and downtrodden, and when they passed through a crowded square, they lined up to watch the procession. Many of them held out their hands and spoke a few words. It took a few moments for Cyrus to realize, though he spoke fluent Artylian, they were begging for food. "These people are starving!" he said to Lord Byrd indignantly.

Byrd winced. "Uriya has raised our taxes and squandered it all. The people in the city are most affected. The granaries are empty, and they survive primarily off of the fishing industry. If the catch is poor, there is not enough to go around. Some of the lords like to appear magnanimous and throw them a few coins. Not that there is anything to buy."

Cyrus felt himself becoming angry at the injustice he saw around him. Sewage and refuse filled the streets, and everything was in a state of disrepair. The gate of the castle itself was the only thing that seemed to be in complete working order. Cyrus was in no mood to humor anyone, so he urged his horse faster and surged through the gate. His men followed him, quickly surrounding the handful of surprised castle guards. The infantry jogged in behind him, and they soon filled the courtyard. More guards heard the noise and rushed to the courtyard, but they found themselves facing the sharp points of dozens of swords.

"Take their weapons," Cyrus instructed. "Find out where the guard room is and shut them in there." There were twenty guards in all, and Cyrus left men to watch them, some men to stay with the horses, and took two dozen men with him into the castle. Too late, someone decided to try and shut the door leading from the courtyard to the hall, and Cyrus' men pushed it back before it could be barred.

"Take us to King Uriya," thundered Cyrus to the man behind the door. The man pointed a shaking finger to a doorway across the empty hall.

"Follow me," interjected Lord Byrd. "I know where he can be found." He led them across the hall and down a corridor. He stopped in front of a door, behind which could be heard music and laughter.

Cyrus motioned to two of his soldiers, and they kicked down the door. Cyrus entered imperiously, his men quickly flanking him on both sides, and he stood with arms akimbo surveying the room. Opulent couches and cushions dotted the floor, and many elegant young people languished decadently on the soft surfaces. A small ball of hair, which he presumed was some kind of dog, yapped at the newcomers. A foppishly dressed young man with a ridiculously feathered hat and jeweled fingers jumped to his feet and exclaimed, "What is the meaning of this intrusion?"

Cyrus looked at him sternly and declared, "We are here to discuss the terms of your abdication, King Uriya."

CHAPTER THREE

While Cyrus was riding through the dilapidated city gates, Darius and his fleet of barges were sailing into the harbor. It had taken nearly fifteen barges to hold all of his men. The larger boats were made for carrying heavy loads of grain or textiles and could easily hold a hundred soldiers. The merchants to whom the barges belonged were being sequestered back in Byrd's holding with promises of ample compensation.

They had floated downriver with the current since the wind was blowing in from the sea. However, to navigate the harbor they would need the sails. It was impossible to sail in irons, or straight into the wind, but Darius had handpicked men from Sherish and the port for this mission who were experienced sailors. They could use the triangular sails to zig-zag across the harbor wherever they needed to go. He also had several skilled archers from Berush's western tribes who were renowned for their skill with the bow. They could shoot fire arrows at any ships who tried to escape.

Once in the harbor, their first task was to commandeer the warships. According to the spies Byrd had sent out, at Darius' request, there were currently four. Beating to windward, the sailors chose a tack that would allow them to come alongside the warships. Four barges were assigned to this task, and the rest of them were to tie up at the docks and subdue any resistance.

Cyrus was adamant that no civilians were to be harmed, and soldiers should be given a chance to surrender, if possible. As the sailors prepared to come about, Darius, who was in the first barge, instructed his men to ready grappling hooks. The four barges turned at almost the same time and came abreast of the warships. The men threw their hooks, pulled on the lines, and were soon scrambling up the sides of the ships.

There was one young sailor on watch on the deck of the ship Darius boarded. As soon as he spied the first hook, he descended the other side of his ship and ran down the dock as fast as he could go. One of Darius' archers raised his bow, but the prince signaled him to let the boy go.

A quick tour of the ship uncovered an inebriated captain and first mate who were summarily thrown in the brig to sober up. When Darius disembarked, he found that two of the other ships had been taken just as easily, and the fourth was completely deserted. It appeared that it had been sitting there for some time with mildewy sails and a hull in desperate need of cleaning.

With the barges all secured, the Berushese sailors, and most of the archers, were assigned to the seaworthy warships and sent to blockade the harbor. Darius set a watch on the docks and headed to the harbormaster's office.

The harbormaster was a balding, portly man, and the bottles on his desk indicated he spent a majority of his time in the same state as the ship captains rather than overseeing the proper maintenance of the Artylian navy. The boy from the docks had tried to warn him, but he was nearly insensible. Darius confined the man and boy to the office, under guard, and headed from the port into the city.

At the customs house, which served as the main gate into the city from the port, a couple of disheveled guards slouched in the shade. On seeing Darius and his men marching up, one of them straightened up with some idea of making an attempt to do his duty. "State your business," he said pompously.

Darius could not even condescend to speak to these poor specimens. Effan and a couple other soldiers quickly pinioned their arms and hustled them into the customs house and left them under guard. A soldier, at Darius' shoulder, stifled a snicker. Darius gave him a quelling look. It was no laughing matter to have such poor defenses.

Once inside the city walls, Darius sent the rest of his men on patrol to assess the state of the city and round up any Artylian soldiers they happened upon. With Effan and a small guard, he headed up to the castle. Finding everything under control, Darius went to speak to the Artylian soldiers Cyrus had shut in the guard house. He looked them over and walked to one particularly scared-looking guard. He picked him up by the collar and forced the man to look him in the eye.

"Somewhere in this castle is a Berushese prisoner named Yarin. Do you know where he is?" the man's head bobbed up and down in the affirmative. "Show me," Darius demanded, and pushed the man toward the door. The man moved quickly, rightly afraid that Darius would prod him if he hesitated. They made their way down to a lower level of the castle, down narrow stairs that hugged the castle's rock foundation. Arrow slits in the outer wall provided enough dim light for them to find their way.

At the bottom of the steps, several small rooms were cut into the rock. Most of them were being utilized as wine cellars, and barrels were stacked from floor to ceiling. The last room was empty of casks, and the door was locked. "Where is the key?"

The man shrugged, and Darius broke the rusty lock with one swift kick from the side. He pushed open the door and rushed into the room. It took him a few moments for his eyes to adjust to the darkness before he finally spied the limp figure on the floor. "Yarin!" he rushed over to his friend and felt for a pulse. It was there, but weak.

The figure moaned and pleaded hoarsely, "Water."

Darius looked around and saw nothing but filth. The stench in the room was overwhelming. He carefully picked the frail man up in his strong arms and quickly retraced his steps back to the surface. There he found an unused sitting room and laid Yarin on a couch. He sent the Artylian guard with some of his own men to find water and clean clothes. They returned with water very quickly, though to Darius it seemed to take an eternity.

Gently he held up Yarin's head so he could take a sip of the cool liquid. Cyrus had brought several healers and herbalists along with the army, and one of the soldiers had gone back to the camp to fetch one. Darius would not trust Yarin to one of Uriya's healers even if one could be found. When the healer arrived, they removed Yarin's soiled clothing so they could clean and treat any wounds. Purple and yellow bruises covered his torso. His lip was cut and festering, and it looked like his nose was broken. They washed and cleaned him carefully, and the healer gently rubbed some ointments onto his bruises. He prescribed water, wine and broth, and most importantly rest. A close eye would have to be kept on him in case he developed a fever.

"What are his chances of recovery?"

The healer pursed his lips. "In a case like this, with possible internal injuries, when the body is weak from starvation, it is impossible to tell. His ribs appear intact. They may be cracked, but not broken. His breathing is shallow, but not labored. He may recover, but it will take time. I will stay with him and do everything I can."

"Thank you," replied Darius. If they had arrived just a day later, it might have been too late. Yarin's condition made his anger rise, and the red haze began to cloud his vision. He wanted to hit something. He wanted Uriya to feel the pain Yarin felt. He left Yarin in the healer's care and went to find Cyrus. And Uriya.

∞∞∞

"Where is he?" roared Darius when he found Cyrus in the hall dictating to a table full of scribes. "I'll kill him!" he raged. There was only one 'he' of any note in the castle, so Cyrus knew Darius must be looking for Uriya.

"You found Yarin? Is he . . ."

"He is alive, but only just. They beat him nearly to death, threw him in a cell and left him there to die. It is amazing he survived. They did not even give him water." Darius imagined Yarin licking the condensation from the cold, stone walls to get a small amount of moisture. "Where is Uriya? I want him to know what it feels like."

"That will not give you peace, brother. Uriya is safely disposed of. We have a much bigger mess to clean up. You have secured the port?"

Darius reported on the state of the port and the status of the ships in the harbor. He knew Cyrus was making him go through the motions until he could calm himself, but it still worked. His anger began to recede and he was able to think clearly again. "I will go and hear the reports from my patrols, if you do not need me for anything else."

Cyrus nodded and dismissed him. Darius had to struggle to keep his thoughts from becoming morose. Cyrus was not immune from the allure of vengeance. He had saved Darius from a situation similar to Yarin's once before. It was true that Darius had never lost a battle or called a retreat, but he had been betrayed.

Over a decade ago, when their father was still alive, Darius had been sent to mediate a dispute between two clans over a watering hole. He had been on a peaceful mission and was a guest in their territory. The two clan leaders had been summoned to a neutral location for a meeting. One of the clans had decided to take things into their own hands and set an ambush.

While Darius and the leaders were conferring in a meeting tent, men rushed in and subdued him and killed the other clan leader. Even then, Darius had been a competent swordsman and got in a few good cuts, but he had been surprised, and he had gone into the tent alone. They had wanted him alive, to hold him hostage and try and force the king into a ruling in their favor, but to take him down they had nearly had to kill him.

He was unconscious two days from a blow to the head. When he awoke, he found himself tied to a cot, unable to move. He was spooned tepid water and soggy bread and came down with a fever. His father had sent Cyrus with an overwhelming number of men to rescue him, and they had wiped out the entire clan. Darius had never been so glad to see his brother. Cyrus had been incensed at the condition he was in.

King Kalin had deposed the leader of the tribe to which both clans had belonged for letting things get so out of hand. The experience had taught Darius to be more wary. Cyrus had learned that there was a time for diplomacy and a time for brute force. He had tried to explain to Darius that just because something was necessary, it was not always going to give you satisfaction, but Darius still didn't believe him.

Over the next few days, Cyrus sent messengers with letters to all the Lords and major land holders in Artylia as well as the shipyards in the harbor further down the coast by the southern cedar forests. He informed them of Uriya's abdication, ceding control of the country to Berush, and called them all to a council in ten days' time.

Darius facilitated the reopening of the port and allowed merchant barges to resume going up and down the river under the supervision of Berushese customs officers and a new harbor master recommended by Lord Byrd. When the first warship was sighted returning, he took a longboat out to the blockade which was still in place. Fishing and merchant boats that had been cleared by the harbormaster were allowed to pass through, but the fleet of warships still at sea could present a problem. The blockade ships still flew the Artylian flag to indicate they were friendly to the returning navy vessels.

When the ship was within range, Darius hailed them and his men rowed the longboat alongside. Darius boarded the ship and explained to the captain that leadership of the country had changed, but that every man was free to continue his current occupation if he so chose. As long as their own positions were secure, the captain and crew were surprisingly indifferent to the news of Uriya's removal from the throne. Darius directed the captain to check in with the harbor master and conveyed that expectations as to the upkeep of his ship would be raised under the new administration.

With that first encounter out of the way, he delegated the task of meeting the returning vessels to one of his captains. Whenever he could, Darius spent time sitting with Yarin. The first couple of nights, Darius slept on a cot in Yarin's room in case he should need anything. However, Darius awoke both nights in a cold sweat, having flashbacks of his own imprisonment. He decided his presence might cause more disturbance than comfort, so once he was sure Yarin was stable, he moved to another room.

Once he was able to receive nourishment, Yarin started to recover rapidly. His ribs were still sore, but he was able to sit up and even to walk around a little. When they found him, it was too late to reset his nose without breaking it again, so it would be a little crooked from now on. Other than that, it seemed he had suffered no permanent damage. By the day appointed for the council, Yarin was able to take a seat in the hall and resume his role as advisor to Cyrus.

There were seventeen lords and land holders present at the council, including the master of the shipyards, the harbor master, and mayor of Letyna. Most of them took rooms in the castle, but a few, including the mayor, which was an appointed position, owned their own houses in the town. Many of them looked nervous as they took their places in the hall. They did not know what to expect from this foreign king who had magically seized the throne from under their noses.

Cyrus had wanted to strike a contrast with what they had experienced with Uriya, so he had dressed very simply, but his lack of outward decoration merely served to accentuate the strength of character and confident authority he had on the inside. When he took his seat, everyone became silent and gave him their undivided attention.

"My lords," Cyrus began in a clear voice that carried easily to every corner of the room, "thank you for responding to my summons. "I find myself in a place I had no idea of being a month ago. Tensions on the border between Berush and Artylia came to a head and we were forced to take action to ensure the safety of our people.

"After taking the mountains, we discovered that King Uriya's negligence and mismanagement were even worse in the confines of his own country than they were on the border. We decided that it was in our best interest to aid in forming a stronger government in Artylia rather than leave it open to invasion by the Cerecians." Murmuring was heard at the mention of the Cerecians.

"In the days since my arrival here I have sent men to scout Artylia's southern border and spy on King Chysh's movements. They have discovered that Chysh has indeed united his lords and is gathering an army. Artylia's defenses, we have found, are woefully inadequate." More murmuring. "Also neglected are many of your fields, your roads and your people," he said more sternly.

"It is my intention to give you one year to mend your fences, cultivate your fields, shore up your defenses and train your soldiers. If you fail to make satisfactory improvements in these areas, your position will be given to someone more worthy. I hope it will not be necessary to take that step." He looked them all in the eye by turn as he spoke.

When he finished, the room erupted with questions and protestations. Cyrus motioned for quiet. Darius, stationed by the door, moved slightly, just to remind everyone he was there. "Let me continue, and that may answer some of your questions. I do not propose annexing Artylia unilaterally. Artylia shall remain Artylia. It shall be run by a council of lords with a representative of the Berushese throne as the head."

The lords started talking amongst themselves and Cyrus gave them a moment to discuss it. "What about taxes," spoke up Lord Modyn. "Are you going to require a tribute?"

"Right now you cannot afford it! The people in the capital are starving. Uriya has squandered your resources. It may be that you will need a loan from your island colony to get through the winter. Too many fields lie fallow. This first year is probationary. No tribute will be required.

"It is my hope, that under our guidance, this kingdom will become prosperous and our partnership will be mutually beneficial. It will be to our advantage to have a neighbor who respects our borders, and its own, and keeps our enemies at bay. A tribute to repay our expenses and maintain our oversight will be discussed at that time."

"What about the land west of the Eryn?" asked another lord.

"That land will become part of Berush. The Eryn

will be the new border."

"So, we won't have a king?"

"Not for the time being. Any decisions of that nature will be made by the council, with the approval of Berush."

This was an entirely new concept for Artylia. Berushese kings had been calling councils for generations, involving tribal leaders and heads of clans in much of the decision making. Artylian kings had always ruled independently of their subjects. The treaty Artylia had with their island colony gave the islanders more freedom than citizens on the mainland.

Cyrus, Yarin and Darius had discussed at length various options for governing Artylia. They agreed that the country was so large, that it would be difficult to govern without cooperation from the lords, and Cyrus did not want to commit his army to spending years away from home to rule by force. Some of them would have to anyway, but not all. Involving the lords in ruling by council was the best option. It just remained to be seen if they would agree.

"I will give you a day to discuss it, and to ask any questions you might have, and then we will take a vote on this proposal."

"And if we do not agree?" asked Cayern.

"You would need to come up with an alternate proposal that would be agreeable to all present, including Berush."

"What have you done with Uriya?" Lord Dolyn wanted to know.

Cyrus smiled. "I am surprised that was not the first question asked. He has signed, as you have seen, articles of abdication in favor of myself. Lord Byrd was a witness."

"But where is he?"

"He has retired from public life with the assurance that he will be well supplied with wine and will be able to continue to take his daily bath at the seashore unencumbered by the affairs of state. Anyone who wishes may see him." No one wished. They were all happy enough to see him go away. All except for Cayern and a few others who had been lax in their responsibilities and were now going to be held to higher standards.

Cyrus dismissed the assembly, and the lords broke into smaller groups discussing what they had heard. Darius watched with admiration as his brother walked around the room listening to people's stories, answering questions and showing genuine interest in their concerns. No one could work a room like Cyrus. He could accomplish more with his words than Darius could with a sword. Before it was time for dinner, he had most of the country's future leaders excited about the direction they were headed.

The next day, when they gathered for a vote, the lords unanimously approved a government by council under the leadership of Berush. Even Lord Cayern had been convinced when he had been unable to come up with a way to get out of it. The three thousand soldiers in and around the capital may also have been a deciding factor. Once that was decided, they had to really get down to work and iron out all the details.

Darius left Effan on duty in the hall and made his escape. He needed something more active to do. He had already whipped the castle guards into shape and had them fulfilling their duties like Berushese guards were expected to do. The port was running smoothly and Cyrus had made sure the people in the city were provided with food. He had sent those without work into Cayern's fields to hay them in trade for the grain Lord Byrd and others had provided over the last few days. The hay would go to those who had cattle, and the cattle could be used to reimburse Byrd or be traded for more grain for those in the city to eat. This sharing and trading of resources was something any good king would have facilitated, but Uriya did not even try to manage his resources.

Darius had gone to see Uriya at Yarin's request. Yarin could not help but notice Darius' haunted look, and he felt that meeting Uriya might offer him some resolution. He hadn't wanted to, not if he couldn't beat him and throw him in the cell Yarin had inhabited. But when he went and saw for himself what a weak mind he had, he was able to let some of his anger go. Cyrus had known it would be useless to exact revenge from someone with so little understanding. When the former king tried to get Darius to model his hats, he had to leave. He could only be angry that Uriya's subjects had put up with him for so long.

Now Darius was ready to move on. Cyrus didn't really need him here anymore. He preferred to be on patrol, pushing the limits of his horse and his own body, fighting enemies with a sword, not diplomacy. Cyrus lived for this type of mental challenge. Darius busied himself listening to reports from the patrols, checking on the guards and finalizing plans to send their army home in waves. It was very expensive to feed so many men away from home.

Several hundred soldiers would remain at the capital for the next year, at least, but they were taking volunteers for those posts. Some of them would be integrated with the navy, some would make regular rounds of the different holdings to make sure the lords were keeping up their end of the agreement, and some would be keeping order in the city and protecting the Berushese representative. Cyrus had confided to Darius that he would give Tomus that responsibility. Onia was already on her way to join her husband in the castle at Letyna. Darius was relieved. He had been afraid Cyrus would want him to do it.

At the end of the day, Darius was walking along the wall of the castle keep, looking back toward Berush. Cyrus came to find him. "You are missing home, brother?"

"I am chaffing from inaction. I miss riding in the sand."

"Well, I bring you an occupation. A request for a favor, really."

"What is it?" Darius wasn't sure he wanted to know.

"You know of Artylia's island colony, Lyliana?"

"Yeeees."

"Well, I need a representative to sail there and inform them of what has passed, and assure them that we intend to honor the treaty existing between them and Artylia. The island is very prosperous, and Artylia benefits greatly from the tribute they send. They only ask that the navy continue to protect them from Cerecian pirates. It is to Artylia's advantage to maintain the fleet for its own protection anyway, so this is not a difficult obligation to fulfill. We want to continue this relationship."

"Cyrus, you know I'm no good at that sort of thing. There has to be someone else you can send."

"Tomus will be busy here with me. I have to be here to help him get started, so I cannot go myself. Tarin is ruling for me in Berush, and Varus, with the help of his captain, is implementing our government with the Artylian mountain tribes. I am thinking of making him the permanent governor there, if he does well. Even if they were not already busy, I would not want to send any of those young men without knowing exactly what they are getting into. We have never sent an emissary to Lyliana. If I send you, I know that you have the experience to deal with whatever fate throws your way."

"Except diplomacy."

"You can take Yarin with you. The healer assures me he can handle the journey. I will be here until you get back, then I will leave Yarin to help Tomus."

"You really want me to do this?"

"I need you to do it."

"When would you need me to leave?"

"As soon as possible."

There were several capable captains who could oversee the army while he was gone, so he couldn't use that as an excuse. "I can be ready in two days. The abandoned warship in the harbor has been refitted, and we can take it and maybe one other."

"Good." Cyrus turned and watched the sun set behind the mountains. His thoughts turned home to the rest of his family. After they had taken the mountains, he had sent Sashia home. It would be several weeks, maybe months before he felt Artylia was stable enough for him to return. He knew how Darius felt.

There was one other thing he needed to bring up with Darius because no one else would dare talk to him about it. "I hear you are having night terrors."

Darius tensed. Of course he was. All soldiers had them from time to time. He was not in the habit of giving Cyrus excuses or arguing with him, however. "Yes," was all he replied, through clenched teeth. He didn't wonder how his brother knew. He always knew everything.

"I worry about you sometimes, Darius. You need to find some peace, some happiness. Your whole life you have served others, first our father, and now me. I could not have succeeded as king without you by my side. But you are now thirty-four years old. It is time for you to raise a family of your own. Do something for yourself."

Darius scoffed. "No woman could put up with me as a husband."

"Maybe most women could not. You only need to find one. Not everyone has to have two, like me." Cyrus had planted his seed. Now he just let it take hold. "Use this journey to the island to clear your head. Consider what I have said. Perhaps you will actually enjoy the sea air, or the beauty of the island. I hear the land there is even more lush and fertile than Artylia. Maybe you can find some rest. Return with a new perspective and tell me what you wish to do. Whatever is in my power to do for you, I will do it," and with that, he left Darius alone.

Darius was stirred by his brother's words. What did he really want in order to be happy? He didn't know. He turned his gaze from the mountains to look at the sea. The last rays of the sun sparkled on the water. Its vast emptiness had a numbing effect on his senses. Maybe a change would be good for him, he thought. He would keep an open mind.

CHAPTER FOUR

Three days later Darius departed the harbor, taking two warships laden with supplies. It had taken an extra day to prepare the ships to transport horses for Darius and his men. The prince refused to travel without a Berushese horse who would know how to respond to his directions. Stalls had to be built and special slings installed to support the horses and keep them from falling with the waves.

Each ship had a hand-picked crew. Darius chose Berushese captains and archers with a few Artylian sailors who were familiar with the ships. Effan and Yarin came, of course, and over two dozen of Darius' own men who spoke Artylian fluently. His brother had also insisted he take a manservant. Darius had never had use for one before, but Cyrus assured him a personal valet would be of benefit in a strange castle.

Cyrus had also sent a letter on a merchant vessel two days before to give the island notice that they were coming. Darius would put in at the island's northern port, in Lord Kirdyn's domain, and decide from there how to proceed. Cyrus wanted him to tour the island and speak to all the lords and return to give him a full report. He had also given Darius complete authority to make decisions regarding the island, appointing him as governor there now that Varus was installed in the mountain territory. Cyrus only stipulated that he needed to listen to Yarin's advice.

The weather was clear and the wind was blowing from the southeast. The captain assured Darius that they would arrive by afternoon the next day. The prince had made sure Yarin had a comfortable chair on deck under an awning. Due to the horses, the air below decks was not the best for someone still recovering from malnutrition.

Darius had been worried he would feel confined on the ship, but the speed at which they cut through the waves was almost as good as riding a horse. Walking on a sea-going vessel was harder to get the hang of than a placid river barge, but he managed better than most of the soldiers and did not get sick. He slept peacefully in his bunk, without dreams, lulled by the waves.

True to his word, the captain sailed them into the island's northern harbor by mid-afternoon. Longboats were ready to meet them and guide them to a large dock where they would be able to unload the horses. Only one of the warships would be able to unload at a time, and Darius expected to stay with Kirdyn for a couple of days, at least, while all that was sorted out. As soon as the ship was secured and the gangplank in place, Darius and Yarin disembarked and went to greet Lord Kirdyn, who was at the docks to meet them.

Kirdyn was a rotund, jolly looking man a little older than Cyrus, maybe forty-five, but not as physically fit. His light brown hair and beard showed a few streaks of gray. He bowed obsequiously as Darius approached.

"Greetings, Prince Darius. It is an honor to meet you. It has been some time since someone of your eminence has graced our shores. Please, come to my castle to refresh yourself. I am eager to hear news of all that has happened in Artylia."

"Thank you, Lord Kirdyn. I am just as eager to become acquainted with your beautiful island and its people," and he gave a slight bow in return, inwardly chaffing at the role he had to play. Yarin gave him an amused glance.

His host led them up to the castle overlooking the port. They went on foot, as Yarin declined a cart. He felt walking would be more comfortable than being jostled around in a wagon.

"This is one of my smaller castles," Kirdyn explained as they passed through the gate, "but it will have room enough for all your men and horses. It is called The Aerie because of the winged lizards that nest in the rocks below. I have another, much greater one, up the river. My holding is the largest on the island," he boasted.

He led them to a large suite of rooms overlooking the harbor. "From here you will be able to see the sun set over the sea. It is quite a beautiful sight. Much different than a sunrise." Darius felt he was trying to deprecate the view from the Artylian capital. "Please take your ease, and then join me for dinner." He left them alone to rest.

Darius' manservant, Eshan would join them shortly with their luggage, and Effan would seek him out as soon as the men were settled in the barracks. Darius laid down on the soft, down mattress of the four-poster bed and sank several inches into it.

Kirdyn seemed to love his luxury. "I do not know if I can do this, Yarin."

"My lord, you can do anything you put your mind to, as you have always done." Darius sighed and steeled himself for a tiring dinner of conversation with Kirdyn.

Fortunately, his host was not really a bad sort. He laughed and joked and regaled the prince with his entire family history, but with many humorous anecdotes. The hall of the harbor castle was small but very finely furnished. Tapestries adorned the walls and ornately carved chairs were set at the high table. Kirdyn and Darius' men ate in shifts since there were not many seats. Darius explained that Cyrus wanted to continue to honor the island's current arrangement with Artylia and Kirdyn was perfectly satisfied with his assurances.

"How do you suggest I proceed to tour the island from here?"

"Well, it will take more than a day's ride to pass through my lands," he said with satisfaction. "I suggest we travel east, when your ships are unloaded, to my primary residence. From there you may travel south or north around the mountains to see the rest of the island."

Darius agreed to this plan, and Kirdyn promised to send out riders to his neighbors to expect the prince's visit. The next day, Kirdyn showed him all around the port. Then they went over Kirdyn's record of tributes and his crop yields. He seemed anxious to prove to the new governor that he was not derelict in his duties. At every opportunity he drew distinctions between himself and the mainlanders. Darius suspected he had heard something about the ultimatum Cyrus had given the Artylian lords.

And it was true; the island did seem to be very

prosperous. Darius had not realized how much trade his own country did with them. Still, by the end of the day he was glad to retire to the quiet of his own room.

Out of the window, just before sunset, Darius caught sight of one of the winged lizards returning to the cliffs. About the size of a seagull, it flew by with a small fish in its mouth. He wished he could take one back for his nieces and nephews to add to their menagerie. It was just one of several species of animal reportedly found only on Lyliana.

The following morning, Darius and his men set out with Kirdyn to ride to the other end of his land. Kirdyn sat on an elaborate, cushioned saddle and rode very slowly, talking the entire way. He had a surprisingly small guard, only three men. Every field they passed was full of workers. Kirdyn waved benevolently to his subjects as they passed. Their faces showed surprise, and they raised their hands tentatively in return, leading Darius to surmise that it was a show for his benefit. Kirdyn was anxious to appear in a good light.

Other than his obsequiousness, there really was no fault to be found. His holding appeared to be in good order, and his fields were flourishing. Many of the crops were plants that Darius had never seen growing before, only heard of, or eaten in the form of a flour or other end product. They stopped periodically to water the horses. The road to Kirdyn's seat followed the river closely. They ate in the saddle to save time since they were traveling so slowly.

In the last light of the day, they arrived at the castle. It was, indeed, much larger than the one at the harbor, a tall, square keep with large stone walls and two watch towers. The river flowed around the front of it to create a moat. It was very impressive, a fortress really, and very practical, but something in the aesthetics was lacking.

The drawbridge was down in expectation of their arrival, and Kirdyn's family was waiting in an inner ward to greet them. Lord Kirdyn introduced his wife and children to Darius and his party. His family was as rotund and jolly as himself, and his children were loud and boisterous.

Kirdyn picked up one of his youngest progeny. "These are my joy! They help me keep my vim and vigor! You have to be on your toes around this bunch!" he declared. Darius nodded in agreement as two of the youngsters began chasing each other through the adults' legs.

Dinner here was noisy, but Kirdyn didn't seem to mind the ruckus. After everyone had eaten, Darius asked Kirdyn if he could go over some maps with him, and they retired to another room with Yarin and Effan accompanying them. Darius spread out his map of the island, and Kirdyn pointed out his neighbors. "This is the nearest holding to mine, a day's journey southeast."

"Who is the lord of those lands?"

"Lady!" said Kirdyn, enjoying the surprise on the prince's face. "Lady Eemya. Her father was not blessed with an abundance of heirs, as I am. Her husband was lord for a while, officially, but she really ran things. She's a widow now, managing it by herself. No children."

"How is she as a neighbor?"

"Oh, she has some strange ideas, but I have had no real problems with her. Had to chase a couple of her men off my lands recently, though. They told me they were map-making, but that did not sound very plausible to me, so I sent them back. What she thinks she needs a map of my lands for, I have no idea."

Darius filed this information away so he could inquire about it later. "So that is where you suggest I head next?"

"If you went the other way, you'd have to spend a night camping out in the open," he shrugged. "From Lady Eemya's castle there are several holdings within a day's ride. You could see the entire southern half of the island and sleep with a roof over your head."

Darius did not at all mind sleeping outdoors, but he did want to accomplish his tour as quickly and efficiently as possible. Yarin and Effan approved of Kirdyn's plan as well, so they adjourned agreeing to travel the southern route around the mountains beginning the next morning.

∞∞∞

A fine, misty rain kept them cool and damp the next morning. One of Kirdyn's men rode with them to the edge of his lands to start them on their way. The path from there, he assured them, would take them straight to their destination. The weather kept everyone indoors, so they encountered few people on the road.

In the afternoon the mist finally began to clear, and in a few more hours it had completely dispersed, enabling them to catch a view of Lady Eemya's castle as they approached. This castle was unlike any that Darius had ever seen. He knew the geology on the island was different from the mainland due to some ancient volcanic activity, but he was still surprised at the color of the castle.

Built at the foot of the northern end of the mountains, and protected in the rear by a sheer cliff, the castle was constructed almost entirely of blue stone. Most of it was bluish-gray, but some of the stones were very bright. The cliff behind seemed to be composed of the same rock and was probably where it was mined. The brightest blues lined the window arches and the gate.

It was smaller than Kirdyn's, but much more beautiful. It had an artistic asymmetry that gave it added interest. The keep was not in the center, but to the back right of the castle, and there were three towers, all of different heights. There was no moat, but the barbican boasted a strong wooden door and portcullis. The crenellations on the battlements were perfectly proportioned and embellished with more colorful agate.

According to the map, the castle was named Freosyd. Yarin had explained it was derived from an Artylian word meaning 'frozen in time or space.' It was in reference to the blue stones that looked like solid water. A seasoned sergeant-at-arms met them at the gate.

"Prince Darius of Berush, emissary of Artylia, requests admittance," announced Effan. The man bowed. "Please enter. Lady Eemya is expecting you."

She might be expecting him, but whatever Darius was expecting, what he found was entirely different. The word 'widow' had conjured an image of someone middle-aged, gray and careworn. The woman that he saw waiting on the steps of the keep was the most beautiful woman he had ever seen. Her hair was a light red, with glints of gold, piled high on top of her head. Her emerald green eyes and pale skin reminded him of an oasis in the desert. The dress she wore was a different style than the women of either Artylia or Berush, but it suited her perfectly. Darius could not tear his eyes away from her. He was speechless.

Yarin noticed his predicament and dismounted with some effort. The long days of riding were difficult for him. He went to hold Darius' horse. "My lord," he prodded gently. Darius woke up and alighted from his horse. The red haze of anger and bloodlust covered his eyes, but this time with a different objective. "Tread lightly," Yarin's warning fell on deaf ears.

With wooden feet, he walked over to stand in front of the lady. "My lady, it is a pleasure to meet you," he inclined his head slightly.

"Prince Darius, it is an honor to have you on our island. I hope you will feel welcome here," she beckoned to a handsome young man who quickly came to her side. "This is Stelan, the captain of my guard. He can see to your men. Dinner is ready in the hall, if you are hungry, or would you like to see your rooms first?" she spoke Artylian with a lilting, musical rhythm that was common among the islanders, and she seemed completely oblivious of the effect she was having on the prince.

Darius knew the men would be hungry, so he opted for dinner first. He himself was unable to leave the lady's side. Servants had come to see to the horses, and Captain Stelan was directing the men to the barracks to stow their packs, then they would be free to join him in the hall. He and Yarin followed Lady Eemya inside.

The great hall took up most of the first floor of the keep. The kitchen and laundry were in a separate, but connected building. Doors on each side of the hall led into corridors with smaller rooms and stairs to the next floor. The walls and floor of the hall were embedded with mosaics of black and blue stones. A warm fire blazed in the hearth to chase away the chill of the morning's rain. Darius noticed none of this.

As they took their seats, Eemya asked him what he thought of the island so far, and he replied, not knowing what he said. She must have found him somewhat dull, because she addressed herself to Yarin on her other side. He explained about the political situation in Artylia, and the status of the treaty, saving Darius from the effort. By the end of the meal, he could stand it no longer, and heard his own voice speaking words against his better judgement.

"My lady, the moment I laid eyes on you, your beauty cast a spell over me. I would be pleased if you would join me in my rooms this evening."

Lady Eemya's mouth dropped open, and she appeared nonplussed. "I am sorry, my lord, but that would not be seemly," she stammered.

Darius frowned. He had to have this woman, but he was very out of practice with the more courtly forms of pursuit. Before he could say more, the lady stood up.

"Good night, my lord." Eemya motioned to a man hovering nearby. "My steward, Jayred, will show you to your rooms."

"I would much prefer that you show me," he said with a disarming grin. Eemya ignored him and walked imperiously away, exiting the hall by a side door. Darius's eyes burned after her.

After giving instructions to Effan, he and Yarin followed the steward to his rooms and assured him they were satisfactory. His manservant, Eshan, had already begun arranging his things in the bedroom. Yarin, Effan and Eshan would be sleeping in the waiting room next to it. In a keep such as this one, there was little room for guests other than the floor of the hall, and only the most prominent visitors had a room to themselves. Even the barracks were minimal, but at least everyone could find a dry place to sleep with a roof over their heads.

Darius, however, was unable to rid himself of the

lady's image. He was not used to being denied. "I'm going to stretch my legs a bit. Wait for me here." Eshan, an observant young man, gave a knowing smile. Yarin, however, had a frown, and his lips were drawn into a thin line of disapproval.

Darius strolled back down to the hall and across to the door Lady Eemya had passed through. He motioned with his head for one of his men to follow. The door led to another corridor, and he heard Eemya's melodic voice floating down the hallway. The steward replied, and Darius saw him exit a door at the other end of the corridor and disappear through an arch at the other end.

"The lady and I have business to discuss," he said to his officer. "Make sure we are not disturbed." This was said in a tone that left no doubt as to what would happen to the soldier if he failed to follow directions.

Darius opened the door, closing it firmly behind him. He beheld Eemya sitting at a desk, pouring over some papers. Candlelight glinted off of her shiny red hair, and her skin looked soft and white. At his entrance she looked up, and a momentary expression of fear was immediately replaced by one of perturbation.

"Yes, my lord?" she rose with barely disguised frustration. "Were your accommodations not to your liking?"

"They were not, since you refused to accompany me, but our 'business' can be conducted here, as easily as anywhere else," and he quickly strode across the room and caught her by the wrist. His other arm went around her waist and he pulled her to him and attempted to kiss her.

She turned her head, and his lips brushed her cheek, his hot breath blowing in her ear. She felt sickened and struggled to get away, kicking at his shins. "Let me go! I'll scream!" and as she sucked in breath to follow through with her threat, he pushed her away, and she stumbled into the wall. She stood there trembling, leaning against the wall for support and contemplated him, her mind working furiously. Much as she wanted to rub her throbbing wrist, she refused to give him the satisfaction of showing pain.

With slow, deliberate footsteps, he walked over to her and put his hands on the wall on either side of her. His hairy face was inches from hers. She considered attempting to thrust her dagger into his heart, but the consequences of such an action could be direr for her subjects than anything that could happen to herself.

"You realize," he menaced, "you are in thrall to me. I can easily remove you from this position and appoint someone else lord here. I control these lands now, and you will do as I say if you know what's best for you and your people."

Eemya gasped. "If I give in to you in this, what else must I give in to? And when you grow tired of me, then what?" She pause to draw a shaky breath, "No, I will govern on my terms or not at all. Either kill me now and ravish my dead body, or deal with me fairly and my people and I will serve you willingly." She drew her dagger and held the hilt up to him as proof of her words.

Her words momentarily shocked him out of his passion and he took a step back. He gazed at her, bewildered, as if seeing her for the first time. In her eyes he saw no fear, only determination and resignation. He had never killed a woman, certainly never made love to a dead one, and didn't intend to start doing either. Most women, even if reluctant at first, were easily persuaded to receive his advances. Just as often, the women had been the ones pursuing him. None of them had held his attention for long, however, and he couldn't remember wanting another woman, as much as he wanted this one, for quite some time. Having never been in this situation, he was not sure how to proceed. As he hesitated, she took the opportunity to drive her point home.

"Your highness, you don't have the men to depose every lord on the island and maintain power on the mainland. Neither can Lord Kirdyn hold it for you if the rest of the lords unite against him. You need allies here. You need peace and stability." She was breathing heavily, but with great effort was able to speak evenly and persuasively.

"This island can produce a wealth of resources and tax revenue if managed properly. Prosperity cannot be achieved if you alienate and fight with everyone instead of bringing them to your side. You will end up with the island going to war to become independent of Artylia. If you force me and do not kill me, I will ensure that it happens!"

Darius licked his lips as her argument sunk in. Her logic was cooling his ardor. Part of him knew she was right. Yarin had been telling him the same thing the whole way here. He had not brought a conquering force with him, merely a diplomatic one. After having just won control of Artylia, Cyrus would hardly be pleased if he started a war with the island by losing sight of his purpose. But neither could he let people get away with defying him. He also did not expect to have this trouble with any of the other lords. They were men.

No answer was forthcoming that would extricate him from this situation with dignity, and he found his ire rising again. "Very well. I will consider your words. We will speak more of it tomorrow," and he stalked out without a backward glance.

Eemya let out her breath in a whoosh. Her knees buckled under her and she sank to the floor. The dagger clattered on the wood at her feet. Relieved, she cried like she had not cried since she lost her father.

CHAPTER FIVE

Darius stalked down the corridor. The glare he gave his man as he left the room spoke more than any words, and the soldier scurried away from him back into the hall. The man didn't know how the lady had gotten the better of the prince, but he did not want to be the next object of his lord's wrath. Darius knew attempting to sleep would be futile, so instead of returning to his rooms, he made his way up to the wall-walk.

Avoiding the guards, he found a quiet stretch of the wall and stood staring out into the night. The stars and moon were very bright, and standing away from the torches he could easily see the lay of the land. A cool, night breeze washed over him and soothed his nerves.

His men would all know the truth by the morning. Word spread quickly. He would lose face with them if he let this affront pass without reprisal. But the lady was right. He needed to consider the consequences of his actions carefully. He had never before debased himself by using brute force with a woman. How could he persuade her to submit to him willingly? Everyone had a weak spot. He just needed to find hers.

He turned away from the wall and faced the courtyard. A few guards were on duty, but otherwise, it was fairly quiet. A couple of servants bustled about, carrying away the few remains of the dinner to the hog pen and drawing water to wash in. The young captain of the guard exited the keep and made his way to the barracks. With his light, blond hair, blue eyes, and muscular physique, the boy could pose for a painting of male perfection.

Darius had seen the look of adoration the young man had given his lady. She obviously cared about her subjects. Did she perhaps return the captain's feelings? He felt a hot stab of jealously at the possibility. His mouth set in a cruel, hard line as his mind formulated a plan. He made his way back to his quarters to put it into action.

∞∞∞

The next morning, breakfast was brought to him in his rooms. Servants and lower ranked members of the household got theirs in the hall as their duties allowed. When he inquired as to Lady Eemya's plans for the day, he was informed that she was preparing to ride out to review the state of the crops, and he was welcome to accompany her. Darius suspected she was trying to steer him back to his official purpose.

Yarin, the night before, had begged him as well, to let her go and move on to the next holding. Even his captain appeared reluctant to follow through on his lord's plan, but he did not argue. Darius had plenty of men who were happy to do whatever he asked, and his captain had delegated the task to two of his coarser, but reliable soldiers.

Darius felt a slight twinge of doubt as he entered the courtyard and saw Eemya, tall and stately, holding the reins of her chestnut mare. Her head was shaded by a wide-brimmed hat, held on with a scarf that covered her hair and neck. The green of her riding habit brought out the color of her eyes. She stroked the mare's nose and spoke to it softly. Then she turned and looked at him, and his desire came flooding back. He walked forward to meet her.

"Good morning, my lord. I trust you slept well." The woman had nerves of steel, to be able to act like nothing had happened, he thought. Her face was impassive. "Are you ready to survey your holdings?" she continued.

"Unfortunately, my lady, there is a grave matter that needs attention." He signaled to two of his men who grabbed Captain Stelan by the arms and threw him roughly at their feet. Lady Eemya's men put their hands on their swords, but the prince's men remained nonchalant. The lady held her men back with a hand gesture.

"What nonsense is this?" she demanded.

"Your young captain is a thief. The purses of my men have been rifled, and several of their trinkets, and more coins than one person should have, were found in his belongings." At this statement one of the prince's men also threw down a purse, which spilled its contents in the dirt in front of them. "You have heard, no doubt, what we do to thieves in Berush."

The tension in the air felt like the skin-prickling moment before a lightning strike. Lady Eemya's men gaped in outrage at this obviously trumped-up charge, but defying the prince and his men could mean death for all of them as they were outnumbered and grossly outmatched. They watched their lady to see what she would do, but she stood straight as a pole, unmoving.

Eemya gazed at Stelan, who was being kept on his knees by the rough hands of the prince's men. Her face was drained of color, and her hands were balled into fists. Darius also looked at her to gauge her reaction. He could not interpret what her exact emotions were for the captain, but he could see her mind straining to find a possible escape from his trap. He almost felt sorry for her. Almost.

Stelan, surprisingly made no protest. Along with everyone else, he knew that this scene was more than what it appeared. He looked at his lady, and then at the prince, and his face blanched as he realized the dilemma which faced her. As well as he could, he straightened his back and held his head high in defiance, trying to indicate to her that she should not give in and that he was ready to die for her if necessary.

All this Eemya knew and observed unconsciously, as her brain was searching frantically for a solution. Suddenly her chin snapped up, and she turned brightly to the prince. "I have indeed, your highness, heard many things that are done in your country. We have been in the habit of doing things differently here. Perhaps, if we take some time to confer, we can come up with a compromise. My lord, would you have your men escort Stelan to the guard room?

"Jayred, show them the way, and assign two men to guard him until this matter has been decided," she gave Jayred a look that told him she meant two of our men. Stelan obeyed without protest. The tone of her speech had given him hope that she had found a way out.

"My lord, if you would follow me?" she gestured

back into the castle. Darius gave her a slight, mocking bow of the head, and followed her with an amused expression. What did she think she could do? He knew he was only going to give her one way out.

She led him back to her office, the scene of the previous night's encounter. He closed the door, as the evening before, but she did not beg or plead as he had hoped. She removed her hat and cloak and threw them angrily down on her chair, then turned and faced him with her hands on her hips.

"Firstly, you should know, that boy you accused is the youngest son of Lord Yoused, whose holdings are nearly equal to those of Kirdyn's." Darius had not known this, and he began to feel unsure of the success of his scheme. Eemya continued, "furthermore, if you cut off his son's hand, as is your tradition, I will send it to his father by the fastest horse and see that it is set before him before the day is out! He will be none too pleased."

Eemya paused to let this sink into the prince's thick skull. He had to have some wit in there somewhere, she thought, or he could not have been successful for this long. "For the reasons I set before you last night, war with the island cannot be a viable option for you at this time, and that is what will happen if you persist with this madness."

Darius began to feel a chill covering his heart. It was the chill of defeat. He had never felt it before, but he started to understand that he might not be able to get what he wanted out of this situation. It was a completely foreign feeling for him, and he was at a loss for what to do or say.

Fortunately, or unfortunately, the lady was still not finished. She crossed her arms as she continued. "Now, I will not support the island going to war, except as a last resort," she asserted firmly.

"However, I cannot let you continue to harass and threaten my subjects. Therefore, we must reach some sort of accord." Darius viewed her skeptically. What could she possibly say that would persuade him? "Please, my lord," she softened her voice soothingly and motioned toward a chair, "please take a seat and listen to my proposal."

His legs moved and he sat, in spite of himself, as though under her spell. Somewhere in the back of his mind, he realized he had greatly underestimated her. Eemya sat in her chair and leaned forward, resting her arms on the desk. In an earnest voice, she proceeded to offer an absolutely outrageous proposition.

"I can see that your attraction for me is not something that will be easily overcome. I will offer you the opportunity to woo me properly, and make me attracted to you. If you can succeed in making me desire you, then I am yours, but I have to say 'I want you.' In return for this opportunity, you must leave my people alone."

Her words nearly knocked Darius backward out of his chair. He did not see this coming. He opened his mouth and nothing came out. Then, finally, he barked out a laugh. "You are a woman of exceptional cunning! What are you, one of the magi?"

Eemya continued to look at him unblinking, and did not respond to his outburst. She waited patiently for him to think about it and give her a true answer. He took a few moments to study her in silence, stroking his beard.

What would it be like to make love to this woman if she desired him equally? It made his head spin to think of it. Could he possibly accomplish it? His self-confidence had already taken a beating at her hands. Everything he wanted had come to him too easily for too long. He had an inkling that he would have to work harder for this than he had for anything in his life. Would she be worth it? He had a feeling she would.

Darius pointed a finger at her. "You do not think I can do it." A tell-tale twitch appeared in the corner of her mouth. "How much time do you give me?"

"Oh, I don't think there needs to be any time constraint," she waved her hand dismissively and leaned back into her seat. She raised one eyebrow and almost smirked, "The opportunity will be rescinded only if you choose to woo another woman."

There it was. She didn't think he could even persist with her long enough to win her without turning elsewhere for solace. "What about you?" he jerked his chin at her.

She understood his vague question and responded, "It's a little different for me. I can't help it if men try to woo me, *obviously*. But I promise not to encourage or respond to them until such time as I relent or you recant."

Darius was still considering. The uniqueness of the proposition was beginning to invigorate him. For the first time, facing something he greatly yearned for, he had a doubt of his success. But he knew he had to try. "Very well, I accept your challenge."

"And my people?"

"I will not use them as pawns in this game, regardless of the outcome."

"Thank you, my lord," she said sincerely, and offered him her hand. To her surprise, he took it and kissed it tenderly and gave her his arm to lead her out.

∞∞∞

Out in the courtyard, the entire population of the castle waited anxiously for the prince and Lady Eemya to return. When they came out, both smiling, both sides were perplexed. Each side had expected one of the two to come out looking like a thundercloud. Each faction hoped it was the leader of the other who would appear so. But both smiling? What could it mean? Those of the prince's men who thought highly of his prowess might read the wrong thing into it, but most thought such a quick change of heart was an impossibility.

Darius was grinning widely, and Lady Eemya rubbed her hands together gleefully as she waited for the prince's horse to be saddled. She turned to the prince and said low enough that only he could hear, "Stelan?" tucking her scarf back around her hat as she spoke.

"Oh, yes." Bother. He had forgotten about him. "Effan," he called loudly to his captain for everyone's benefit, "New evidence has come to light. Captain Stelan is to be released. Please see that the misplaced items are returned to their owners."

With that, he mounted his horse, and that was all the satisfaction the onlookers would receive. Darius appreciated, though, that she let him be the voice of authority in the matter. She had the most calculating mind he had ever encountered. He suspected that she was capable of being as devious as himself, but she was more discriminating in her use of power. Or more wise.

He reigned in his horse, ready to follow Lady Eemya out the gate. She mounted her horse and the mare pranced as she led her to the prince's side. "Are you now ready to view your holdings, my lord?" "Absolutely. Lead the way, my lady."

They rode mostly in silence, a few select men from

each party accompanying them. Darius frequently stole glances at Lady Eemya. Soon, however, the beauty of the day cried for his attention, and he soaked in the bright sun, clear, blue sky and green fields.

The fields really were impressive. Never had he seen such neat rows and fields free of weeds. Everywhere was bounty. There was evidence of sophisticated irrigation as well.

Most interesting of all, were the farmers themselves. Everywhere they rode, the workers were laboring industriously. As soon as they saw the procession, they spontaneously stopped and waved, or came running to line the road. They bowed and curtsied, happy and excited to see their lady. She stopped to talk with each one and inquire about their progress.

Then she would introduce Darius as the new prince regent of Artylia, and acting governor, come to inspect the island. He was welcomed by one and all, and the farmers brought offerings of fresh produce. The women brought out bread, boiled eggs and fresh cheese. One man who owned a peach orchard was so disappointed that his peaches were not yet ripe, that he asked them to wait while he ran back to his house. He returned with a small pot of peach preserves, made by his wife, and offered them to the prince. Darius was humbled by the man's generosity and eagerness to please.

Around lunchtime, they arrived at a small village, and the people brought the tables and stools out of their houses and spread out a feast for them. Eemya and her men emptied their saddlebags of the offerings received on the way and added it to the abundance. Everyone laughed and talked, and each member of the village came and bowed to the prince and welcomed him to the island. A couple of children recited poems, and he marveled at their education.

Someone brought out a flute, and the children joined hands in a dance. Eemya entered the circle and danced with them. Some of her hair escaped from her scarf, and her cheeks were flushed. Darius had never seen such an entrancing sight.

One of the village elders had been observing the prince and noticed his interest in the lady. He rose and walked slowly, using a cane, over to the table where the king sat. "My name is Masyn, your highness," he bowed low, leaning on his stick, "may I sit with you?"

"Please," Darius waved at a stool, curious and surprised at the presumption by an Artylian. They generally had more formal distinctions in rank than Berush where Darius interacted with all of Cyrus' subjects equally. Those in Lady Eemya's domain were very different from what he had observed in the rest of Artylia. He was going to have to play along if he had any hope of changing her mind about him. The man sat down next to him, but strangely did not speak. He merely observed the activity, as the prince had been doing.

Darius was very good at reading people and understood what he was about. "So," he gave the man an opening to speak his mind, "tell me about her. How does she do it?"

The elder seemed unperturbed that the prince had read his thoughts. "She is a gift to the world. There is no one like her. Her father was a just and fair man, but strong, and she was his only child. He brought her up the same way, to lead with firmness and compassion. She has put in place a system of crop management that has made this holding the most profitable on the island by the acre," he said proudly.

"How does that work?"

"She has us keeping records on the weather, the success of various crops, the best times and methods of planting. Each village is responsible for designating who will grow which crops each year to prevent depleting the nutrients in the soil. We have discovered that some crops grow best when they are planted together with another variety of vegetable."

He paused for a moment. "Last winter, her master farmers predicted that the spring would come late, so we delayed planting for three weeks. We had six inches of snow, and other holdings lost much of their seed and had to replant, while we lost nothing."

"You keep records? So some of you can read and write?"

"Most of us can read and write. Ten or twelve years back, my lady called one or two elders from each village, those of us who had a hard time keeping up with field labor," he raised his cane, "to the manor to learn letters and calculating. Then she sent us back to teach our villages. Every village has at least one elder, or scribe, who keeps the town records and passes on his learning. Everyone studies in the winter months, and the rest of the time I teach the young ones who are too little to help in the field all day. It has been a great joy."

Darius was amazed. The farmers were planning together, studying like scholars and scribes, and educating the children. Most leaders would be afraid that by educating the populace they would become too independent. Every king he knew of, even Cyrus, to some extent, had maintained control by centralizing his knowledge and power and keeping it for himself.

It would have been a grave mistake to remove Lady Eemya from her position. No one else could come in and do what she was doing. Very likely it would cause a rebellion if he appointed a heavy-handed representative who would take away all the freedoms these people had. If the rest of the island were like this, Cyrus would indeed find it profitable to maintain the relationship. To raze the place to the ground over a woman would be a huge loss. But so would be the loss of this woman. Somehow, he had to avoid losing either.

Darius remembered she was a widow, but as yet, he had heard no mention of her husband other than Kirdyn's brief appraisal. He asked the old man about him.

"Ah, he was a wise man, and did not stand in her way," and he closed his mouth as if it was not his place to say more. Darius gathered from that that her husband hadn't been good for much, which agreed with what he had already heard.

"What do the other lords think of her methods?"

"Oh, most of them have copied some of the simpler innovations, like crop rotation, if they had not hit upon something similar already. They are reluctant to give any of the decision making over to the common people, or teach them to read. Except Lord Yoused. The lame young man sitting at yonder table was sent here to copy our records and learn some of our methods to take back and implement in Yoused's holding."

"I assume Lord Yoused thought he would lose nothing by sending that one."

"You have the right of it. Restyn is not fit for labor, nor is he noble. Here he has found something useful he can do using the talents he has for letters and numbers. He has helped us with some formulas for predicting weather patterns." In spite of his disability, the young man seemed comfortable with the villagers and conversed animatedly with other youths. It seemed that a purpose could be found for everyone in Lady Eemya's society.

Everyone had work to return to, so Lady Eemya soon signaled that they must be moving on. Darius thanked Masyn for talking to him, still not quite sure of his motives, and Masyn bowed. "It is a wise man who can listen to his elders, be they of high or low station. I am honored to have met you, my lord."

They left the village and turned back toward the castle, following a different route. They had to travel a little faster to make up for the extra time spent in Masyn's village. This path was shorter than the road they had left by, but they still stopped on numerous occasions to greet farmers and other workers along the way.

In one town, they were met excitedly by a cartwright and a blacksmith. They were practically jumping up and down with eagerness. "My lady! We were going to make a trip up to the castle to see you tomorrow. We have something to show you! Come and see! Come and see!"

Eemya got gamely off her horse and followed them into the cartwright's yard. Before her stood a cart with a curious mechanism under the seat. "What is it?" she asked.

"Well, we were talking with Dod, you see, and looking at his bow."

"It was the bow that started us thinking about it."

"He uses it to shoot rabbits with. He's a good shot."

"He must be," offered Eemya, trying to see where this was going. Darius had dismounted and was looking at the cart as well.

"Well, you know how it bends and then springs back? We wondered, could you do the same thing with some strips of metal?"

"To what purpose?" Eemya was still bewildered as to the application of this principle, but Darius was beginning to understand. He pushed down on the seat of the bench, and it gave slightly, springing back when he removed his hand.

"Yes, you have it, sir! My lady, come sit and try it, then you will see." Eemya allowed the cartwright to hand her into the wagon, and she sat gingerly on the seat. They had no horse handy to pull it, so the two men grabbed onto the hitch and pulled. Eemya rode around the yard on the cart, bouncing slightly in the seat.

"This is amazing!" She laughed aloud. "My lord, you have to try it! Come sit with me!" The men pulled the cart back around and stopped in front of Darius and Eemya introduced him to the men. They were surprised and pleased to have the honor of showing him their invention. Darius climbed up next to Eemya and sat next to her, happy that she asked for him. They rode around the yard again, their combined weight no trouble for the burly blacksmith and his partner.

Darius was greatly impressed. "I have never seen anything so ingenious, and yet the design is superbly simple. It might not be practical for the everyday farm cart, but I can imagine other possible uses for it."

"Usually I am black and blue after riding in a cart all day," exclaimed Eemyn to the inventors. "This seat made the ride more comfortable than sitting on a dozen pillows. Well done!"

"Do you think you could put the mechanism on the wheels as well as the seat?" questioned Darius.

"On the wheels?"

"Could we put it on the wheels?" The blacksmith and cartwright looked at each other with sudden inspiration. "That is an idea! We'll get right to thinking on it! Thank you my lord!"

As they rode away, Darius remarked to Eemya, "They've really got something there. I might have to steal those two from you!"

"We are all your subjects now, my lord," she returned somewhat stiffly.

He tried to mollify her. "Well, at the very least, I'll have to send some of my own people to apprentice under them." He shook his head, and Eemya looked at him inquisitively, but he did not elaborate. What he felt after this short tour could not be put into words. There was no way he would admit to her that he felt inadequate for the task governing this island, even for the short term. His experience was too limited.

They arrived back at the castle and rode through the gate with about an hour to spare before sundown. As soon as they dismounted, the stable boys came to take their horses. Darius walked over to Eemya. "Thank you for riding out with me today," he said with sincere emotion.

Eemya suddenly found his intense hazel eyes to be somewhat disconcerting. She managed to hold his gaze as she replied that he was quite welcome. "If you will excuse me, my lord, I will rest a little before dinner." He bowed his head in reply and watched her walk inside.

Eemya made her way to her chamber, and her maid helped her out of her riding habit. She laid down on the bed to rest, but doubted sleep, let alone peace, would come. Tears stung her eyes as the strain of the day took its toll. Exhausted, she fell into a fitful slumber.

∞∞∞

Darius, meanwhile, made his way to his own rooms. He sat down in a chair and began to contemplate the challenge before him in earnest. However, everything he had seen that day was still swimming around in his head, and he felt the need to act on some of his ideas before He could address the problem of the lady.

He shared his observations with Yarin and asked him to write a letter requesting his brother to send several artisans and scribes to the island as soon as possible. Once the letter was finished, he sent his manservant to ask the steward to ensure it was sent to the mainland by the swiftest route possible. Then he cleared everyone from the room but Yarin. Yarin, he knew, would be discreet, and was one of the only men with him, other than Effan, he could trust to be completely honest.

"Yarin," he took a moment to figure out how to phrase what he had to say. "Yarin, I find myself in unknown territory, and I am in need of some advice."

"I am at your service, my lord."

"I want you to be honest with me." Yarin sat patiently in earnest expectation and nodded his assurance. "You are married, aren't you? Happily?"

"I might say so, yes, my lord." Yarin raised his eyebrows.

"So, you would say you have some experience with women?"

"A little, my lord. With one woman in particular."

"Which is a very different type of experience than anything I have to reflect on. What can you tell me about winning the heart of a lady like Lady Eemya?"

Yarin leaned back in his chair and put his hands together. He looked down his nose at Darius, evaluating him. "You are in earnest, my lord?"

"I am."

"It will not be an easy task."

"I am aware of that, believe me."

"It may take some time, my lord," Yarin persisted. "You will need great patience."

"And you feel that is something in which I am lacking?" replied Darius sarcastically.

"You have not had much reason to exercise it."

"I cannot disagree with you, but how to proceed? I am in the desert with her."

Yarin hesitated. "You will not be offended? You said you want honesty."

"You cannot possibly offend me more than I have already been today unless you continue to refuse to answer me!" Darius sighed. "There, I have already lost my patience with you. This is going to be difficult!"

"My lord," Yarin placated, "I think I can get you started in the right direction, if this is truly what you wish." From a nearby table he grabbed a metal goblet with a shiny surface and handed it to Darius. "Your outward appearance is the first thing people notice. Sometimes it is a reflection of the inner man, sometimes it can be deceptive, but you get to decide how best to present yourself."

Darius looked at his reflection in the goblet. Sure, the curved surface distorted the image, but he could see what Yarin was driving at. His hair was wild and unkempt, and his untamed beard was wiry and grizzled. It had been some time since he had taken notice of his looks. He had been told he was handsome, but no one could tell under this mess.

"Well that's easily attended to. When Eshan gets back, I'll send him to find some scissors, a razor, and a comb." He sniffed. "And I suppose it would not hurt me to have a bath. Anything else?"

"I would suggest that you try to treat her like a

man."

"What? That's the furthest thing from my mind."

Yarin put up his hands. "I mean, treat her like an equal. Like you would any of the other lords subject to you. Do not make her feel of less importance because she is a woman." Yarin waited until it appeared Darius understood what he meant, then continued. "One last thing. Try to get her to talk about herself. That is where you will learn the most about what she wants, from her own mouth."

Darius nodded. "Thank you, Yarin. That seems like sound advice. Now where's Eshan?"

∞∞∞

Just a few minutes late for dinner, Darius arrived in the hall. His beard and mustache were trimmed, his side-whiskers shaved, and his wavy, black, shoulder-length mane of hair was pulled back and tied with a black ribbon. Eshan had combed and even oiled it a little to make it shiny. He was dressed in a clean shirt and gold-colored tunic that brought out the flecks of gold in his hazel eyes.

Feeling slightly nervous, and smelling a little too much like a flower, he thought, he hung back at the door and searched out Eemya before she saw him. They had ridden horseback all day, but Eemya still managed to sparkle like a ruby. Dressed in a dark red gown, her hair, in contrast, seemed almost golden instead of its normal red. The glossy locks were styled elaborately on top of her regal head. White lace was at her throat and wrists. His heart lurched in his chest, and his feelings of desire began to give way to something deeper.

Eemya had just taken a bite of dinner when she saw him enter out of the corner of her eye. She turned her head and looked again, and nearly choked on her food. A violent fit of coughing overtook her, and a servant and the steward rushed over to aid her, but she waved them off. Her coughing subsided. "I am fine. Something just got stuck in my throat."

She made to rise and greet the prince, but he motioned her to remain sitting. Her reaction was more than he could have hoped for. Eemya's surprise at his appearance was very evident. Darius couldn't help the smile of satisfaction on his face as he took his seat.

Part of her wanted to ignore the obvious effort he had made, but she couldn't help acknowledging it. The words came out anyway. "My lord, I hardly recognized you."

"I will take that as a compliment, my lady. I was hoping we could have a fresh start."

"As we agreed this morning."

"I wanted to convince you that I was sincere."

"I see."

Darius decided he had best leave it at that. He set himself to be attentive to her. If her goblet was empty, he filled it. He made sure she had the choicest cuts of meat. He offered her the honey and the salt. No table in Eemya's hall was below the salt, he noticed, though their table was still physically higher; everyone had the same accessibility to the prized seasonings and sweeteners. It was less formal than many halls. Darius complimented Eemya on this and tried his hardest to make polite conversation.

Eemya did not know what to make of this complete reversal. A person could not really change this quickly. It had to be an act, and she viewed his behavior with complete distrust. On the other hand, she had to admit, the new look was quite attractive. He had a handsome face and strong jawline, now that one could see it, and his overall appearance was much softened. No longer did he look like the wild animal he had seemed at first.

He caught her looking at him, and she turned away quickly. Too quickly, and now she looked conscious. Oh dear, now she was blushing, of all things. She tried to replay the events of the last day so she could be angry with him again.

Darius ignored the temptation to call attention to her blush, much as he wanted to tease or gloat. Instead he brought up the subject of the state of the island, taking Yarin's advice to treat her like an equal. "Who would you suggest that I visit next, or do you have more that you would show me?"

"If you would like to go over our accounts, I could show you those, but you have seen most everything of importance here. Sir Gryn has a minor holding next to me. You might save time if you send ahead and request Sir Gard and Lord Gern to meet you at Gryn's manor. They are brothers, and share the same interests. Then Lord Yoused would be the next thrall in your path. His castle would be a good place to stay the night, if needed."

"Ah yes, Lord Yoused. What is he like?"

"He is a good lord. Fair. I don't have to worry about him encroaching on my lands."

"But you do with others? Do the island lords war amongst themselves often?"

"It has not come down to actual fighting for several years, but there are often disagreements." She gave him a brief history of the land boundaries and how often they were contested. One lord had actually diverted the flow of a stream to try and usurp control over a fertile valley. Some of her people were working on creating a more accurate system of maps for the island. They could eventually be a basis for proving ownership. "But I would prefer it if you did not share that information with any of the other land holders at present. Some of them have resisted letting my men on their land. They view it as spying."

"I can understand that," he remembered what Kirdyn had said about it.

"Do you have any recommendations for approaching them with this matter?" she asked, genuinely curious. Being a man, like them, he might see more clearly how to present the issue than she.

Darius thought for a moment. He wanted to give a good answer. It was the first time she indicated that he might have something to offer her. "Most people need to see how something will benefit them before they will accept or invest in it. If you approach the lords personally and explain how a system of maps would be to their advantage, they might be more willing to allow it."

Eemya nodded. "That makes sense."

"The border between Berush and Artylia has been in dispute for generations, and now that my people have conquered Artylia, that border has been moved to a more advantageous location. But I can see how that solution would not appeal to you."

"As I said, I have no wish to go to war. How will you maintain order over such a large area? And the people are so different. How will you keep peace?"

"It has been my experience that a swift and strong response to any dissent is the best way to prevent uprisings. My brother is delegating governance of Artylia to his son-in-law and a council of Artylian lords, but they will be on a short leash. You have given me some ideas for improving their agricultural system, and people's lives in general, but these changes will take a long time to implement, and it will be much more difficult over a larger area."

"By swift and strong response, you mean killing anyone who opposes you," she said harshly.

"Sometimes it is necessary, yes."

"Not if you treat people fairly to begin with." Now she was able to see the real Darius. Their ideas on this matter were entirely opposed. For a moment she had felt there might be some danger of losing her resolve. However, she felt compelled to make a small concession, "I can see, though, it could be different trying to rule this whole island, for example, rather than one holding."

Darius inclined his head. He felt it was best to abandon this subject for the moment. It brought to mind his earlier attempts to get his way, and he did not want to keep those fresh in her memory. His objective was different now. Or was it? No, his objective was not different, it was more.

Most of the castle ate dinner at the same time, but as at Kirdyn's Aerie, the lower tables had to eat in shifts depending on how many guests were in attendance. With the prince's extra men, it would be some time before everyone was finished eating.

At this moment, Stelan came in from his turn at watch to take his meal. His first thoughts, though, were for his lady, and he sought her eyes. He had not seen her since his brief imprisonment, and the accounts of what ensued were conflicting. He needed to reassure himself that all was well. Eemya saw him, and though she did not turn her head, she winked at him. He visibly relaxed and found a seat. His relief at her apparent well-being was indescribable.

Darius saw Stelan enter as well, and though he could not see Eemya wink, he knew there was some communication between them. He could feel the jealousy rising in him like bile. She had said she would not encourage or accept any other suitors, but what was going on between her and the captain? She had called him 'that boy' this morning. That was hardly a term a grown woman would give to a paramour, was it?

He knew he could not leave her castle without knowing how things stood. If he became too angry or jealous, he was in danger of doing something he might regret. There had to be some way he could get to the bottom of it. He had a sudden inspiration. "When I leave tomorrow to visit Lord Yoused, I'd like to take Captain Stelan with me. I feel it would be useful to have someone in my train who knows the area."

"Stelan?" Eemya was incredulous. "Absolutely not. You were ready to chop off his hand this morning!"

"You know I did not expect that it would actually come to that."

"I know what you expected." She was becoming very angry and on the verge of losing her temper. She didn't think she could take any more of this.

"I can leave you one of my men in exchange," he tried to appear calm and detached.

"And what would I do with one of your men? I cannot think of any enemies that I need to frame for theft at the moment," she said scathingly. "No. I do not trust you. I have several other men who would be able guides, and for whom you do not already have animosity."

"All the more reason I should take Stelan, so I can have an opportunity to earn your trust."

Eemya closed her eyes and rubbed her forehead in exasperation. She was done with thinking for the day. She had done her best not to cry in front of the prince, or show him any weakness, but if she did not leave now it would all be in vain. "I can speak of this no more this evening." She rose to leave. "Good night, my lord." She had to use all her will power not to flee the room at a run, but make a graceful exit.

Darius rose as well and followed her into the corridor. "Lady Eemya!" She turned and faced him, suddenly looking very weary and fragile. "If it means that much to you, I will not insist. Just tell me why."

"Why what?" All the fight had gone out of her, and she would happily answer any of his questions if he would just leave her alone.

"Why does he mean that much to you?"

"Stelan?" she asked stupidly, not comprehending why he was asking. Then suddenly it dawned on her. "You think Stelan and I are lovers?" She had the effrontery to laugh.

"You mean to say that you are not?" Darius crossed his arms as though he doubted her.

"Stelan is like a son to me! He has been with me since he was ten years old." Eemya began to raise her voice, "My marriage was childless, so when his father sent him here as a squire, I took him under my wing. Our sergeant-at-arms trained him, but I supervised the rest of his education, taught him to read and write. He sees me like a mother!"

"He does not look at you like a mother," Darius sneered.

"You think everyone's thoughts are as impure as your own."

"They usually are."

Eemya threw up her hands. "Take him with you, then, if that is the only way to satisfy you! Now that I know the reason for your dislike of him, I have no fear, because it is completely unfounded."

Her emotional outburst convinced him that, for her part at least, she was telling the truth. When people were at their breaking point, they found it difficult to keep up a pretense. "I promised you that I would not use your people as pawns, and I will not. If you will lend him to me, I will take him and be glad of it. If you truly wish it, then I will leave him with you. I just had to be sure you were being honest with me."

"If you knew me, you would never suspect otherwise."

"I am trying to know you, and this is the only way I know how."

"Then I pity you. You will have a lonely life."

Darius was about to give an angry retort, but Eemya swayed on her feet and threw a hand out to steady herself. He stepped forward and caught her just before she fell to the floor. As he gathered her in his arms, Stelan came into the corridor looking for Eemya. Before he could get the wrong impression, Darius called to him. "Help me. Where are my lady's rooms? She has fainted."

Stelan led the way down the passage, through an archway, and up a flight of stairs. Darius ascended the stairs carefully, and went through the door Stelan held open for him. He went inside, and much as he relished the feel of her against him, he gently laid Eemya on the bed. A maidservant clicked her tongue as they brought her in. Stelan and Darius both appeared to want to stay by her side, but the maid shooed them away. "Out, the pair of you! I will take care of her from here. She needs rest!"

They exited into the hall and stood there sizing each other up. Stelan regarded the prince with evident mistrust. He obviously did not have much practice hiding his emotions. If Eemya truly viewed him as a son, then Darius would do well to win Stelan over. "You comport yourself well under pressure, captain," he offered as an opening.

"I knew I had done no wrong." Stelan ground his teeth, obviously wanting to say more, but restraining himself.

Darius tried another tack. "You seem to put much trust in your lady."

"It has never been misplaced."

"Is that the best you can do, boy?" he goaded. "Come on, show me what you've got."

"Though I would lose, I would challenge you to mortal combat, my lord, if I did not know my lady would disapprove, and I will not call a man names if I'm not going to back it up with my sword. I will only say that you do not have my lady's best interest at heart, and if you knew her as the rest of us do, you would have no wish to do her harm!" Stelan said vehemently.

"I do not wish to harm her," Darius put up his palms to calm the young man. "I am trying to understand her."

Stelan's expression became one of skepticism. "That is not how it appeared this morning."

"Lady Eemya and I have agreed upon a change in tactics." The captain raised an eyebrow, but Darius did not explain. Instead he asked for Stelan's assistance.

"You want me to help you? I don't understand."

"Travel with me when I ride out tomorrow. I could use someone along who knows the geography and the politics of the island. You can represent Lady Eemya's position to me and perhaps help further her agenda. I will also be visiting your father, and it might predispose him in my favor if you were riding with me."

Stelan considered the prince's words. They were very persuasive. He and his father were not exactly close, but they had mutual respect for each other. It would be good to see him again. However, the prince had already proved that he was not above deception, and Stelan was not sure he could take his words at face value. As had been the case in the morning, there might be more going on than he was aware of. On the other hand, if he travelled with the prince, he could keep an eye on him and report on his movements. Eventually the captain replied, "If my lady gives me leave, I will accompany you."

"Excellent!" Darius clapped him on the back. He was enjoying the young man's befuddlement. He gave Stelan instructions on when he intended to depart, and then left him. The captain waited a few moments to make sure the prince was really gone, and then went to arrange a guard at his lady's door, just in case. Darius returned to his rooms satisfied with the events of the evening. He recounted everything to Yarin, who had only caught part of the conversation at the dinner table.

"My lord," Yarin protested, "this is not the way to win a lady's favor!"

"Why not? I did exactly what you said."

"You hounded her into a faint!"

"I needed information. I cannot proceed if I don't understand the lay of the land." He reflected a moment, and then felt slightly abashed. "Perhaps I pushed too hard, but that is the only way I know to get the truth out of people." Yarin sighed and slumped into a chair. "I found out what I wanted to know. I discussed subjects at the table that I would with any other lord, and I got her to talk about herself. You are the one who told me it would take time. I don't expect her to view me favorably by the end of one day."

"Time will not be your friend if you cannot change your behavior."

"Once I know what to do, I shouldn't have a problem doing it. The more I know about her, the better I will be able to predict her responses. I have to gather information and regroup, just like in battle. 'Knowing your opponent is the key to winning a contest,' father always said. I may have lost a couple of skirmishes, but I will not lose this war." He was becoming fond of this analogy. "I have not lost a war, yet," he growled.

Yarin harrumphed. "There's always a first time."

CHAPTER SIX

Eemya woke before dawn and called her maid. She did not want to be caught unawares by anything this morning. She thought about feigning illness, which would not be unreasonable after her ignominious exit the night before, but was afraid to leave the prince to his own devices. He might insist on seeing her anyway.

Her heart stirred with motherly gratefulness when she discovered the guards at the door, and she sent one of them to find Stelan. Her maidservant, Maygla, had told her Stelan had been with Darius when he brought her to her room. She shuddered to think what might have happened if he hadn't been there. Darius had agreed to her terms, but she didn't know how good his word was. He had a strange way of wooing, that was certain.

She remembered how he had looked at dinner, but pushed the image from her mind. She could see that she would need to be more proactive about a defense of some sort from his attentions. Not that she was afraid she would succumb. Certainly not. But who knew what kind of mischief Darius would invent in the meantime. What if he became impatient and frustrated and decided to disregard their agreement?

Fortunately she had thought to build a safe-guard into the terms. She pressed her lips into a thin smile. She needed Lydima.

Lydima was a distant cousin with no lands of her own who lived off of her relatives. She had been a lady-in-waiting to Eemya for a time, but Eemya had had to send her away for causing havoc in the barracks. She had been worried about Stelan, who was young and impressionable. Even now, she had reservations about exposing him to her, but maybe she could keep him out of the way long enough for Lydima to take the prince's attention away from herself.

Maygla finished helping her dress just as Stelan knocked on the door. "Follow me," Eemya directed. "We will breakfast in my study."

They walked downstairs to the office in the corridor off of the main hall. The guard who had been outside her room followed and stationed himself outside the study. "The prince has asked me to accompany him on the rest of his tour," Stelan informed her once they had closed the study door.

"He has?" Eemya looked at him sharply. "What did you say?"

"I said I would agree if you gave me leave."

Eemya let out a long breath as she sat down. That would solve the problem of keeping him away from Lydima in the prince's absence. "I hate to put you in his hands, but the situation could turn out to our advantage."

"I thought it might be a good idea to keep an eye on him. Jayred and Byden can handle anything that needs doing while I am gone."

"You would go even though he accused you of theft only yesterday?"

"It appeared that he was using me as leverage against you, not that he had a personal vendetta against me."

Eemya was glad he was able to read the situation clearly and that she didn't have to explain it to him. She had been proud of how he handled himself.

"I need to thank you, my lady, for saving me yesterday."

Moisture pooled in the corners of her eyes, and she blinked it back. "It was nothing." They both knew that to be a lie, but neither said anything. Maygla brought breakfast, a simple meal of porridge, bread and milk, but it was very nourishing.

After a few moments of silence Stelan ventured, "The prince told me you had agreed to a change of tactics."

"Yes." She thought it strange that he had spoken of it so freely. "This has now turned into a prolonged game of strategy." She had eaten quickly, and as she spoke, she moved her dishes from the table and brought out a paper, pen and ink. "Now I must implement my next move. You have my leave to accompany Prince Darius. You had best go and prepare. Pick one more man to ride with you." She looked up at him from her writing. "Watch yourself." He nodded solemnly and left the room.

Eemya finished composing her letter to cousin Lydima, asking her to come at her earliest convenience and help her entertain the new Prince Regent and his entourage. Let her read into that what she will. Eemya sealed the letter and went into the hall in search of Jayred.

ꝏꝏꝏ

Darius assembled his men in the courtyard. Stelan had come and informed him that he had leave to ride with him. The prince was pleased with this, as he felt it kept a tie between him and Lady Eemya. Her thoughts would turn his way if only to wonder how he and the captain were getting along.

Stelan and another man-at-arms brought out their horses and joined the rest of the men. Darius smirked at the thought that Eemya felt the captain needed a babysitter. They wore no armor, because the island was at peace very few guards wore any, but they carried their swords as a mark of their station. Their cloaks were packed in their saddlebags since it promised to be a warm, fine day.

Darius had decided to ride directly to Yoused's, stay at least one night there, and then take Eemya's advice and see the three brothers together at Gryn's manor. After that, he would return to Lady Eemya before touring the other side of the island. He was just wondering when she would make an appearance, or if he would have to go in search of her, when she walked through the door of the hall.

She wore a simple brown dress with a green overskirt, and she was hatless. Her hand came up to shade her eyes, and her hair glinted in the sun. Darius's long, firm stride quickly closed the distance between them. "I thank you for your hospitality, my lady," he smiled boldly. He explained to her his plan of travel. He leaned as close as he dared and promised, "I will return in a few days to see you again before continuing my tour."

"I have not a doubt of it." Really, the audacity of the man knew no bounds. Darius noticed the fire had returned to her eyes and wondered what would be in store for him when he came back. "Safe journey, my lord," she said, and he knew she was trying to dismiss him. He nodded to her and turned to mount his horse. He signaled his men to move out, and he resisted the urge to turn and look at her once more. It would be embarrassing if she was no longer there.

Stelan rode up next to him. "Take the right-hand road at the fork, my lord, if you plan to go directly to my father's castle," he instructed.

"Thank you, captain. Tell me, are there any bandits on this island? Should we be on the alert for anything?"

"We have occasional problems with petty theft, but no bands of outlaws. There's no place for them to hide. Every man belongs to one lord or another, and the lords are currently at peace amongst themselves. I can foresee no trouble on the road, my lord."

"What about visitors from the mainland?"

"It is mostly just our own merchant vessels and fishing boats that travel back and forth. Since Lyliana's agreement to become vassals of Artylia in exchange for the protection of its warships, we no longer have trouble with raiders from Cerecia. Once in a while, someone with family on the mainland will make a visit. Do you have a particular concern?"

"No, but one should never take anything for granted. I always assume there is danger ahead. That way I am ready for it."

"Constant strain of that kind must take a toll."

"It does, but it's better than dying. You've never been in a battle, have you?"

Stelan shook his head. "My lady keeps a number of guards as a deterrent to any lord that might decide her holding is fair game, but we have not yet been called on to defend her with our lives, though I would do it willingly."

"That's easily said, but not as easily done. There's no telling what a man will do until he's tested. I've seen plenty of men turn tail and run at the sight of my sword. Others lose their senses and fight erratically. You can be glad if you never have to stare death in the face in battle. Killing a man puts a mark on your heart that cannot be erased. It changes you."

They were silent for a while as Stelan contemplated the prince's words. Darius felt himself in danger of becoming melancholy, so he said more lightly, "If your behavior yesterday morning is any indication, you would be able to do your duty if ever called upon. I am surprised," he glanced appraisingly at the captain, "that you agreed to come with me."

"Sometimes sacrifices must be made for the greater good," replied Stelan with a look on his face like he had eaten a sour grape.

Darius laughed loudly at his grimace. "Ha ha. You know, I may begin to like you after all."

They continued to ride for some time, passing through farms and several villages. It was a different route than he had taken the previous day with Eemya, but the scenery was just as pleasant. Stelan took over the role Lady Eemya had played, waving to the workers, accepting offerings of food or refreshment and introducing Darius to the people. The prince could see her influence in him, and deduced Stelan was in the habit of riding out with her regularly. He had the same openness and generosity that Eemya had.

Darius wondered briefly what it would be like to have a son. Since he was not the eldest, he had not had the pressure to marry and produce heirs like Cyrus had. Neither had he taken seriously his brother's suggestion that that a family would make him happy. Cyrus had once talked of giving him his son, Ashin, to train as a soldier when he was old enough. Darius had not been sure he wanted that responsibility, but as he saw Eemya's reflection in Stelan, he felt an emptiness in his life that he had not noticed before.

Then he had an even more uncomfortable thought. What would a boy look like who was emulating his behavior? He didn't know if he would want to see that.

Eemya must feel her childlessness keenly, he thought. She definitely seemed the mothering type. He remembered how much she enjoyed playing and dancing with the children in Masyn's village yesterday.

It was nearly noon, and the horses needed a rest, so Stelan led them to a stream where they could water them. The men pulled food out of their saddlebags and took the opportunity to stretch. The line of thirty horses at the stream was more than Stelan had ever seen together at one time. He wondered that Lord Kirdyn even had that many to loan out. He decided to try and be friendly with the Prince's men and asked Effan about them.

He was told they had sailed over in two large boats and brought the horses with them. Stelan made a mental note to be present at Kirdyn's port when the prince returned home so that he could see how they were loaded. He nodded at Rhed, the man-at-arms who had accompanied him, to let him know that all was well.

When they resumed their journey, Stelan again rode next to the prince, guiding them on the swiftest way to Lord Yoused. They also sent a rider ahead to inform them of the prince's imminent arrival.

Something had been on Stelan's mind, and he had been debating whether to speak of it or not. "My lord, you were right when you said that taking a life changes a person. I have not experienced it myself, but I have observed it in others." Darius raised his eyebrows and waited for him to continue. "I do not know if Lady Eemya would want me to tell you this story, but I feel that you might be able to offer me some insight."

"I will if I can," Darius said, encouraging him to speak. He was curious to hear anything Lady Eemya would not want to tell him.

"A couple of years back, we had a series of grisly murders. They involved children. One or two happened in my father's holding, but most were on Lady Eemya's land. The man who did it was eventually caught in the act and Lady Eemya had to deal with him.

"On the island, you know, if a man kills another accidentally, or in a passion without premeditation, the family can take monetary compensation rather than executing the killer. But with something like this, the man had to be put to death. Rather than have one man carry the weight of it, my lady had any relation of the victims who wanted to, form a line of archers and shoot him on command, together. There were about half a dozen men who participated."

"Well, that is an interesting way to do it," Darius mused, but he was unsure what insight Stelan could be wanting from him.

"My lady also shot an arrow." Now Darius was truly surprised. "She doesn't practice archery, but as this was an unusual occurrence, she felt the need to lead by example, so she used a crossbow."

"Ah. And how did she handle it?"

"She was very solemn, but she was in command of herself. One of the men threw up after, but she checked to make sure the condemned man was dead, and kept them from desecrating the body afterwards." Stelan felt he had to be completely honest and confided, "I felt a little queasy myself, just watching."

Public execution was evidently not very common here, thought Darius. It was fairly frequent back home. "How was her aim?" he asked. That could be telling.

"It was true. Straight through the heart."

Since the bolt of a crossbow was much different than the arrow for a longbow, it would have been easy to tell which was hers. "So, what is your question?"

"Well, at the time, my lady felt the need to explain to me what had happened, and why she decided to deal with it that way, but she never talked about how she felt, though I could see it affected her. Her eyes were shadowed for weeks. What I want to know is, if I ever do have to do my duty in this area, how does one deal with it afterwards?"

"Honestly," Darius laughed hollowly, "if you can, you drink yourself into oblivion! I do not have that luxury. Like I said, I always consider that I am in danger and try to stay alert. There are some, like my brother, who believe that they can do no wrong and can go home with a clear conscience. What they have done is justified in their eyes. Some actually enjoy the thrill of battle and having the power of life and death. Others find solace in the arms of a woman."

The prince's expression clouded and it seemed like his thoughts were far away. "Some become angry at life, and some become constantly afraid and try to hide from the world." He wriggled uncomfortably in the saddle.

"And which are you?" Stelan wondered.

"Me?" he scoffed. "I'm a little of everything." Darius fell silent. He had revealed more of himself than he intended. At least, he hoped, if Stelan could understand him, then there was a chance that Lady Eemya could come to understand him as well. "So, what do you think of how your lady responded?"

"Well," Stelan thought it over carefully, "I know she believed she did the right thing, and I agree. But then, I think, maybe she did hide herself away for a while. Inside, at least."

"I imagine the deaths of the victims involved weighed on her just as much."

"You are probably right. It was a terrible time. I hope nothing like that ever happens again."

Darius shook his head. "Where there are people, there will be evil. That is why you must always be alert. Sometimes the evil can come from inside yourself."

The words came out before he realized what he had just said. The truth hit him with almost physical force. It felt like falling off a horse and having the wind knocked out of him. Just as he had let his physical appearance go, he had let his inner self go. He had let evil grow inside of him until he could not even recognize it for what it was. He had dealt with all the death and pain he had seen and caused by ignoring it, pretending it didn't affect him, and filling the void with constant activity, but he had only fed the darkness in himself, and now he was losing control of it.

Stelan broke into his thoughts. "I guess that's why a person needs good friends and family, to recognize when you are in the wrong, and tell you. Or stop you from hurting others, as in the case of this man. His family refused to acknowledge his evil, and it just got worse."

Darius realized now that his brother had seen the darkness growing in him. That's why he had sent him away for a while: to give him something constructive to do instead of spiraling downward. He had been in danger this whole time, and it was from himself. He had almost failed in the mission Cyrus had given him because he could not control his desires.

Darius was so absorbed in his self-discovery that he did not notice Stelan had stopped talking. The young man had observed something in the demeanor of the prince that made him hang back and give Darius some space.

Stelan's own mind was busy trying to piece together a picture of the prince's true nature, and he couldn't quite do it. The man he was conversing with now seemed completely different from the one who had done such outrageous things the previous day. Maybe he was unstable? Or maybe he was just used to cutting down anything that stood in his way. Stelan thought the latter was more likely. Lady Eemya had taught him to try and bring out the best in people, that they were capable of great things when you expected greatness from them. If he looked hard enough, maybe he could even find it in the strange prince ahead of him. He decided he would give it a try, over the next few days, if Darius would let him.

It was now very late in the afternoon, and as they crested the next hill, they saw Yoused's castle, glowing orange in the light of the lowering sun. Stelan came abreast with the prince once more. "There it is. My father's castle. It is called Sonefast." They rode down the hill and across the wide valley without speaking, taking in the scene.

Yoused's home was much more spacious than Eemya's. Like Kirdyn's fortress, its outer walls were of gray stone, and the keep was tall and wide. There was no moat or drawbridge, but as at Freosyd, the gatehouse contained a portcullis, which was raised, and strong wood doors. The courtyard was larger than Kirdyn's, and paved with smooth stone. The horses' hooves clattered as they entered it.

Lord Yoused stood on the steps of the keep to receive them. Darius dismounted and walked over to him. Yoused was a lean, graying man of medium build. His stance and posture were dignified, but not haughty, and his eyes looked kind. The clothes he wore were of plain and simple cut, but the fabric looked to be high quality, most likely imported from the mainland. Darius was glad that he had made his own appearance more acceptable.

"Welcome, your highness! It has been some time since we have had the pleasure of receiving a dignitary of your stature." Yoused introduced his older sons and their wives, who were also in attendance. He nodded at Stelan, standing a pace behind the prince. "It looks like you already know my youngest."

"Yes, he has been an invaluable guide." Darius introduced Yarin, who was a little stiff from the ride, as his advisor. "Yarin is more knowledgeable than I about the history between Lyliana and Artylia. However, I have already learned much during my visit here."

"Well, we are glad to have you. My steward will show you to your rooms so you can refresh yourselves, and then we can speak more over dinner. My men will see to your horses."

The castle was large enough to have a stable inside the walls, but some of the horses would have to be housed elsewhere, since there were so many of them. Stelan moved to go with the rest of the king's guards to the barracks, as befitted his current station, instead of into the castle with his family. Darius found that curious, and he called to him and motioned that he should follow. "You'll stay with me," he told him.

Stelan hesitated, and glanced at Rhed, but he obeyed.

The two rooms assigned to the prince were spacious and comfortable. A large, curtained bed and fireplace filled one room, with a table and chairs against one wall. The windows looked over the curtain wall into the wide, green valley. The other room had a smaller bed and several cots set up in it, with extra bedding, for however many retainers the prince had brought with him. Both had pitchers of water and basins for washing and bowls of exotic fruits.

Everything a guest might possibly need seemed to be provided for. Yoused really knew how to make visitors feel at ease. That in itself would normally put Darius on the alert, but his instincts told him that Yoused's hospitality was genuine.

After washing up and making themselves presentable, Stelan led the way down into the main hall. Dinner was an elaborate affair. Yoused's kitchen staff had come up with a variety of delicacies on short notice. The wine was of high quality vintage. The atmosphere in the hall was relaxed, and was not as noisy and chaotic as at Kirdyn's. Still, it did not quite achieve the gaiety and camaraderie of Eemya's hall. Here there was still a great deal of formality and strict separation of rank.

"So, your highness," began Yoused, "I understand your brother intends to honor our previous agreements with Artylia?"

"There seems no reason to change it at this juncture," Darius replied. They conversed for some time about politics and Cyrus's plans for Artylia. Darius asked about the state of affairs on the island, and Yoused explained about the system the lords used for bartering, trading resources and labor as needed, and how they determined each lord's share of the taxes due to the mainland each year.

"How do you solve disagreements between yourselves?"

"If we cannot come to terms with a neighbor, we will assemble a meeting of the lords and it will be decided by the group."

"Do you use a simple majority?"

"We try to come to consensus, but that is not always possible. Then we go by majority, but dissenting lords have always had the option to appeal to the king of Artylia, though we like to keep our problems amongst ourselves."

"So you currently have no problems with your neighbors?"

"None at all."

"I hear not everyone is happy with the way Lady Eemya goes about things," Darius persisted. He was interested to find out what other lords said about her.

Yoused made a strangely sad smile. "She definitely has a mind of her own, but she has proven herself an able leader."

"Your son, Stelan, has certainly turned out well. He has many of her notions about things."

"Yes. I considered recalling him when Lord Faryn, Lady Eemya's husband, died, but Stelan wished to stay, so I let him."

"What happened to Faryn?"

"He died of a fever. We lost quite a few to illness that year." Yoused did not seem quite comfortable with this subject, and he began to propose an itinerary for the next day. Yoused controlled the only other natural harbor on the island, and it was because of the competition he offered Kirdyn that export prices remained reasonable for the other land holders. Darius agreed that he would like to see the port, and it looked like Yoused would keep him busy the entire day. That gave him one more night before he could return to Lady Eemya, and now he was grateful for the delay. He needed to arrange his thoughts before seeing her again. He told his host of his plan to visit the three brothers next, and Yoused promised to send riders out to call them together on the appointed day.

Yoused had scheduled some entertainment for the evening, and though the jugglers and singers were quite talented, the prince was unable to pay them any attention. When it was over and he could finally retire to his rooms, he was relieved. During the entertainment, he had had some time to think without being required to converse with anyone. In order to remove the darkness from himself, he decided, he would need some help. He had gotten to a point where he was not sure he could tell the difference between right and wrong. The people best suited to help him were Effan, Yarin and Stelan, and he called them into his room.

They had no idea what he was going to say, and he felt sure it would surprise them. Effan already did as much as he could to help Darius with his night terrors. Yarin would be willing to help him, but he was not sure about Stelan. If their roles were reversed, he doubted he would do it. If someone had treated him the way he had treated Stelan, he probably would have killed him.

Darius motioned them to have a seat and he summoned his courage to speak to them. "I have come to the realization that I am a very selfish person." The men were visibly surprised at this opening. "I bully everyone into getting my way, and when I don't get it, I act like a spoiled child, but with much greater ability to do harm. Yarin," the prince turned to him as he spoke, "you were right that I need to change my behavior, but I need to change more than that. I need to change my very thoughts. I need to know what is right to do, before I can do it." Yarin's eyes were shining with emotion. He had never thought he would hear anything like this from Darius.

"Stelan, I treated you very badly yesterday, and I hope you can overlook it. Take time to think it over, if you need to, but I would like all of you to help me to change myself for the better."

"I do not need time to think about it, my lord," answered Stelan. "I had already resolved to do that very thing."

Darius shook his head in wonderment. "You are a greater man than I. That is why I asked for your help. Effan, you are already invaluable to me. I know you would do anything I ask, but I ask you anyway, as a friend, not a superior, to continue as you have been. I would be lost without you." Effan nodded solemnly, too emotional to speak.

Darius looked at Yarin. "I also, my lord, will help you in any way I can, as I have always intended."

"With greater success, now, I hope!" Darius grinned. "If any of you see me doing something purely self-centered, please tell me. You can remind me that I promised to listen. What do you recommend for my next step?"

The men considered carefully. They hoped Darius was sincere, but would he be able to keep to his purpose when faced with temptation? When faced with Lady Eemya? None of them wanted to be the one to say her name.

Finally, Stelan felt it his duty to the lady to put her ahead of his own discomfort if he was to be an example in unselfishness. "The others know you better than I, but it would seem that there is really only one other person on this island to whom you have behaved improperly—Lady Eemya."

"I know." Darius's face fell. The anguish he felt could not be described. Once she was no longer before him, he was able to see more clearly the wrong he had done. "Do you think it is possible for her to forgive me? Will she give me another chance?" To truly show his contrition, he was afraid that he must release her from their current agreement.

"It will take more than mere words to convince her," cautioned Yarin.

"I don't need to convince her of my sincerity right away, but just to give me a chance to prove it."

"If you go to her as you have to us, she will forgive you, I am sure of it," assured Stelan. Darius admired his youthful optimism, but feared that the boy's faith in her might be disappointed.

"Even the most forgiving lady will only take so much. She may forgive you but be unwilling to give you the chance to show you can really change. You must resign yourself to follow her wishes in this matter, even if she asks you to leave her alone," proposed Yarin, knowing this would be hard to hear. "That may be the only way to truly prove yourself to her."

Darius held his head in his hands. "At least I have a day to think it over and prepare what to say."

Yarin rose and placed his hand on the prince's shoulder. "Making the choice to do right is the first step. I am . . . proud of you, Darius." He used the prince's name in a fatherly tone that he would never dare to do under normal circumstances. Then he bowed, and left the prince to his thoughts. Stelan and Effan followed him out. There seemed no more to say.

Darius sat staring and thinking for some time. Eventually he laid himself down on the bed, but sleep did not come. His heart ached, and for once, he let himself feel the pain. Distorted images of those he had killed in battle swam before his eyes.

So many times, he had worked himself into a furious frenzy before a fight, that the anger was now a constant companion. He could not rid himself of it. But for tonight, at least, the anger retreated and was replaced with sorrow. When his emotions had finally exhausted themselves, the beautiful, comforting face of Eemya appeared before him, and he fell into a dreamless slumber.

CHAPTER SEVEN

In the relief of the prince's absence, Eemya had had a gloriously peaceful sleep. Now that he was gone, even if it was only for a day or two, she could relax. The last couple of days she had been completely on edge.

Now Eemya had just received word that her messenger had found Lydima only one holding away, with Lord Woldyn. She would be arriving that evening. Eemya felt sure that the prince would not be able to resist Lydima's charms. Then, if he was a man of his word, of which she was not entirely convinced, he would leave her alone. She felt somewhat ashamed as she arranged for Lydima's rooms to be near Darius's. They deserved each other, she rationalized.

Several other items of business needed attention, then she rode out with Yula, the castle healer and herbalist, to visit a sick family. When she returned, she sent one of the castle guards to help the family with the farm work until they were better. Her 'guards,' since they were not often called on to actually defend the castle, helped wherever they were needed. That included everything from breaking up brawls to becoming migrant workers during harvest time. This particular guard was married, and his wife went with him to help nurse them back to health.

Eemya thought it would be nice to have a partner like that. Faryn had let her do as she wished, but he did not help her. He was content with riding and hunting and spending his days in leisure. Which was fine. She had been content with that. It had been their agreement, after all. Her father thought she needed a husband to legitimize her hold on the land in the eyes of the other lords, and Faryn had promised that he would let her make all the decisions in regard to management of the holding. The responsibility was something he had gladly let her keep.

Two years after their marriage, her father had died, content that all would be well for her. As far as the holding went, all was well. In fact, it prospered. But Eemya still longed for more. There was no spark between her and Faryn, no passion. They had not been in love when they married, but she had hoped that it might grow. It did not. In the end, she had become somewhat disgusted with his laziness.

Still, he was kind to her. He had not been a drunkard or carouser. He had expressed regret that, for whatever reason, they seemed unable to have children, though they had tried. She had even consulted with renowned healers from Artylia, but to no avail.

Five years after her father had died, Faryn contracted an illness that kept him fevered and delirious for days. No matter what she and Yula had tried, they were unable to bring it down. Eventually he had succumbed. Eemya felt guilty that she did not miss him. Sometimes she wished she had someone to lean on, but she had determined that she would not make another marriage of convenience. She had proven to herself that she could manage the estate alone, and she had done it alone for four years now.

At least she had Stelan. He was a constant joy to her. She was so proud of the man he had grown into. Someday, he would want to marry. She hoped that his wife would join him here, and they and their children could be her heirs.

Of course, at only thirty, she was still young enough to have her own, but the prospect was bleak. There was no man on the whole island who had captured her interest. Most of them considered her innovations and methods to be outlandish. She wanted a partner who would respect her and support her. And love her. The handsome face of prince Darius came to her mind. The lecherous wolf! He certainly had passion, but he couldn't control it. Why couldn't she have both respect and passion? Was that such an impossible thing to ask? She put the question to the universe at large.

The herb garden beckoned her through the window of her study, and she went out to take a walk in the warm, afternoon sun. The healing rays helped to raise her spirits as she strolled around inspecting the various plants.

"My lady," Jayred came and found her. "Your cousin Lydima has arrived."

"Already? All right, thank you." Eemya steeled herself for the unpleasant task of welcoming what she deemed a necessary evil. She hoped this was not a case of swallowing the spider to catch the fly! No, much as she disliked Lydima, Darius was a far greater threat.

"Lydima," she welcomed her in the hall with open arms. "It is wonderful to see you!"

"It has been too long!" gushed Lydima, and she kissed Eemya on both cheeks. "You are looking a little tired. Are you well?"

"Just a little worn out, that's all. You look lovely, as always!" Lydima was slightly shorter than Eeyma, and definitely more voluptuous, with a creamy complexion and honey-colored hair. Her curls hung scandalously loose around her face for a woman of twenty-seven years. The head of every man within the hall was turned toward her.

"I will give you some of my eye-ointment. It will do wonders for those circles." Eemya had to refrain from rolling her eyes. She ushered Lydima into a receiving room and ordered refreshment. For the next hour, she was regaled with stories of Lydima's conquests until Eemya blushed for her. "Your invitation comes at a very opportune time. I have my sights on Lord Woldyn. He is almost to the point of proposing, I am sure. Hopefully he misses me enough while I am gone to consider taking the final step."

"Really? You are considering settling down?" Eemya was surprised. Especially since Lord Wolden was a widower in his early forties, and paunchy. He was the only eligible lord at present, though, besides Lord Yoused, and Eemya knew Yoused had no interest in Lydima.

"I won't be young and beautiful forever, you know," Lydima scoffed. "Plus, I don't have the security of my own holding, as you do. I can't afford to play around forever," she sniffed. She took a sip of the wine that had been brought. Then she gave Eemya a shrewd look. "Now, why did you really send for me?"

"What do you mean?" Eemya questioned defensively. Inwardly she squirmed a little.

"I mean, I know that you don't like me. You don't

approve of me at all, so why am I here?" Eemya looked uncomfortable and opened her mouth to say something, then closed it again. "You said you wanted my help entertaining the prince. Well, you know what type of entertainment is my specialty." Eemya flushed as Lydima studied her. "The prince has designs on you, and you want me to draw him off. That's it, isn't it?"

"Yes," Eemya sighed. "It was wrong of me to ask you."

"Not at all. I just find it very amusing. You could do worse than to keep him happy, you know. I would say it would be politically expedient." Eemya glared at her. "Not to worry cousin, I know your prudish sensibilities. I'll help you if I can," she grinned. "It should be fun."

"What about Woldyn?"

"Pish. Most men would be pleased to have a prince's cast-offs. It may even make me more desirable. Maybe Woldyn will get a little jealous." She leaned back in her chair and put her feet up on a stool with an air of satisfaction. "So, tell me about this Prince Darius. Is he really so terrible? I have heard that the Berushese could be quite barbaric," she said with a sparkle in her eye.

Eemya gave her a favorable description of his appearance but explained that he had a temper, was used to getting his own way, and would go to great lengths to get it. She avoided going into detail or telling Lydima about their 'agreement.'

"Really, he sounds quite fascinating!" Lydima rubbed her hands together. "So when is he returning?"

"He sent word today that he would be returning tomorrow evening."

"Perfect. I don't suppose you could draw me up a

mineral bath? I need to look my best."

There was a hot spring on the island that was loaded with salts and minerals prized for their healing and cleansing qualities. It was located on Lord Olged's property, and he charged a high price for bottles of it, but she did have some. Eemya felt that, considering what she was asking her to do, she should give Lydima whatever she required. She tried to squelch the mortification she felt at being in this ridiculous position. She would be glad when it was all over.

∞∞∞

Darius had a very busy day looking over Lord Yoused's holding. Yoused had prepared an ambitious itinerary, starting off with his agricultural concerns, farms, mills and livestock, then heading downriver to the port. They travelled this section by boat, the current doing most of the work so that they could admire their surroundings. Yoused kept a running commentary. Occasionally Darius would ask a question or make a reply, but everything was in very good order, and his thoughts kept him too busy to hold a conversation. Yarin had begged off the expedition, not having an affinity for boats and being tired from travelling all the previous day. Darius brought only Stelan, Effan and two of his other men with him.

Everyone they saw stopped and bowed. They were very respectful, but not as exuberant as in Eemya's holding. Yoused did not feel it necessary to stop and introduce him to every common peasant they came across. Though Yoused's lands were vast, it seemed his primary industry was fishing. When they reached the mouth of the river, they entered a natural harbor bordered by land on three sides. Everywhere were docks and piers and small fishing boats. There were no large boats like Darius had sailed in, but there were several merchant vessels and what looked like a fair-sized pleasure craft.

"The fishing between here and the coast of Cerecia is quite good," Yoused explained. "Ever since Artylia began patrolling the straight, we have been able to sail unmolested."

The island didn't have the tall, straight trees that were necessary to make larger ships capable of carrying more men. The Cerecian raiders had many such boats. The island was lush and fertile, but the variety of trees that grew in the dense vegetation of the mountains was not large enough to build ships greater than those currently seen in the harbor. The oarsmen guided their boat to a nearby dock, and they disembarked.

Next they walked around the docks inspecting the day's catch. Many of the fishermen were cleaning nets, and their boats were empty. Yoused explained that most of the fish were sold on the mainland, since they took in much more than what they needed for themselves. Records were kept of all sales, and the appropriate amount of tax sent to Artylia each year with the annual tribute.

They stopped for a meal on Yoused's personal boat, the pleasure craft Darius had seen when they arrived. During the lunch they discussed the possibility of a couple of warships harboring on the island for added protection. Yoused told him that he would consider it. After eating, they returned home on horseback. The men who brought the horses to the port would return by boat.

Darius appreciated Yoused's hospitality and the efficiency of his enterprises, but he was becoming a little tired of all the politics. He had to work not to show boredom or impatience. How many holdings did he have left to visit? Nine or ten, he thought. Could he endure visiting that many more? Maybe he would ask several more of them to a central location to meet, as he was going to do tomorrow, rather than visit them all personally.

They returned to the castle just as night was falling. Darius wished he could go straight to bed. His body screamed for rest to make up for getting so little last night. However, Yoused had prepared an even larger feast than the night before. Since the cooks had enough notice today, they had roasted a pig, and all of Yoused's family, plus his most prominent merchants, and the port-master were invited. Several women flirted with him at the dinner, including one of Yoused's daughters-in-law, but he ignored them all.

As soon as he deemed it would not be insulting, he excused himself with needing to prepare for the next day. He asked Stelan to give Yarin a summary of the day's events, and he barely had removed his boots before he fell back on the bed, asleep.

∞∞∞

Darius woke before dawn the next morning with the realization that he would see Eemya again that evening. He jumped out of bed and made himself ready by candlelight, feeling that the sooner they left, the sooner he could see her. Then he remembered what he had resolved to do.

He sat at the table and took the writing instruments that had been provided and started to compose what he would say. The words he wrote on the paper seemed completely inadequate. Afraid that someone might come upon them, he set fire to them and burned them in the fireplace. His nervous energy found an outlet in pacing around the room.

At dawn, he woke up his companions and told them to get ready as quickly as they could. Yoused had requested that Darius take breakfast with him, so he did, but did not linger. As soon as his men were ready, they prepared to depart. Yoused came to the courtyard to see them off.

Stelan came to say farewell to his father. "Goodbye, father. It was nice to see you again."

"And you, son. I hope it will not be so long until the next time we meet." Darius felt like their farewell lacked some of the proper emotions. Maybe they were just a very reserved family. "And you, Prince Darius. I believe that our relations with King Cyrus will be peaceful and profitable ones. Please feel welcome to visit any time."

"Thank you, Lord Yoused." They parted with feelings of mutual respect and optimism.

The journey to Sir Gryn's holding only took a couple of hours. All they had to do was follow the river inland from Yoused's. They still had a long way back to Eemya's holding afterward, so he hoped the brothers would not keep him long.

Yarin brought him up to speed on their situation. "Their father, Lord Godyn, decided that all his sons needed land, so he divided his holding into three smaller estates. Lord Gern, the oldest, was given the castle, and the other two have built manors on the parcels they received."

"There are no land title restrictions on the island?"

"Each lord may do with his own land as he sees fit. As long as the taxes were paid, Artylia didn't concern itself with the island's governance."

Sir Gryn's manor was built entirely out of wood. His land went right up to the northern peak of the mountain, so he had the resources of the dense forest available. He had no wall around his dwelling, but it appeared well built and ample for his needs. Darius presumed it had been built recently, after the division of the holding. Gryn probably felt he had no need of defensive measures since the island had not been invaded in many years. If nothing else, he could take refuge in his brother's castle during a crisis.

Darius instructed his men to water the horses at the nearby river. Yoused had had the foresight to pack their saddlebags with provisions, and Darius was grateful, as he got the feeling the brothers might not be prepared to feed all of his men. Three very similar looking men came out of the manor to meet him. They were short and barrel chested, and two of them were balding.

"Good morning, my lord," said the one who looked the oldest. He confirmed that he was Lord Gern, and gave all the customary statements of welcome and introduced his brothers. "We are glad, indeed to hear that someone more forceful will be in charge. Perhaps now, some of the issues we have been having will be resolved."

Darius raised his eyebrows. "I was not aware that you had any grievances."

"Oh, nothing much. Just some minor irritations here and there. Please come in, and we can discuss everything."

Darius entered with Stelan, Effin, and Yarin behind him. This was not looking to be the quick visit he had hoped. They entered a very small hall and sat around a table in the center with benches on each side. A maid brought in wine and some simple refreshment of bread and cheese. Darius gave them what were now becoming his standard assurances that relations between the island and Artylia would remain the same for the time being. Then he asked them to tell him their concerns.

"Well," said Sir Gryn, "one of the problems has to do with the digging of wells." He looked at Darius meaningfully, as if he should know what he was talking about.

"Wells?" Darius encouraged, hoping for an explanation.

"Yes, wells! Lord Eklyn had an agreement with me, and my father before me, that he would compensate me for watering his goats in my river."

Darius put a hand up. "Sorry, Lord Eklyn? His name is not familiar."

"The father of the current Lady Eemya," Sir Gryn waved impatiently.

"Ah, I see," said Darius, although he didn't.

"Yes, well, when he died, I told Lady Eemya I would need more compensation than I had been getting. She refused to pay! Instead, she built a well on her own property, as close to the river as she could get, and is sucking my water right out of the ground! With some kind of fancy wind-power, no less!"

Darius's moustache twitched. "So what did you do then?" He looked sideways at Stelan to find an accomplice in his humor. He saw the captain had put his hand over his mouth. The brothers evidently didn't know that he served Lady Eemya.

"Well," Gryn huffed, "I marched over to Lord Yoused, to get his opinion. Do you know what he told me? He said that there was nothing he could do about it. There are no rules against digging wells. Now, I ask you, shouldn't she have to pay for using my water?"

"Unfortunately, I'm afraid Lord Yoused is right. Anyone can dig a well on their own land. It is the same in Berush."

Sir Gryn expressed his frustration and disappointment that Berushese policies were no different than the lax Artylia's had been. Darius was highly amused. Lady Eemya was not one to give in to anyone it seemed. She had definitely put Sir Gryn in his place.

The prince had to listen to several more complaints the brothers had about their various neighbors. A couple of their assertions would have to be looked into, since he had only heard one side of the story. Others were easily settled by reinforcing that the current rules would stay in force. Soon enough, Darius was able to take his leave, exhort the brothers to keep up the good work on their lands, and head back.

To arrive at Freosyd at a reasonable time, they would have to ride straight through. Stelan guided them through some less populated areas, stopping at fewer villages. Darius decided to try and get as much insight on Eemya as he could before they returned, so he asked Stelan to tell him more about her. "Why has Lady Eemya not remarried? I would think she would still want to have children," he inquired, since this was one of the things he was curious about.

"I don't know," replied Stelan. "My father asked her, you know."

"Really," Darius was taken aback. "Why did she not accept? I would think it would be an advantageous alliance." This information explained some of Yoused's mood the night he arrived, and his willingness to defend her to other lords.

Stelan shrugged. "Neither of them talked to me about it. I only know because all the castle was whispering about it the next day, that he had been rejected. He had seemed very disappointed when he left."

"Hmm." Youased evidently did not respond to rejection the way he did. "Well, what about you then?"

"Me?" Stelan looked at Darius like he was crazy. "Why would I marry her?"

"The same reasons your father would. You obviously admire her."

"Yes, but not that way. She's like my mother." Stelan had such an expression of shock on his face that Darius believed him.

"So you would have no objection to her marrying me, if she chose to?"

"Nothing would please me more than to see her happy, by whatever means she wishes. It is really not my place to influence her in this matter. But aren't you getting ahead of yourself, my lord?"

"She will most likely throw me out on my ear if I give her the choice," he tried to say this cheerfully. "I just wanted to know where you stand."

"I will stand with my lady, no matter what her decision." Stelan looked at the prince with encouragement. "But I will stand with you, as long as the two positions do not conflict. I believe you can be strong enough to continue on the right path, even if it is not the one you want."

Darius was somewhat bolstered by the young man's confidence in him. He would stick with his resolve. "I'll remember you said that. I may need you and Yarin to douse me in a water trough later." Yarin was back at the rear of the procession, so he was not a part of the discussion. It was hard for him to keep up the pace.

"It would be my pleasure, my lord." Stelan kept a straight face for a second, and then grinned widely.

They crested a hill and saw the azure towers of Freosyd before them. They rode the rest of the way in silence. Darius slowed them down so Yarin could catch up with the front of the column. "I feel I need you beside me, my friend," said Darius simply, and they rode the remaining distance three-abreast.

Once they rode into the courtyard they were in complete shade, and it took a moment for their eyes to adjust. When he could see clearly, Darius's eyes found Eemya standing in her customary place on the steps. He stood still on his horse, gazing at her, searching for some sign of emotion. There was none.

He noticed that she was dressed very simply. Even her hair was tied back in a plain knot at the base of her neck. She might be trying to look less attractive, but it emphasized her high cheekbones and green eyes, and she appeared just as beautiful to him.

Eemya was already uncomfortable enough at this moment, and the three men staring earnestly at her began to unnerve her. Finally, Stelan made strange jerk of his head toward Darius that she was at a loss to interpret, and then he turned his horse toward the stables. Yarin likewise moved off a ways and dismounted.

Without taking his eyes from her, Darius got off his horse and walked up the steps. There was some great significance to this scene of which she was unaware. "My lady, I must speak with you at your earliest convenience."

Eemya hesitated. She had no wish to speak with him at all. "Very well. I can see you first thing in the morning." He nodded and was about to walk away when she continued, "Let me introduce to you my cousin, Lydima."

Only then did he notice the woman beside her. She was a beauty, and she knew it. Her dress and hair were styled demurely, but there was something seductive about her. Instantly he knew what Eemya was up to. If the woman had been there the day he had first arrived, he might have fallen for it. Not now. He had to give Eemya credit for creativity. Were the situation reversed, he might have done the same thing.

"What a pleasure to meet you, your highness," she drawled. Her eyelashes fluttered and she made a low curtsy.

"The pleasure is all mine," he replied courteously, then withdrew with the excuse, "I must see to my men."

"Cousin, you are insane!" Lydima hissed as soon as he was out of hearing distance. "He is even more handsome than you described, and there is nothing lacking in his manners."

"You should have seen him before. In private he is not so guarded. He really has quite a temper."

Lydima shrugged, "Men are supposed to have a few rough edges. That is what they need a woman for. You could polish him up really nicely if you wanted."

"That is not what I want out of a relationship."

"Well, if you're sure, I'll try my best. It appears he has only you in his sights. He didn't even notice me."

"You can make any man notice you. He's not an idiot though, so do not overplay it." Eemya cautioned.

"Do you observe my modest attire and simply dressed hair? I'll have to be more like you to catch him if you're his type."

Eemya thought Lydima did not quite understand the definition of 'modest,' but she left it alone. The cousins returned to the hall and waited the men to join them at dinner.

∞∞∞

Darius could not find Stelan, but he was able to

corner Yarin and ask his advice on how to proceed at dinner. Should he ignore Lydima, or play along? Part of him wanted to annoy Eemya, but Yarin insisted that now that he had set himself on a path of doing right, he should behave honestly and completely ignore Lydima. Eemya expected him to respond to her cousin. What better way to show his sincerity than to refuse her cousin's charms?

It turned out that Darius was able to ignore Lydima and annoy Eemya at the same time. If the stakes had not been so high, he would have thoroughly enjoyed it. Even being polite to Lydima could be easily misconstrued, so he decided not to worry about being polite. If Lydima had not known better, she would have thought she was invisible. Darius ignored her questions, and when answering was completely unavoidable, he answered with a monosyllable and immediately addressed a question to Eemya.

Lady Eemya was both fascinated and perturbed with his behavior, and she had difficulty making conversation. She was amazed at his ability to forestall Lydima's advances. Lydima tried to brush his hand with hers, and he moved it out of her way. He filled his own goblet before she could get to it. She asked him a question and he directed his answer to Eemya as if Eemya herself had asked it. Eventually Darius excused himself and said he needed to see to his men.

Yarin, who had been watching the scene from further down the table, got up and followed him. "I think, my lord," he said as they walked down the length of the room, "that it might be best if you were never alone while that woman is here if you want to stay above any suspicion of wrongdoing. If the Lady Lydima is anything like you, she will not give up easily."

Darius smiled at the thought. "'Send a thief to catch a thief,' as the saying goes. Thank you, Yarin, you are probably right."

Most of the men were still in the hall, and though they were a little rowdy, they were not causing any real trouble. Eemya had her men keeping an eye on them as well. Some of her men were curious about Berush, and several of his soldiers were busy weaving tall tales of their skill in battle. Most of the servants waiting on the tables were men. Perhaps Eemya had hidden all the women away in the kitchen.

Darius made his way to the barracks with Yarin behind him. Only a couple of his older guards were resting in the barracks, sleepy after dinner and tired from the day's long ride. Eventually Darius found Effan in the stables rubbing down one of the horses. "At least here's one female who does not shy from male attention," Darius joked half-heartedly as he stroked the mare's nose.

Effan snorted. "The men aren't used to such peaceful missions. Inactivity will make them restless."

"I sympathize with them heartily, believe me. My brother is adamant that it remain peaceful, so ensure they restrain themselves. Roust them out of the hall and into the barracks if necessary, but I hope it won't be. I will have Yarin to keep an eye on me."

Effan nodded. "I will stay with them tonight, to be sure." Darius clapped him on the shoulder and headed back toward his rooms.

Once there, Darius made plans to sleep in a cot in the adjoining room instead of his own bed. He had a feeling that Lydima might make a more direct attack later that evening. Yarin protested that the prince should take the poster bed, and he would sleep in the cot, but Darius knew the older man would have difficulty sleeping comfortably anywhere but a real bed. Darius could sleep just about anywhere, as long as his dreams didn't bother him. He moved the cot to block the door from the other bedroom, so it wouldn't open.

Darius was concerned for his men, but he also preferred that Effan not be present for this little charade. He directed Eshan to place his cot in front of the door from the passage. Eshan spent more time with the castle servants than anyone else in the prince's train, to make sure the prince had everything he needed, so he had heard a lot of gossip. He did not want to be impertinent, but he could not keep a straight face.

Darius observed his dilemma. "Yes, I know, Eshan. This is the exact opposite of what one would normally want to do." Eshan put a pillow over his face to cover his laughter. Yarin grinned, and Darius chuckled. "All right, that's enough of that, now!" he said sternly, not really meaning it. "Not a word of this to anyone, Eshan!"

Once their amusement calmed down, Eshan and Yarin were easily able to fall asleep. Darius was too anxious. He rehearsed what he would say to Eemya in the morning. He listened for an intruder in the other room. His loudly beating heart was the only thing he could hear.

Finally, after quite some time had passed, he heard the door of the other room push open. Soft footsteps padded across the floor. After a few moments, the feet padded back, and the door closed. Eemya's cousin was lucky, for her own sake, that she had not surprised him in his sleep. Lady Eemya would never have forgiven him if he had killed her cousin, mistaking her for an enemy, he thought grimly. Now that the anticipation was over for one event, he was able to get some rest.

CHAPTER EIGHT

Eemya woke the next morning with the unpleasant remembrance that Darius had requested a meeting. She cringed slightly, wondering what he might have to say about last night's awkward dinner. Then again, why should she care what he said about anything? After dinner, Lydima had told her she still had a couple of tricks up her sleeve. Maybe, after all, she was successful last night. A week ago, Eemya would have thought such a hope on her part was impossible.

Eating sparingly, she rushed through her morning rituals. She had continued with Stelan's idea of having guards at the door, and kept them with her down to her study. Darius must have been lying in wait nearby, for as soon as she sat down, he knocked on the door. "Enter," she sighed, and rose to meet him.

The prince entered the room and walked around the table to stand before her, but not close enough to make her nervous. Then he amazed her by falling to his knees in front of her. He completely prostrated himself, with his face to the floor. "My lady," his voice broke, "I have treated you in a most offensive manor. My actions were completely dishonorable, yet through it all you have shown great strength of character. I . . ." he stumbled here, in agony, fearing her response, "I release you from our agreement, and I pray that you will be generous enough to forgive me."

Eemya stood in shocked silence. His remorse was so unexpected, that she had nothing prepared to say. Darius dared to look up at her face. His eyes pleaded with her. "If you tell me to go, I will go, but . . . I would like to stay," he choked out.

"I want you to go," she whispered, but the words sounded like thunder in his ears and crushed his hopes. His face turned ashen. He stood shakily.

"Farewell, my lady. I am truly sorry." He bowed and left.

Eemya realized she had been holding her breath and sat down, feeling a little faint again. She put her hand to her forehead and tried to process what had just happened.

Stelan was waiting for Darius in the passage. One look at the prince's face told him the outcome. "Let me talk to her," he offered, but Darius shook his head.

"It is no more than I deserve. Thank you, Stelan, for your faith in me."

Stelan gripped the prince's arm. "Do not give up on your resolve. You can still be worthy of her, even if she should never know of it."

"I hope I will see you again, my friend." Darius smiled sadly at him and left to gather his men.

Stelan sorrowed for him and for his lady as well. It was unlike her to be so hard, but he understood she had been sorely tried. He followed Darius into the courtyard to see him off.

∞∞∞

Lydima found Eemya in her office, staring vacantly. She told her cousin what had transpired, and Lydima's eyes widened. "Eemya, you have to forgive him! Never have I heard of any man, let alone a prince, humbling himself in such a way!"

"That is not what he is really like. He is an animal. A man's heart can't change overnight."

Lydima considered her next words carefully. "My dear," she sat next to Eemya and patted her hand, "what if this *is* his true nature, and his boorish behavior was out of character?"

"What are you saying?"

"I am saying that everything I have seen shows him to be a man of self-control and restraint. Eemya, he did not even sleep in his room last night." Eemya looked at her uncomprehendingly. "I had a servant watch him and tell me when he went to bed, and when I crept into his room last night, he wasn't there. He had moved into the next room and slept in front of the door in order to avoid me. The servant told me he found them all in the one room this morning."

"So, he is smarter than you are," Eemya argued obstinately.

"If he really was as you picture him, he would not have run from me! I do not get rejected often, trust me."

Lydima's words started to sink in. Was it possible that Darius was not as bad as she had painted him? She had been able to reason with him, after all. She shook herself. An honorable man would never have been tempted. Why should she forgive him? Then she began to feel a little guilty. She was always practicing mercy, forgiveness, and generosity with others. Why not Darius? Because his offense was so much greater?

She thought of a farmer in her holding who had killed another man in a fit of anger. He had been very contrite, and the family of the man had been persuaded to take restitution instead of exacting the death penalty. The farmer had been so grateful, and part of his restitution had been to take over responsibility for the man's family. Was Darius's crime worse than that? Certainly not. She remembered his pleading gold-flecked eyes.

"The prince obviously cares deeply about you," continued Lydima, driving her point home. "Enough to resist me, enough to apologize, and enough to obey your wishes."

Eemya felt her heart begin to stir at Lydima's words. He was leaving! He deserved forgiveness at least. She stood up. Without another glance at Lydima, she left the room. Lydima sat back in her chair and put her fingers together in satisfaction.

Once she began moving, Eemya fairly flew to the courtyard. She wanted to catch him before he left. She arrived to see the men mounted and ready to move out. Darius turned around in the saddle to give an order to his captain. He saw Eemya and froze. His heart leapt into his throat. Every head turned to look at her.

"My lord, a word?" she spoke tremulously.

If the yard had not been completely silent, he might not have heard her, but he would have gone to her anyway. He dismounted and quickly closed the space between them, his eyes hopeful.

Eemya would not have chosen such a public setting for this, but she gathered her courage and spoke in a whisper, "I forgive you."

Darius made a loud gasp of relief and pressed his hand against his eyes to try and prevent the tears that threatened. He fought to regain his composure. "Thank you, my lady."

Eemya was moved by his response. Perhaps Lydima was right, for once. "You may stay," she found herself saying softly. She drew herself up and added in a firm voice, "on approval." Then she turned and went back inside.

The tension in the air dissipated and the normal noises of the castle resumed. Stelan, who had been watching with the rest of the crowd, couldn't resist letting out a loud whoop. Effan took the liberty of dismissing the men, and they headed their horses back to the stables. Darius was rooted to the spot; his sudden rise from despair to hope had immobilized him. Yarin let a servant lead away his horse and went over to Darius. "What do I do now?" the prince asked him.

∞∞∞

What do I do now? Eemya asked herself. Lydima was no longer in the study to advise her, but she probably wouldn't agree with the advice anyway. If the prince was going to continue to use her castle as home base, with the intent, she assumed, of continuing to win her over, she needed to figure out how she was going to proceed. Why couldn't she have forgiven him without asking him to stay? He had nearly thirty men who would wander around causing trouble as well. She must figure out some sort of occupation for them all. She could hardly send them to work in the fields. That might be demeaning to seasoned warriors such as Darius's men.

An idea dawned in her mind and she rose and went in search of Darius. She found him in the hall, conferring with Yarin and Stelan, of all people, who had seemed on unexpectedly good terms with the prince since they returned. When she walked up to them they abruptly ceased speaking and rose to greet her. Suspecting that they were discussing her, she flushed slightly but managed to stay calm. "May I ask you, my lord, if you have considered your itinerary? It would be helpful for me to know when you and your men are to be quartered here so my staff can be prepared."

"We were just discussing what the best plan might be. I would value your input." Darius motioned for her to have a seat in front of a map of the island that was spread on the table. Eemya noticed it was not a very accurate map, but it was good enough for their purposes.

"What are you considering?"

"I would like to continue your suggestion of seeing several lords at once. Since I don't know the land, or the personalities of the various lords themselves, I don't know the best place to meet. I also want to be sure that if there is something I should see, the iron mine on Retand's holding for example, that I don't miss it."

"Lord Retand's castle is pretty centrally located. We were thinking of calling the lords on the eastern side of the island together there," put in Yarin.

Eemya looked at Stelan. Darius noticed her hesitate when Yarin mentioned Lord Retand. "What is it?"

"Well, it's probably nothing you would need to worry about, but . . . there have been rumors of a few suspicious deaths at his castle the last few years."

"Suspicious in what way?"

"Just unexpected, unexplained deaths. All women. I would suspect poisoning."

Darius raised his eyebrows. "I'll bet you suspect a

little more than that. What do you think is really happening?"

Eemya sighed. "I hate to say anything without more proof, especially if you plan on staying with him. I wouldn't want people saying things about me without evidence."

"I promise I can listen with an open mind. If I am walking into danger, I would like to have an idea where it might come from."

"It is not likely that you would be in any danger, my lord, but at least three women working in the castle have died in the last five years. Lord Retand has a wandering eye, and his wife is very jealous of her husband."

"You think she's eliminating her rivals?"

"That is what I fear," said Eemya uncomfortably. "The only way I can possibly see that being a problem for you is if she somehow sees you as a threat to her husband. I have met her once, and she struck me as being somewhat unbalanced."

"Would you recommend that the prince stay elsewhere?" Yarin interjected.

"The iron mines are on his land, so if you want to see them it might be expedient to stay there for at least one night. His castle is also the largest and best able to accommodate the other lords who would be coming. But I would employ a food-taster."

Yarin and Darius weighed the convenience of Lord Retand's castle against the possible threat from his wife and decided to go ahead with their plans. Lady Eemya volunteered to send out riders taking the prince's request to the lords concerned to meet in five days' time. Darius would depart in three days. They agreed that would give everyone enough time to prepare.

This brought Eemya back to her original purpose

in seeking them out. "With three days of idleness ahead of them, your men may become restless, so I would like to request a favor."

"I am all ears," said Darius, curious to hear what she would say. He prepared to be surprised, as he had been every time they had conversed.

"My men have had very limited training and no experience in combat or castle defense. The times ahead may be uncertain as the people of Artylia adjust to their new ruler. It would ease my mind if you and your men could hold some training sessions and help my men improve their fighting skills. Perhaps you can find some ways to bolster our defenses as well."

Stelan became considerably excited at this prospect. "That is an excellent idea! Byden is the only one of us who has seen real action, back when the Cerecians were still raiding our shores. We could all use some pointers."

Darius leaned back and considered the idea. Slowly he nodded his head. "It's not much time to work with, but we could definitely show them some drills and techniques that they could practice to help them improve and stay sharp." He looked at Eemya with a twinkle in his eye. "You are lucky that my men and I are some of the best warriors in the whole of Berush."

Stelan stood up. "Shall I tell the men to prepare for training and assemble in the courtyard?"

"Hold on a moment. Let me call Effan and have him go with you to see what we have to work with. We will need wooden swords and some leather gauntlets to protect their hands, at least."

"I can go find him, my lord, and take him to the armory."

"Very well. Both of you report back to me before

we gather the men."

Stelan was out the door almost before he had finished. Darius and Eemya shared an amused look, and then suddenly Eemya burst out laughing. Darius wanted to be let in on the joke, but Eemya just shook her head. When she tried to speak, she just laughed more. The tension of the last few days had built up and found a release. Now that she had a plan to keep everyone busy the next few days, she became more relaxed.

Finally, she was able to explain her mirth in a guarded enough manner, "I was merely remembering an absurd assumption you had had the other day, my lord."

Darius smiled wryly. He understood that she was referring to his misplaced jealousy over the nature of her relationship with Stelan. "I apologize for that, my lady. I can see, now, how absurd it really was."

Eemya smiled, enjoying the humor at his expense. Darius' heart skipped a beat at the thought that he had made her laugh, even inadvertently. Seeing her happy suddenly became one of his goals. It was a more selfless one than any he had had so far. Winning her over was a goal he had thought would make him happy, not her.

Eemya observed his intense look, but remained ignorant of its cause, so she returned to the task at hand. "If you would like to compose a letter to the northern lords, I would be pleased to help Lord Yarin make copies for my riders to take with them. Or you could send one of your men with each of mine. Either way, it will let the message be given more directly from you, and will have more authority."

Both Darius and Yarin appreciated the wisdom of this suggestion. It would not look good if it seemed that Eemya was unduly influencing his decisions or receiving favoritism. Of course, he admitted to himself, in reality she was influencing every decision he made, but it wouldn't be good politics for that to become general knowledge.

In the end, they decided to do both, that way nothing could be misconstrued. The men would return by the route the prince intended to take so his men could rejoin him, and Eemya's would continue home. Darius and Yarin retired to their rooms to write the summons, and Yarin promised to meet her in her study to make the necessary copies.

Out in the corridor, Lydima was waiting. "Eemya, my dear, I am so proud of you!" she gushed. "You have become very open-minded."

"Which I am sure I will come to regret."

"You may be surprised. I hope, instead, that it will bring you great happiness." Eemya looked at her like she was crazy. "At any rate," Lydima put her arm around Eemya, "you do not need me here. If you can lend me an escort, I will get back to Lord Woldyn." After extorting a promise from Lydima not to trifle with her men, Eemya arranged for her to leave that afternoon.

Eemya had not been in her study very long before Yarin knocked on the door. She had her writing implements ready, and they each made two more copies of the letter. Even though she knew Yarin would probably report their conversation to Darius, she couldn't help prying a little. "So how long have you been serving Darius?"

"I have been serving the royal family of Berush since the time of Darius' father. I am well acquainted with both Darius and Cyrus, but this is the first time I have been specifically attached to him. Most recently I was the ambassador to the court of Artylia."

"Oh! That must have been very difficult."

"Indeed. At the end I was imprisoned for several days before Darius and his men overthrew the capital at the end of the campaign." Sympathy for his suffering showed on her face. "It was not so bad. Infinitely preferable to risking your life in battle, in my view. I am not a soldier. The king of Artylia was both arrogant and ignorant. If the Artylians had had a wiser leader, we could have avoided all this."

"I have heard that the reverse could be true as well."

"Cyrus is a very wise and fair ruler, but he can also be very hard. When he chooses a course, he will not turn from it. He will not have to, because he has Darius to carry it out. In this case, their actions were justified. Artylia provoked us into action," was his diplomatic answer.

"Hmm." Eemya could see that further conversation in this direction would be futile.

"You are a politician as well, I see."

"No, I am not a good liar. I would say I am more of a thinker, or strategist."

"I can definitely see that, my lady," Yarin smiled.

"Unlike Prince Darius, perhaps, I can see when a course of action should be abandoned because its outcomes are no longer desirable."

"Like this morning?" suggested Yarin impertinently. Eemya narrowed her eyes at him.

"I admit that particular reversal was very quickly done, but I will not discuss my reasons." She was still not completely sure of them herself. At least, she could not yet put them into words. Certainly, she would not want the prince to know of them. She decided to be more blunt and see what she could get out of Yarin if she put him on the spot. "So, then. I'm sure Prince Darius has informed you of our interactions, to some extent. Tell me, what would he want me to know about him?"

Surprised at her directness he replied, "I'm sure whatever he wants you to know, he will tell you himself."

"Do not try and deflect me. Here is your chance to put in a good word. Sell me on his good qualities, if there are any."

Yarin could not help but rise to the bait. If he refused to say anything, it would be seen as a sign that there was nothing good to say. After a short hesitation he began, "Darius would much rather have the chance to show you who he is without outside bias, but I'm sure there are many conflicting," which Eemya interpreted as meaning negative, "reports, so maybe I can sort it out a little for you. Let me start by saying that Darius' greatest quality is loyalty. He is extremely loyal to his family, to his friends, and to his men. He would do anything for Cyrus."

"That is a rare thing among royal brothers."

"It is indeed, and Cyrus could not do without him. His men are loyal to him as well. In battle, he is a leader men would follow anywhere. His heroism and bravery are inspiring. If believes in the necessity of what he is doing, he is unstoppable.

"The border between Artylia and Berush has been in dispute for some time. It is difficult to draw lines on a mountain. This war started because raiders from Artylia killed a young goat herder and stole his flock. Darius was on patrol and found him. The boy's father begged him for justice, and Darius gave it to him. Instead of ceasing their aggression, the Artylian mountain tribes sent an even larger invasion force, but we were ready for them. Darius chased them all the way back to the Eryn."

Eemya wondered what a man who could drive himself that way was like on the inside. It must be very dark, she thought, to be able to cut people down in battle like that, day after day. "What about women? Has he had any special relationships with anyone? Has he been married?"

Yarin huffed into his mustache. "He has not been married. Beyond that I cannot say."

Eemya knew she would have difficulty getting anything else out of Yarin. In her mind she saw Darius as a man bloodthirsty for vengeance who needed victory to sustain him and could not stand losing. His apologies were just an attempt to win another way. But, she had forgiven him, and she would have to give him a chance to show her she was wrong. "So, you have nothing else to add that might convince me to see him in a more favorable light?"

The prince's advisor racked his brain to think of what he could say. "I don't think anything I can say would convince you. You will just have to form your own opinion."

"My opinion is already formed. I am trying to un-form it, but I do not think it is possible." She rose from her seat. "Thank you, Yarin. I will have five men ready to depart within an hour if you can ask Prince Darius to do the same."

Yarin took the copies of the letter, and Eemya went to talk to Byden since Stelan was busy. Byden chose five men who he felt would not mind missing the Berushese battle training and had them prepare to ride out. Eemya asked Jayred to make sure their saddle bags were supplied with at least three days' worth of food.

The courtyard was full of men clearing the space of carts and tools for the training exercises. After the messengers left on their mission, Eemya had about fifteen men-at-arms, plus Stelan, and Darius had twenty-five soldiers. Effan was in charge, with Darius supervising. Byden observed, not having the energy to keep up with the younger men.

First, they ran through some drills that a man could practice alone to strengthen his arms. Then they assigned each of their men to one or two of Eemya's as a coach, and the rest served as opponents. There were not enough wooden swords for everyone, so half of the group would work on wrestling techniques while the other half fought with swords. All the men were glad of the activity and went to work with a will.

Eemya had put on her hat, since she sunburned easily, and was watching from the top of the wall. It was easy to see from her vantage point that her men were mortifyingly deficient compared to Darius' soldiers. Captain Effan was instructing his men to hold back and go slowly as if they were starting from the beginning. Eemya hoped the training would make her men more confident and not demoralize them.

By the end of the afternoon, there were many bruised knuckles, but most of the men were smiling from the exercise. Training was to resume immediately after breakfast the next morning. Eemya felt quite warm, just from watching. She retired to her room and decided to have a cool bath before dinner. The bath consisted of standing in a tub of water while a maid assisted by pouring water over her, but it felt refreshing.

Then she had to consider what she would wear to dinner. Now that Lydima was gone, and that scheme had failed, should she continue to be drab, return to normal, or something else? She decided to be normal. Why should she change her habits? So she dressed her hair simply, but attractively, and wore a nice green and gold dress. It was not her fanciest dress, but the colors were very flattering.

Darius was already waiting when she arrived in the hall. He had also cleaned up and looked very sleek and suave. "I look forward to the one time of the day when you are not avoiding me." Eemya wanted to make a caustic reply, and could only keep herself from it by remaining silent. Of course she wished to avoid him. "Is your cousin Lydima no longer with us?"

This promised to be an extremely uncomfortable line of questioning, and Eemya was annoyed with the prince for bringing it up, but she looked into his twinkling eyes and her mouth started twitching. "She had business elsewhere."

"Oh, is that what it's called?" he grinned.

"I regret inviting her," she gave into his teasing. "I'm sorry."

"Sorry that it did not work?"

"My lord, please," she was extremely embarrassed to actually be discussing Lydima with him.

Darius sensed it and relented. "I bear you no ill will for the attempt. I would have tried it myself if our roles had been reversed."

She looked at him skeptically. Darius turned his attention to the meal, for which she was grateful, but he continued to be attentive to her and made sure she had everything she needed before she could ask. "It seemed like the men enjoyed the training exercises today," she offered in an attempt to be polite.

"They did. Stelan, in particular, was very enthusiastic. If I can take him with me to Lord Retand's, I can continue his training on the way."

"I am sure he would be pleased to accompany you. My men can benefit from any training they can get."

"Do not feel badly that they are deficient in their battle skills. It is a blessing to be at peace." Darius spoke these words quietly, but with such strong feeling that she felt chastised for having those very thoughts. They ate in silence, each deep in contemplation.

Darius' thoughts turned to a way to spend more time with her, other than dinner. Eemya had cleverly contrived a means to keep them all busy and out of her way. "I hate to leave you out of the training. Is there anything you would like to learn, maybe the longbow?"

Eemya arched her eyebrows and pursed her lips in surprise and thought for a moment. "Actually, I would like to learn some wrestling techniques for escaping from someone's grasp."

"You know you don't have to fear that anymore from me," replied Darius softly.

"No? Well, you are not the only man in the world. It might still be beneficial."

The prince nodded. "All right. When would you like to practice?"

"Any time that does not interfere with your schedule for the training of my men."

"How about as soon as our meal is finished?"

"That is fine. Is what I'm wearing appropriate for this exercise, or should I change into something else?"

"Assuming that dresses are your normal attire, I do not think your style of clothing matters for our purposes," he smiled.

Eemya ignored his smile. "The solar should be a large enough room. I will have the furniture moved to the side. Let me fetch Stelan to help us." She rose. Darius rose and followed her, determined not to let her shake him. He wanted to see her as much as possible.

Eemya walked around the room to where Stelan sat eating. "Stelan, we need your assistance. The prince is going to hold a special training session for me." Stelan shoved another bite of food into his mouth and rose with curiosity.

They exited the hall and went down the corridor and up the stairs toward Eemya's rooms. She stopped in front of a door Darius had not yet been through. "Wait here," she instructed the men. She went inside and shut the door behind her. Darius heard hushed conversation inside the room. Shortly the door opened again, and four women he had not seen before exited quietly, made quick curtseys and hustled down the hall to another room. Eemya glared at him with a look that did not need explanation. He could not blame her for hiding her ladies-in-waiting from him and his men.

She reentered the room and motioned for Darius and Stelan to follow. They pushed all the chairs against the wall, and a large space was created in the center of the solar. Eemya looked at Darius and stated firmly, "If you would demonstrate with Stelan, then I will try it with him afterward."

Darius understood that she did not want him to touch her, but he summoned enthusiasm for the lesson anyway. At least she was permitting him to be in the same room. If she allowed him to teach her something, it would be a step toward trusting him. "Stelan, come behind me and put your arm around my neck, like this." Darius demonstrated a head lock on the captain. He released Stelan, and Stelan came behind him and did the same.

"Most people pull at an attacker's arm, and you can almost never get free doing that alone, especially if your attacker is stronger than you. You have to find a way to get him off balance and use leverage to get away. Go ahead and squeeze harder, captain!" Stelan put him in a hard, firm hold.

Darius reached up and pulled at the thumb of

Stelan's dominant hand, causing his arm to twist slightly. This allowed him room to turn his head toward Stelan's chest so he could breathe. Then he bent forward while stepping backward and twisted his head out of Stelan's arm, pulling it down, and pushing Stelan's face back with his left arm.

It all happened very fast, so he repeated the maneuver again slowly, explaining it step by step. "If you are having trouble reaching the thumb, poke at the man's eyes, and he will at least loosen his hold, if not let go altogether. When you are able to bend over, you can reach behind with your other hand and hit a man here also," he mimicked punching Stelan's groin.

"Let me see Stelan get out of it when you are choking him," Eemya demanded. The men reversed their roles, and Stelan mimicked Darius' movements. Stelan also was able to twist away.

"Let me try." Stelan put his arm around her neck, and Darius helped her through the steps slowly. Then he had her repeat them by herself. "Pull harder," she instructed Stelan, and she followed the steps and twisted away again. She still doubted that Stelan was trying his hardest, so she steeled herself to endure being close to the prince again, and tried to put aside the fear the memory raised. If she could escape from him, maybe it would actually help her to put those feelings aside.

"All right," she took a breath and turned to Darius, "If I can escape from you, I will be convinced."

Darius was a little concerned. He did not want her to feel threatened by him again. "Are you sure?"

Eemya nodded and motioned him over. When he put his arm around her neck, she had a brief moment of panic. The man was solid as a rock. He didn't squeeze too hard, but his muscles were tense, and it felt like nothing could move them. Nevertheless, she repeated the sequence of moves successfully and was able to get loose. She stood and stared at him with her mouth open. "That is amazing!" she panted.

Darius nodded. Maybe she would feel safer with him now. "Now let me show you how to escape someone trying to choke you from the front." He demonstrated with Stelan, and she repeated it with the captain.

"If someone has a knife to your throat, it is a little different. You want to avoid being cut." He took a knitting needle from a nearby sewing basket as a substitute for a knife. With Stelan as the role of attacker, he showed Eemya how to unobtrusively move her hands into position to pull away the knife-wielding arm. "One hand should pull his hand downward, and the other hand should push his arm up. Then you back under his elbow this way." They practiced that move until she was comfortable with it.

"What if someone just grabs my wrist and tries to drag me somewhere, and I do not have an angle to kick or poke his eyes?"

"Well, most people try to pull away, and again, if your attacker is stronger, that will not work. Instead, you put your other hand over his and push toward him, throwing him off balance. He will release you to try and steady himself. It is a reflex."

Eemya tried it with Stelan several times. It was too easy. "Pull harder," she urged. "I do not want to hurt you, my lady," he said uncertainly. "I want to know how well it works," she insisted. He reluctantly gripped her wrist as tightly as he could and pulled hard. She resisted for a half a heartbeat and then followed Darius's instructions to push forward. Stelan lost his balance and fell to the floor.

"I think it works," he said, rising to his feet.

Eemya felt exultant. She was used to ordering men around, but this feeling of physical empowerment was something else. No longer did she feel completely defenseless. Darius' heart warmed at her look of confidence. His burden of guilt eased a little. Eemya turned to him, flushed with success and offered him her hand. "Thank you, my lord. This was very instructive."

Darius took her hand and pressed it to his lips. As it had been the first time she offered her hand, his touch was so tender that it took her by surprise. He held it just a little longer than necessary. "You are welcome," he affirmed sincerely and released her hand.

She turned from his gaze to speak to her captain. "Thank you, Stelan, for your assistance," she said, effectively dismissing him. She was sure he was tired from the afternoon, but did not want to embarrass him by saying so. Then she turned to Darius.

"Good night, my lord. I look forward to observing the men progress in their training tomorrow."

Darius knew that meant he was dismissed as well, even though he, by rank, should be dismissing her. It was her house, however, and that changed the rules a little. He was trying to be unselfish and give in to her wishes, but it was hard when she kept pushing him away. She curtsied and turned to retire to her room.

"Lady Eemya," he called out to her. She stopped and looked back over her shoulder. He took a couple of steps closer to her. "If there is anything else I can do for you, you have only to ask." She looked at him and dipped her head in acknowledgement and left him standing in the corridor. The longing he had for her was as strong as it had ever been.

CHAPTER NINE

Eemya awoke with the same thought that had been in her mind when she fell asleep: if Darius had begun with the attitude he had now, she might have given in to him. His behavior now was exactly what she could wish for in a suitor. But she still could not believe that this was his true self. Let her see him thwarted again, or angry, and see if he would act consistently. She would continue to observe him with an open mind.

The morning did not afford her the opportunity, however. Representatives from a couple of villages had come to her to consult about some difficulties with their irrigation systems. After some discussion, it was decided that a couple of new wells needed to be dug. Diverting water from their few streams was not very efficient, and the amount of rainfall so far was less than average. It took until nearly lunchtime to work it out, so she fed the villagers before sending them on their way.

By the time she was free to go outside, the day had turned hot. She took a fan and found a seat in the shade of the gate house. Most of the men had stripped to the waist and were glistening with sweat. She was grateful Lydima was no longer here to voice comments.

Effan was driving the men harder today. The Berushese soldiers were really giving them a workout. He had them repeating several simple techniques and principles of leverage over and over until they were proficient. Those who were slow on the uptake were berated soundly. "You have just lost an arm!" or "You are dead!" she heard over and over.

She saw Byden take a young man aside who was looking particularly harassed. She imagined him instructing the boy not to give up in front of these strangers. They were expected to learn from this, and he needed to do his job.

Darius caught her eye and nodded at her, but did not approach her. Now and then, he gave quiet directions to Effan, who would then change tactics. The men were tiring, and Effan called a break for everyone to get some water. During the break he went over to confer with Darius.

When the men returned, Effan directed them to form a circle. "We have been telling you how swordplay is all about attack. You want to control the battle. There is attack and counterattack. Your best defense will turn into an attack on your opponent. Prince Darius and I will now give you a demonstration of some of the principles we have been talking about."

He and Darius also stripped off their tunics and shirts. The Berushese soldiers had been instructing them in unarmored combat anyway, since there was little armor on the island to go around, and most of it was leather, not metal. In unarmored swordplay the object was not to be struck at all. When wearing armor, there was a little wiggle room and a fighter could use his body as leverage in some cases.

Darius and Effan began by holding their swords with both hands at shoulder height in a middle guard, and circled each other at wide range. Those of Darius' men who had been coaching stood next to their 'students' and explained what was happening.

Byden came over to Lady Eemya to do the same thing. "A good swordsman will not make the first move," Byden told her. "Instead, he will evaluate his opponent and wait for him to open."

The fierce expressions on the two men's faces belied the wooden weapons in their hands. Effan made the first move, and Darius' sword moved so fast Eemya could hardly see it. Effan deflected Darius' counterattack and spun out of reach again. Darius had been careful not to overcommit himself, so he was not thrown off balance.

The prince evaded Effan's next strike and then thrust toward his exposed side. Effan quickly turned his sword and slid it along the flat of Darius' blade to turn it away. Darius used his wrists to twist his blade around Effan's, working his way into Effan's near guard. The captain pushed the flat of Darius' blade against his chest with his own and managed to push him back. They retreated and circled each other again.

Eemya had never seen anything like it. The Berushese had been defeating her men easily, within two moves when they were trying, but the level of skill Darius and Effan had achieved was more than she imagined was possible. Her knuckles turned white as she gripped the edge of her seat, completely engrossed in the action.

This time, Darius attacked first, Effan parried, and sword met sword with move after move. Openings were not given by either man. Each countered with a move calculated to draw the other into a vulnerable position, but both were so experienced that neither was taken in.

Effan thought he saw an open line and made a rising cut, but Darius had merely feinted and expected Effan's move. He slid his blade inside Effan's with a flick of his wrists, spun around, hooked his foot around Effan's leg and took him to the ground. With the wind knocked out of him, Effan let go of his sword and found Darius' wooden blade at his throat. Loud hoots and applause were heard as Darius helped Effan off the ground. Both men were dripping with sweat, but grinning widely.

"I do not let him win just because he's my prince!" Effan proclaimed. "He's really that good! You only get that good with constant practice, so let's go to it!" With renewed energy, the men resumed their exercises.

"We are very lucky to have them here, my lady," said Byden. "This training was an excellent idea," and he walked off to observe one of the pairs of wrestlers.

When she had suggested this activity, she had been thinking of avoiding trouble without considering that something could actually be gained. Neglecting the defense of her domain was an omission she had not considered to be a great problem. The sudden change of circumstances in Artylia made her look at the situation with new eyes. There was no guarantee that their present peace would last. She would have to speak to Darius about establishing a more defined defense system for the island that did not rely soley on the Artylian navy.

The exercises were having the added benefit of building camaraderie between her men and Darius'. They all appeared to be enjoying the activity, and Byden made sure his men appreciated the fact that they were learning from the best so there were no hard feelings.

So absorbed was she in her thoughts that Eemya did not know Darius stood next to her until he spoke, "Are you pleased with the training?" She jumped. "I did not mean to startle you."

"Sorry, I did not see you. I was thinking."

"And what were you thinking?"

"That we need more of this training than just three days. The whole island does. We are extremely vulnerable."

"A conclusion I have come to myself. When I return to Artylia I will leave some of my soldiers here to travel to different holdings and train the men. We will also send you more weapons and armor. Yoused and I discussed harboring warships here on the island and not basing them solely on the mainland. I think I will write my brother tonight to send one to each harbor, whether Yoused and Kirdyn like it or not."

"Does Berush have a navy of its own?"

"A small one, but this war was won without involving the navy at all. The warships that were in port were virtually unmanned. The ships that were out to sea were informed of the change in government when they returned to port. They were so low on supplies that they little choice but to accept our terms. Where else would they go?

"According to their records, there are two ships unaccounted for. One is assumed lost at sea. The other, we suspect, may have decided to turn pirate rather than submit to Berushese authority. So, to answer your real question, the Artylian navy will continue to function as it always has, just under new management."

"I am surprised they gave in so easily. It seems like

they could have made a stand together somewhere."

"If they had been able to communicate with other ships, they might have. They had no plan in place or way to coordinate. And with no king to fight for, they had no motivation."

Eemya turned back to observe the activity in the courtyard, but she was imagining what the sailors must have felt returning home to find everything they knew had changed. She was also very aware of Darius standing next to her. Thankfully, he had thrown his shirt back on, but she could feel the heat emanating from his body.

After seeing him fight, she could somewhat understand his aggressiveness and see that he had to work to control it. She was beginning to believe he was sincerely trying. She stole a swift glance at him and he smiled down at her. Quickly she returned her gaze to the fighters.

Stelan was sparring with one of Darius' younger soldiers, and he appeared to be learning quickly. Eemya could see that he was putting the principles that he had been shown into practice almost as aggressively as Darius had done, but without the perfect execution. She wondered at how quickly he had begun to idolize Darius after their rocky beginning. Boldly, she decided to ask. "How did you win him over?"

Darius looked confused, and then he followed her gaze. "Stelan?" He shrugged. "I asked him to forgive me, and he did. He has a very clear sense of right and wrong, so I also asked him to help me . . . to see again, and he agreed. There are not very many people like him in the world. He is very pure. When he was younger, my brother was like that."

Eemya acknowledged to herself that he was right about Stelan. "And what were you like?"

"I was the palace terror. I still am, although some of my nephews are vying for the title." Eemya tried to imagine Darius as an uncle and failed. "My father started my combat training early to give my energy some direction. What were you like as a child?"

"Pretty much the same as I am now, only smaller."

"You were always so serious?"

She nodded. "My earliest memories are of accompanying my father when he visited the fields or helping the herbalist. I had no brothers or sisters to play with. Do you have any sisters?"

"I do. She is ten years younger than me, so we never played together. Now she is married with her own children."

Each of them considered how their lives would be different if they had children of their own. Eemya wished her marriage had resulted in a child. Darius, however, wondered what it would be like to have children with Eemya.

Stelan's coach yelled some directions at him and he obeyed. He found an open line to his opponent and was able to score a hit. His coach congratulated him briefly but made him get right back to work. This time, his opponent attacked harder, challenging him to react more quickly.

Byden had seen Stelan's potential long ago, and he had encouraged Eemya to promote him. Byden was getting on in years, and he was no longer comfortable in the saddle, so Stelan replaced him at Eemya's side whenever she rode out. The older man taught him everything he knew about maintaining the castle and leading other men. No one resented Stelan's promotion. All the men, even if they thought he was too idealistic and sometimes poked fun at him, knew he was completely trustworthy.

Most people, at first impression, thought Stelan

would be extremely gullible. A person so good-natured and optimistic would not be able to see faults in others. But that was not the case. His desire to protect his lady and do his duty, along with the wisdom Byden imparted to him, had helped him develop a keen sense of discernment. He could tell if something was off. If someone said or did something different than what Stelan would do himself, he noticed it and wondered why.

If Stelan thought Darius was sincere, thought Eemya, then it was most likely true. She would try to follow Stelan's example and operate under that assumption. Even Lydima's observations concurred, and she had cultivated her discernment skills in an entirely different manner. Eemya could almost hear her exhorting her to give Darius some encouragement. Eemya sighed audibly.

"What is it?" asked Darius with concern.

"Just thinking." There was no way she was going to repeat to him her thoughts, so she had to say something else. "Thank you, my lord, for willingly following my suggestion. This has turned out better than I could possibly have imagined."

She had placed her hand on his arm when she spoke, and Darius had hardly heard a word she said. It was the first time she had voluntarily touched him. Learning escape moves and giving him the privilege of kissing her hand didn't count. He tried not to read too much into it. She curtsied and left before he could think of anything to reply.

The rest of the afternoon passed for him in a blur. Fortunately, Effan was in charge, not him, so his absentmindedness was not obvious. They wrapped up early due to the heat to let the men have a break before dinner. If it was only his own men he was training, Effan would have kept them going, but

Eemya's men were not as well conditioned.

Darius found Yarin and composed another letter to his brother requesting warships be reassigned to the island. Letters to Yoused and Kirdyn were also composed informing them of his intentions. While they were working, Jayred knocked on the door. "A messenger from Lord Kirdyn has arrived, my lord."

"Send him in." The messenger entered.

"My lord," he bowed. "Lord Kirdyn sent me to inform you that some workers have arrived from King Cyrus, along with supplies. He wishes to know your directions for them."

Darius had almost forgotten his request for blacksmiths and cartwrights. His brother had acted very quickly. Conveniently, he was able to instruct the messenger about the workers, give him the letter he had just written, and instruct him to return to Lord Kirdyn first thing in the morning.

Darius was excited to discuss these developments with Eemya. Following Yarin's suggestion to treat her like an equal was not difficult at all. He was learning that she was his equal intellectually, and he was pleased with the discovery. He appreciated her insight as much as any man's. Never had he thought to find a woman like that. Never had he thought he would look forward to talking with a woman in general.

Before dinner he used the pitcher and basin in his room to rinse himself clean of the dirt and sweat from his demonstration with Effan. With combed hair and clean clothes, he entered the hall. When Eemya saw him, she smiled. She smiled at him. Happier than he could remember being in a long time, he took his seat next to her.

Over dinner he told her of the workers' arrival, and they discussed plans for building a special facility to start producing the unique springs her men had invented. As he conversed with her, he wondered again what it would be like to receive her love. The more he came to know of her, the more she seemed out of reach.

Winning her was no longer just a challenge. It was his dearest hope. He didn't just want her. He loved her. He would love her whether she ever returned his love or not. This realization overwhelmed him, but at the same time, it gave him both purpose and peace. He would convince her of his love if it took his entire life.

∞∞∞

The next morning the men started their training early to beat the heat. Eemya's guards were sore and stiff, so they started out with some jogging and stretching to warm them up. Then they practiced the techniques they had already learned and introduced some more advanced footwork and fencing theory.

As they took their first break, there was some commotion at the gate. A woman driving a cart was screaming for help. Byden quickly took charge and discovered she had an injured man in the back of the cart. He sent a man to fetch Lady Eemya and directed two others to carry the man to the infirmary.

Eemya had heard the noise and appeared in the courtyard almost immediately. She listened to the woman for a moment and gave some directions to Jayred, who had followed her. Then she rushed to follow the men to the infirmary. She called for Stelan to accompany her and instructed everyone else to resume their activity.

Darius waved at Effan to carry on and took the liberty to follow Eemya. When he entered the infirmary, he found one of Eemya's ladies-in-waiting comforting the woman, who was evidently the man's wife. Inside the next room, which looked like it was fitted out as a surgery, the man was laid out on a table, moaning loudly.

"Where is Yula?" Eemya asked one of the men who had carried in the patient. The other had already returned to the courtyard. The man shrugged.

"She went out this morning to check on that sick family," he replied between gags. The man was about to lose it.

"Well, we can't wait for her." Eemya looked at the man and said, "Get out." She spied Darius in the doorway. "I assume your stomach will not balk at this. Can you help?" she asked crisply.

He nodded and entered the room. Right away he saw what had disturbed the other man. One ankle of the patient on the table was completely crushed. The foot was connected to the leg only by some shreds of skin and muscle tissue. Jagged shards of bone stuck out from the leg and blood was staining the table. The blood was only dripping, not gushing, or the man would have died before he arrived. It appeared he was lucky enough that his arteries had not been severed.

Servants sent by Jayred brought buckets of clean water and towels. One of them waited outside in case anything further was needed. Eemya mixed some wine with a pinch of opium and handed it to Stelan. "Get him to drink that." He held the man's head up and helped him to drink it, a swallow at a time.

She tore the pant leg away and tied a tourniquet tightly around the leg just above the injured section. Then she poured some wine over the man's wounds. Darius knew this was believed to help prevent the wound from becoming septic. She set a bucket under one end of the table, which was slightly elevated on the opposite end, and grooved, so the blood would drain in one direction. Darius thought that was a clever design.

Next, Eemya readied several lengths of what looked like cat-gut guitar strings and set them close by. Finally, she took a bone saw and a knife off the shelf, doused them with wine as well, and directed, "Hold him down and keep him down."

Stelan, who had never assisted in an operation so serious, was nevertheless used to following directions without question and he laid himself across the man's arms and chest. Darius positioned himself to hold the legs in place. Stelan closed his eyes and turned his head away, but Darius watched closely. Sashia was the only other woman he knew of who had the stomach for this sort of thing. She had followed Cyrus into battle and run the field hospital on more than one occasion. Many hardened warriors could not stand to assist an amputation.

Eemya gave them a glance to make sure they were ready. Her look at Darius was inscrutable, and he wondered what she was thinking. Did she find it ironic that she was the one removing a man's limb, not he?

Using the knife, she quickly cut away the dangling foot and excess flesh and scraped it into the bucket. Then, she trimmed around the jagged leg bone leaving two flaps of skin that could be stretched over the end of the leg when it was all done. This took almost no time, and next she took the bone saw.

Eemya's face was grim, and her mouth was drawn into a thin line, but she looked determined. With a strong, slow back and forth motion, she cut a clean edge through the bone. The man had been still up to this point. Cutting away the mangled foot did not cause any more pain than he was already experiencing. Sawing the bone was something else. The opium dulled his senses, but he still moaned and tried to squirm. Darius held his legs firmly and thought the man lucky that he didn't have to experience the full amount of pain.

What Eemya did next was something Darius had never seen. She took a length of the string and carefully tied off the ends of the blood vessels in the exposed stump. In Darius' experience, surgeons, or executors of justice, sealed the vessels with a hot iron or merely bandaged the patients, or convicts, up and hoped for the best. Both of these methods had a high mortality rate.

Finally, after bandaging up the leg, she took a deep breath and removed the tourniquet. Every time he had seen this done without an iron, the bandage was quickly soaked with blood. They watched the wound for a few moments until Eemya appeared satisfied and nodded at him and Stelan to let go.

"Let's carry him to one of the beds," she directed. "Careful."

Stelan and Darius gently picked the man up and followed her through a door to a third room. The several cots were all empty, and they laid him down on the first one. Eemya wiped her hands on a towel and walked back through to the room where the wife was waiting. She handed the slop bucket to the servant who took it without looking at the contents.

Eemya then turned to the wife. "Cyla," Darius noted that she knew the woman's name, "his foot could not be saved," the woman gasped a sob, "but I hope I have saved his life." To her lady-in-waiting she instructed, "Take her in to see him. Stay with her until I send someone to relieve you. It is very important that he keep still and calm." The lady nodded and put her arm around the woman to guide her to her husband. "Thank you for your assistance, gentlemen, we are done. The servants will clean up."

With that she walked out a side door into the herb garden. Stelan looked to Darius for further direction and he tilted his head toward the door to the courtyard. "You go on back. I'll stay with her a while," and he patted Stelan's shoulder as he went out.

Darius had been awed by Eemya's calm and presence of mind. However, he knew that once the crisis was over, the strength that kept you going would leave you. Then you would feel all at once the emotions you had kept at bay.

The door to the garden was open, and through it he could see Eemya sitting on a bench, staring at her hands. He knew what she needed. He filled a bowl with clean water, grabbed a towel, and went outside. Without speaking, he sat down next to her and held out the bowl. Her eyes stared without seeing, but mechanically she placed her hands in the bowl and let them soak.

When the dried blood from under her fingernails began to color the water, she swished her hands around for a moment and then scrubbed at them with the towel. When she was finished, Darius took the bowl and poured the water out on a row of small, green, sweet-smelling plants. Then he returned to her side.

Eemya shuddered and let out a choked sob. Darius ventured to put his arm comfortingly around her shoulders, and she leaned into him and began to cry on his shoulder. He didn't tell her everything would be all right. The man might still die. But he remembered what his father had told him after his first battle when he was fifteen. The words had helped him then, so he adapted them to the current situation.

"You did what you had to do, Eemya. You did it better than anyone I have ever seen. It had to be done."

"I know," she sobbed, "but I still feel terrible!"

"What you are feeling is normal. Let yourself feel it." Thinking about the depths he had let himself sink to, he admonished, "Trust me, it's better than keeping it inside. Let it out."

He wanted to stroke her hair and kiss her tears away, but he dared not without her permission. It was not the time for that. He just lent her the strength of his shoulder as long as she needed it. Eventually her sobs ceased and she stopped shaking. Darius wanted to hold her forever, but he was afraid she would remember herself and become angry at his presumption.

He removed his arm, put one hand on each of her shoulders and gently set her back. "Come," he said, standing up, "You need to get out of these soiled clothes and take a rest."

Eemya was too numb to argue and followed him mutely as he led her back to her room. He handed her off to her maid who clucked over her like a mother hen. Outside her door, he stood for a moment feeling bereft. Caring for her had filled a need in his heart, and he now felt himself to be less without her, like she was one of his own limbs that had been cut off. He picked up his leaden feet and pointed them back toward the courtyard.

All day, he kept an eye out for Eemya to return to check on the patient. Once she had recovered, he was sure she would come back to evaluate the effectiveness of her work. A few servants went in and out, and a lady came to relieve the first, as promised. It wasn't until late in the afternoon that he saw

Eemya return to the infirmary. He headed over to hear her assessment of the patient's condition.

It wasn't long that he had to wait. When she came through the surgery she found him leaning against the doorframe. Eemya felt more than a little embarrassed about crying in his arms earlier, but he put her at ease by asking about the patient. "How is he doing?" Darius asked as he stepped back out of her way.

She walked through to the waiting room and let out a relieved breath. "So far, so good. There is no severe bleeding. Now we just have to watch that the wound does not fester."

"I have never seen the vessels tied off that way. Have you done it before?"

Eemya shook her head. "I assisted with an amputation a few years ago. A man had cut his leg with an axe, and it festered until the flesh began to rot. It had to be removed. Yula bandaged him up as well as she could afterward, but he continued to bleed. He died.

"Yula refused to use an iron to close the wound. She said he would die of shock. Ever since then I have been thinking of ways to stop the bleeding and decided to try tying them off. We will see if it works."

"The idea is definitely worth putting to a larger trial regardless of how well this man recovers. How did the accident happen?"

"Evidently he was walking beside the cart, he slipped, and the cart wheel ran over his ankle." The cart wheels had been reinforced with iron strakes. "If he lives, he will still have a big adjustment ahead of him. His life will not be the same."

"How is his wife handling it?"

"She is distraught. She blames herself for the accident since she was driving. He told her it was not her fault. It is very sad." Eemya needed a change of subject, so she asked how the combat training was going.

"Very well. I am pleased with how eager your men are to learn. Some men resent having others point out their deficiencies, but yours are all working with enthusiasm. In three days, they have improved more than I had hoped. Effan is planning to end with a short tournament, if you would like to come and watch."

Eemya was excited to watch and followed Darius into the courtyard. He brought a chair from the infirmary out for her to sit on and placed it in the shade of the wall. Effan had divided the men into two brackets, Eemya's fifteen men and fifteen of Darius'. Most of the matches were over quickly, but a few pairs of fighters were more judicious with their movements and took their time.

Stelan very quickly showed himself to be the most advanced of Eemya's men. He waited for the last of the Berushese to finish so he could fight the winner. A young warrior named Halem defeated all the men Effan had chosen to participate on Darius' side, and Stelan prepared to face him.

Halem attacked first, but he was testing Stelan out and letting him show what he had learned. Stelan countered more quickly than Halem expected, and Halem had to adjust his guard and step back to regroup. Stelan fought aggressively with solid technique, but his opponent was much more experienced. Halem was able to anticipate Stelan's moves and worked his way inside Stelan's guard until a line opened up.

With swift movements Halem was able to knock Stelan's sword out of his hand and deal what would have been a deadly blow. Effan signaled that the match was over. All the men came to congratulate both Stelan and Halem.

Effan signaled for quiet and Darius went to join him. "Congratulations to all of you who have participated in this training. You have all improved. You have also been wonderful hosts and made us feel welcome on this beautiful island. For dinner tonight, with my lady's permission," Darius looked at her and she nodded graciously, sure that whatever he was proposing would be fine, "I will provide a cask of fine Artylian wine as thanks for your hospitality." The men cheered. "Continue practicing what you have learned!"

The men were dismissed and they set about restoring the courtyard to its normal state. Byden oversaw the return of all the practice equipment to the armory. Darius parted from Eemya with the promise to see her at dinner.

After the tournament, Eemya felt that she should turn the dinner into a special occasion to celebrate. There was not much she could do at the last minute, but she instructed the kitchen to bring out everything they could. A nearby village had a couple of competent musicians, so she sent someone to fetch them.

After some consideration, she threw caution to the wind and dressed in her finest dress. Her ladies dressed her hair in elaborate braids. Eemya told her ladies they could attend dinner in the hall as long as they left together. She felt she could trust Darius to keep his men in line. Just before dinner, she sent a message for Stelan and Halem to join them at the high table.

When she entered the hall, Darius' eyes shone his approval. "You look beautiful, my lady," he whispered in her ear as he helped her to her seat.

Everyone was in good spirits and heartily enjoyed the meal. The men toasted each other with the imported wine, and they talked and joked animatedly. Everyone enjoyed the musicians, and by the end of the night the revelers were full and drowsy from wine. Some of the men, tired from the exercise of the last few days, some perhaps having drunk too much, fell asleep at the table.

"Stelan, are you ready to set off tomorrow?" Eemya inquired. "Yes, my lady. I have never seen the northern side of the island. It should be quite an adventure."

"You are already down five men carrying my messages. Since I'm taking Stelan and Palyn with me," Palyn was Eemya's most knowledgeable island guide, "will you have enough men left? Do you want me to leave a few of mine here in case you need them?" Darius asked Eemya.

"Thank you, but that should not be necessary. They will not be needed to assist with the harvest for some weeks. Those who are left should be able to handle anything that arises."

"Well then, will you have breakfast with me in the morning before I leave?"

"Yes," she was finding it harder and harder to refuse those hazel eyes. If the eyes truly did show the intents of a man's heart, then she no longer had anything to fear from Darius. "I would be happy to have breakfast with you."

"Then I will bid you goodnight. We have all had a long day and deserve some rest."

Eemya watched him depart, and then she rose and took her ladies with her. Jayred would be the responsible one this evening and keep an eye on everyone in the hall. When she finally got into bed, she fell asleep peacefully with a smile on her face.

CHAPTER TEN

The next morning Darius was instructed to meet Eemya in her study. When he opened the door, he was surprised to see an elderly gentleman sitting with her. Did she still mistrust him enough that she needed someone else in the room? He had noticed the guards at the door had been dismissed.

Eemya showed no distrust when she eagerly jumped to her feet to greet him. "Good morning, my lord! Come in! Let me introduce you to Elder Staid. It would please me if you allowed him to accompany you to Lord Retand's as your food taster." Elder Staid stood and greeted him. The man looked like he was nearly ninety, but he stood straight and moved like a much younger man. "He is an herbalist and a healer and has experience with many medicines and poisons."

"Can you ride?" Darius asked the man skeptically.

"Yes, my lord."

Darius looked at Eemya. "Do you really think it is necessary?"

"It would greatly ease my mind about you staying

there."

Darius would happily do anything she asked if only she was truly concerned about him. "Very well, then. I will gladly accept any offering of yours."

"You must promise not to taste or drink anything from that castle unless Staid has tasted it first," she said sternly. She looked at him, expecting him to answer.

"I promise," he swore solemnly.

Eemya nodded at Staid. "Thank you, Staid. You may make preparations to depart with the prince." Staid bowed and exited the room leaving Eemya and Darius alone.

"Come sit and eat, my lord," Eemya said, suddenly shy.

Darius sat down at the table which was covered with choice fruit, cheeses, bread and cold meat, but he didn't want to eat anything. He just wanted to look at the woman he loved. This amazing, talented, intelligent, beautiful woman. "Eemya . . ." he could not continue.

Eemya stared at her hands and could not meet his eyes. "My lord, I . . ." she looked distressed, and he could not bear that. She had suffered enough at his hands already.

He forced himself to speak. He had to be honest with her, even if she did not yet return his feelings. "Eemya, I told you on that first night that I had power over you. Over the last few days, our roles have reversed. You have already forgiven me, which is more than I deserve, but you now have power over me. When I leave today, I leave my heart with you. All I ask is that you will allow me to return and see you again."

Lady Eemya's feelings were in turmoil. Darius, from what she had seen of him, was an all or nothing type of person. Once he committed to a course of action, he did not divert from it, and he gave it his all. She was not quite ready to do that. She admitted to herself that she was becoming attracted to him, even becoming fond of him, but she could not yet give him her heart. She did not want to discourage him, neither did she want to give him false hope. So she merely said quietly, "I would like that."

Darius took her hand and kissed it with a passion that startled her. "Thank you, my lady. You have no idea how much that means to me." He continued to hold her hand. "You will be in the forefront of my thoughts every moment I am away."

He stood, still holding her hand, and she rose with him. He raised her hand to his lips again and kissed her palm. Turning it gently, he held her hand to his cheek, letting her touch him instead of touching her like he wanted to. Slowly, he moved his hand away as they stood close together, her fingers gently exploring the side of his face.

Eemya was trembling, and breathing heavily. Her hand moved down his neck to rest on his chest, over his heart. He placed his hand over hers and reiterated, "It is yours. For as long as I have breath, it will be yours."

"I . . ." she was choked with emotions she did not understand and could not speak.

"You do not have to say anything," Darius whispered. "I cannot expect you to return my feelings. It is enough to know that you will allow me to come back to you."

She nodded, looked into his eyes, and was unable to tear herself away from them. The love that shone out of them was unmistakable.

Darius smiled at her. "I will return very soon."

"I have not a doubt of it."

∞∞∞

On the way to Lord Woldyn's, where they would stay the night, Darius' stomach growled, trying to remind him that he had eaten nothing for breakfast. His thoughts were so full of Eemya that he didn't even notice. All he could think of was the feel of her hand caressing his face. Palyn was sent with them as a guide since Stelan was not familiar with this side of the island. The guide rode with Effan, and Stelan chose to ride with Halem to discuss sword fighting techniques. That gave Darius the freedom to relive those precious moments uninterrupted.

Lord Woldyn's welcome was in keeping with the hospitality he had been shown by the other island lords thus far. Lydima hung onto Woldyn's arm. He was a middle-aged widower, with no children, and seemed quite taken with her. She attempted some playful banter, but Darius could not summon any enthusiasm for a witty reply. If she had hoped for help with securing Woldyn's affections, she was on her own.

At dinner, Staid insisted on beginning his duties as food taster. "It would not do for you to employ me with one lord only. My lady would not want us to show we suspect anyone in particular."

Darius recognized the wisdom of that, so he submitted. It was embarrassing to have to wait for Staid to taste or sip everything before he could eat, however. Poison was rarely employed in Berush. If you had something against someone, you went to war with them, challenged them to a duel, or slit their throat in their sleep. To use poison was considered cowardly. Berushese did not hide behind the anonymity such a tool provided but took credit for their actions.

Fortunately, dinner was not protracted unduly, and Darius and his men were able to retire to a good night's sleep. Before climbing into bed, the prince composed another letter to his brother. He took some time over it, writing it himself, and then sealed it before finally lying down to rest.

The next morning, they set off early for Lord Retand's holding. The quickest road to their destination took them through the forest at the foot of the mountain. Here again was a great variety of vegetation that Darius had never seen. The large amount of rainfall the island received supported many tropical plants. There had been rain the night before, and the ground was still damp and mist-covered. Though the soil was rich, it was not deep, especially on the mountains, so the trees did not have the root structure to support trunks as tall as those on the southern border of Artylia.

The undergrowth showed evidence it had been thicker, but had died back. "We had an unusually cold winter this year. It killed off some of our more delicate shrubs and flowers. Normally we only see snow on the tops of the mountains," explained Palyn.

The forest floor was thick with rotting leaves and vines, but some flowering tendrils and plants were already making a resurrection. There was one particular flower, a red-dipped lily whose white center was striped with green, which reminded Darius of Eemya. Both of them were bold, but delicate at the same time.

The guide found some ripe red berries, and he offered them to Darius. They were tart, but very juicy, and had a good flavor. Later, they passed by a bush with shiny, round, black berries. Palyn told him never to eat them, or even touch the leaves, as it was extremely poisonous.

The wildlife on the mountain was also different from what he was used to. Colorful birds gathered seeds and nectar from the flowering trees, small reptiles chased insects around the branches, and several unusual varieties of rodent nosed around on the ground. He was informed that there was one species of small deer native to the island, but they had been over-hunted and were rarely seen. Darius was sorry when they finally left the forest and began to pass through cultivated cropland again.

This was one of their longest days of riding thus far, and everyone was glad when they finally rode up to the gates of Lord Retand's castle. It was large and square, like Kirdyn's, and equipped with both an inner and outer ward. Wrought iron embellished the woodwork and towers. It was aptly named Adamantine. The fortress would easily be able to accommodate the remaining five lords with whom Darius still had to meet.

Lord Retand was a handsome, genteel looking man, but he did strike Darius as somewhat nervous when he introduced himself. His wife, Lady Aylusia, had a self-satisfied look like a cat who had just eaten a mouse. Her pupils, he noticed, were strangely dilated. The prince wondered briefly how many rivals she had taken out in order to secure her husband. His first impression agreed with Eemya's assessment of the lady.

The other island lords had arrived at various times that day as well, and a large, elaborate feast had been prepared to welcome them and the new governor, Prince Darius. Staid tasted every dish and drink Darius was served, and he noticed at least one other lord took the same precautions. None of them brought a lady with them. Nothing untoward happened, however, and the meal was well-prepared with a wide range of dishes. All went to bed satisfied.

After breakfast the next morning, Darius and Yarin, with Stelan and the other lords, met in a large library to discuss conditions in Artylia and the island's status. All were relieved to find that the current treaty would remain in force.

"We had heard rumors that Uriya was going to raise our tribute again. We are glad to find that Cyrus does not deem it necessary," stated Lord Paynid.

"Artylia is not in as good of condition as the island. It is possible that they may require a loan," Darius raised his hands over their objections. "A loan, not a tax. It would be repaid with interest over a couple of years, once their production level has returned to normal."

Darius and Yarin explained the terms of the possible loan in more detail. The island lords agreed that was far better than raising the tribute, and they would have more than enough to share, as long as the recent rains kept up, even with the late spring. Darius conveyed that King Cyrus would be happy to know they were agreeable to it, should it be necessary.

The lords talked through their lunch, then Darius spent the next several hours in individual interviews with each one, listening to reports from their holdings and hearing any grievances or concerns. Lord Paynid was one of the ones who Lord Gern had mentioned having issues with, and he and Darius were able to come up with an acceptable solution to their difficulties.

Another ample dinner filled everyone's stomachs, and the lords made ready to depart home the next morning. Darius would tour the iron mines after breakfast and return to Eemya a day later. The thought of returning to her was different than he had ever felt about returning to his childhood home, now Cyrus' domain. He was always happy to go home, but it was just a visit.

The idea of having someone waiting for you, just for you, in a home of your own was an intoxicating thought. Hope stirred in his heart that it might be possible for him. Cyrus was correct. The right woman could completely change your life. He slept deeply, and in peace.

CHAPTER ELEVEN

The entrance to the mines was about an hour away from Retand's castle. There were several profitable silver mines in the Berushese mountains, but Darius had never been inside of them. Yarin stayed back at the castle to rest, but Stelan and Effan went with the prince.

On the way, they stopped by the bloomery where charcoal was used to reduce the iron to a workable state. The bloomery was a large clay oven with special ventilation pipes that allowed air to fan the flames and achieve greater temperatures than could be reached by a normal wood fire. After being smelted in the oven, the sponge iron was taken to a forge to be reheated and beaten to release impurities.

The iron wrought there was then sent to forges around the island or traded on the mainland. Blacksmiths and metal workers, like Eemya's, could then use crucibles to create steel by combining the wrought iron with carbon, or they could continue to work the iron until it became stronger. It was very hot, smoky work.

Mining was work of a very different sort, but just

as difficult. Retand's mines had several entrances, and the tunnels went deep into the mountainside. Iron was a very important and widely used metal, and the retrieval of it from the bowels of the earth could be a very lucrative enterprise for those who knew what they were doing.

Retand introduced his foreman, Ayree, who would take them on a tour of one of the newest shafts. Ayree explained the careful process of digging out the tunnel and shoring it up with supports as they went along. "This is a vein of iron ore, right here," Ayree pointed out. Its reddish color looked nothing like the final product.

Stelan and Darius went forward to look at it. As they investigated the vein, a low rumble reached their ears, became gradually louder, and the ground started to vibrate. "Is that a cave-in somewhere, or an avalanche?" wondered Darius.

The others stood mutely, slow to realize what was happening. Stelan reacted first. "Earthquake! My lord, we must get out of here!" and he pushed Darius toward the entrance.

At his words, everyone began to run. The floor of the tunnel began to shake, and Stelan lost his footing. As he fell, the roof began to cave in. Darius turned to see a beam from the ceiling fall and the roof started to cave in. He started back to help Stelan, but Effan pulled him forward. "The whole tunnel could collapse, we must get out," he urged.

Darius did not want to leave, but it would do no good for them all to be lost under the rubble. They emerged, coughing, from the mouth of the tunnel as plumes of dust billowed around the entrance. As soon as the dust settled, Darius went back into the shaft.

"Take care!" Ayree warned. "It could still be unstable."

"Sometimes there are aftershocks, my lord," cautioned Retand. "We should wait."

"I am not leaving him in there," insisted Darius, and he ventured back into the tunnel. When he reached the site of the cave-in he called out, "Stelan! Stelan, can you hear me?"

Ayree had gone back in with him to assess the damage. "The debris is too thick, my lord. He will not be able to hear you." Darius started moving the rocks, but Ayree held him back. "Let me get my men. We will dig him out, but we must do it carefully so we do not cause more of the tunnel to cave in," and he hurried back to gather men and tools.

"He is right. The miners know what they are doing. We must let them take charge," affirmed Effan. Darius could not stand inaction, but he let himself be influenced by those with clearer heads.

Ayree soon returned. With him were men carrying tools, wooden beams and lamps. The miners quickly added new joists and cross beams to support the roof before they began working. Then they began methodically clearing out the rocks and loose soil and carried it out in wheelbarrows. Darius insisted on helping, and moved the heaviest rocks at a pace that amazed Retand's workers. Every few feet, they shored up the walls with additional supports.

All day, they worked unceasingly. Darius had sent Effan back to call more of his men to help wheel out the rubble. With fresh men, the work continued at a rapid pace. Near nightfall, a small space appeared at the top of the pile with pitch black on the other side. The prince shouted Stelan's name again and was rewarded by a faint groan from the other side. "He's alive! Keep digging!" shouted Darius.

The men would have persevered anyway because the tunnel had to be cleared, but Darius felt like he had to do something. Yelling at least eased his tension a little. He knew what it was like to be a prisoner. Trapped by men or by a mountain, the panic and the helplessness had to feel the same.

It took a little longer, but eventually enough space was cleared that Darius was able to scramble through the opening. Ayree handed him a lantern, and Darius looked around for his friend. A beam had fallen across his chest, and his head and right arm were all that was visible. Descending slowly, so as not to knock loose any of the rocks, Darius made his way over to Stelan. He was breathing shallowly, but had passed out.

Ayree came through the opening and picked his way down behind Darius. Together they removed one piece of wreckage at a time. They had to avoid causing more dirt to slide down on top of the injured man. When they were finally able to safely remove the beam, Stelan shuddered and took some ragged breaths. Darius was afraid to move him, but Ayree instructed that they move him a short distance from the debris so that the men could clear it without endangering him further. They would need a much larger hole before they could carry him out on a stretcher.

Water and clean rags were handed through the opening, and Darius put a damp cloth on his friend's forehead and washed his face. Stelan had regained consciousness, but was having trouble breathing and could not speak. The prince and Ayree checked him over for injuries. It appeared his left forearm was broken, and when they touched his ribs, he groaned in pain.

The air in the shaft was damp and cool, so Darius removed his tunic and laid it over Stelan to keep him warm. He kept up a soothing monologue, describing to the captain what was happening. Slowly and steadily the hole in the tunnel widened enough to safely bring in a stretcher. A healer came with it and supervised the lifting of the patient onto it.

Once they were safely back at Retand's castle, Darius waited by his side while the healer assessed Stelan. Fortunately the earthquake had not been strong enough to disturb more stable structures like the castle. Lord Retand assured him that his healer was the best and offered his apologies for the catastrophe.

"An earthquake can hardly be considered to be your fault," dismissed Darius with some impatience.

"It has been at least fifteen years since our last earthquake. Your young captain would have been a very small boy at the time. I wonder that he recognized what was happening so quickly."

"He's pretty sharp."

The healer finished his examination and came over to speak to the two men. "It will take some time, but he should be able to make a full recovery. His arm is too swollen to be set today, but it looks like a clean break. I have immobilized it and will set it as soon as the swelling goes down," he took a breath and looked at them gravely. "That is the good news. Unfortunately, he has fractured a couple of ribs, and is having trouble breathing. I think the lung is punctured. It will take several weeks of rest and close care to make sure it does not become inflamed."

Darius let out a long breath. "Can he be moved? Lady Eemya would no doubt wish to nurse him herself."

"It would be highly inadvisable," said the healer, glancing back at the patient. "The pain to his ribs alone, on such a journey, could kill him. I have given him something for the pain, and he will sleep for a while now."

"Very well. I will send messengers to her at once to inform her we will not be returning as planned." He considered going to fetch her himself, but decided he could not abandon the captain. Stelan's quick thinking had saved all the rest of them. Darius excused himself from Lord Retand, and went to compose a letter to Lady Eemya. She would be expecting them to return in two days, but now that would not happen. He wanted to inform her of the situation without unduly alarming her. His heart wanted to say so much more to her, but he tried to restrict himself to what was necessary.

My Dear Lady Eemya,

Let me first assure you that all is well, or will soon be well. However, we will not be returning tomorrow as planned.

In order to recover from injuries received in a cave-in during the earthquake, Captain Stelan must rest and is unable to be moved at present. One of his arms was broken, and some of his ribs were fractured when he realized an earthquake was underway and pushed the rest of us toward the exit. I owe my life to his alertness.

The healer assures me that he will make a full recovery, and I will stay by his side until I see that it is so, but I am confident that it would be accomplished all the more speedily if he was nursed by your own hand.

I hope that this missive finds you well, and that your holding did not suffer any damage. Effan will be delivering this letter with instructions to place himself at your disposal. If you wish, he can remain there to assist your steward in any way necessary while you are away. I eagerly await either a letter confirming your good health or the honor of your esteemed presence.

Your Eternal Servant,
Darius

He labored over the closing, finally deciding to keep it simple. Darius found Effan and asked him to take the guide, Palyn, and several other men and deliver his letter to Lady Eemya as quickly as possible. At dawn, he returned to sit by the captain's side until he awoke.

∞∞∞

When Prince Darius left, Eemya felt restless and irritable. She could not understand her emotions. She was impatient with her ladies, could not attend to her tasks, and had to ask a messenger from a nearby village to repeat himself twice. Once, her feet even took her by the rooms he had used, and she stood there listlessly for several moments before she realized where she was and what she was supposed to be doing. She would not admit to herself that she missed him, but only that she noticed his absence.

The encounter after the breakfast they did not eat had unsettled her greatly. She had experienced feelings she had never felt before, not even for Faryn. There were none among her ladies with whom she felt comfortable speaking about it. Her mother had died birthing her stillborn brother, and Eemya felt her absence acutely.

Several times a day, she checked on her amputee. When Yula returned she was amazed at his excellent progress. The healer was tempted to be jealous of her pupil's success, but in the end, she could not help but be proud of her protégé. The man was recovering well, and the wound was not festering. It would only be a few more days, and then he could return home. He would have to walk with a crutch for some time, but when the leg had healed, he would be able to tie on a wooden peg.

The day of the earthquake, Eemya was out riding. Her horse skittered a little, but she was able to maintain control. The messengers she had sent out with Darius' summons had, by now, all returned. She sent them out again to check each village for damage or injuries, particularly to windmills or wells that might need repair.

The quake was weak enough that it did not appear to have inflicted any structural damage to her castle or any other buildings. Most of the messengers had returned by evening, and aside from a few minor injuries, everything seemed to be well. One of Darius' blacksmiths had suffered a burn when the shaking caused him to drop the iron he was working into a vat of water prematurely. An elderly woman carrying a load of washing had fallen and hurt her back. No one seemed to have suffered any worse harm. Eemya wondered briefly if all was well with Darius and his men. They were scheduled to tour the mines that day.

The next day passed as had the previous days, and it was not until the middle of the night that Jayred knocked on her door with urgent news. She pulled on a robe and opened the door.

"My lady, Captain Effan has returned with news from Prince Darius. He awaits you in the hall." Eemya rushed past him and ran down the stairs. Something must have happened! "He rode through the night, my lady!" Jayred called after her. That was normally a two day ride. He would have had to get fresh horses from Lord Woldyn, she thought.

Before she entered the hall, she tried to compose

herself and slowed to a walk. She opened the door and saw Effan, looking haggard, but he stepped toward her and bowed while holding out a letter. "My lady."

Eemya snatched it from him and tore open the seal. She read it so quickly that she had to read it again more slowly before she understood it. Turning to Jayred, she commanded, "Wake Byden and have him ready four men to ride out with me immediately, then come and see me for further instructions." She turned and contemplated Effan abstractly.

"I am at your service, my lady," he bowed again under her scrutiny.

"Prince Darius is very generous. It would be prudent for you to remain here to support Jayred and Byden if both Stelan and I are to be absent. You and your men go and get some sleep, and you may report to Jayred in the morning." He bowed a third time and started to leave when she added, "Thank you captain, for delivering this message so swiftly."

In under an hour, she and her men were on the road. The moon was nearly full, so there was plenty of light. At midday, they reached Woldyn's castle, and they took the horses Darius' men had left. They were just enough rested to ride again. Lydima encouraged Eemya to stop and rest, but she knew that worry for Stelan would never allow her to sleep, so she continued.

Near midnight, they arrived at Adamantine. Darius must have been on the lookout, because he met them in the outer ward. Eemya clutched his arm. "How is he?"

"He is stable. His breathing is still labored, but he has been able to sleep most of the day. He is awake now."

"Take me to him."

He led her into the castle. Lord Retand met them inside looking like he had just been roused from bed and thrown on some clothes. "I am sorry, my lady, to be meeting under such circumstances. I have sent for the physician, so he can explain more thoroughly your man's condition."

"Thank you," she said, hurrying on to Stelan's room. Darius opened the door for her, and she rushed in. Stelan saw her and tried to sit up, but winced in pain. "Do not move!" she ordered him. A tear escaped her eye and she wiped at it with her finger. "How are you? No, do not try to talk. Let me hear the healer's analysis first."

The healer had just come in, and he explained to her Stelan's condition. The pressure on his lungs had subsided, and he was able to breathe more easily. The swelling on the arm had gone down, and the bone had been set. Eemya inspected his work and found it satisfactory. She helped Stelan to eat some broth, and when he fell back asleep, she gave in to exhaustion herself and fell asleep in her chair.

Darius had a couch moved into the room and gently lifted her and settled her onto it. She stirred slightly, but did not wake. For a while, he sat in the chair and watched her sleep. Then, having gone without sleep himself for most of three days, his chin dropped to his chest and he too, slept.

CHAPTER TWELVE

For the next week, Eemya nursed Stelan unceasingly. Lord Retand brought books from his library and Eemya read aloud to the patient. Darius sat and listened, and sometimes took a turn to read himself. The books were mainly dry histories of Artylia and the island, but they helped to fill the time since Stelan was able to do nothing else.

Once in a while, Lord Retand would come and sit with them as well. He seemed to enjoy the society, but was ill at ease and didn't stay very long. Lady Aylusia was conspicuously absent. Darius, however, enjoyed spending so much time in Eemya's company.

"My lord," Stelan said to Darius one afternoon, "would you speak in Berushese? I would like to learn it."

"Oh, yes, that would be very interesting," chimed in Eemya, "and useful as our countries are now more closely connected."

"Certainly, if you wish," replied Darius, and he began by teaching them a few simple greetings and introductions like 'my name is,' and 'good morning.'

Yarin joined in on the lessons as well, and proved himself to be a natural instructor. He wrote out an alphabet for them, and found a book in the library that was written in Berushese so they could practice reading.

Both Stelan and Eemya were quick learners and took to the language easily. Talking still made Stelan tired, but he listened carefully. The time passed very pleasantly for all. Once, when Yarin was resting in his room, Eemya remarked on his delicate health. Darius described the conditions in which he had found his friend in Uriya's castle. Eemya was shocked, as Yarin had greatly downplayed his suffering during his captivity, and he rose in her esteem.

More importantly, Eemya finally had to admit to herself that her feelings for Darius were undergoing a complete transformation. When she had woken on the couch that first morning at Retand's and seen the prince asleep in the chair, she felt warmth and gratitude toward him wash over her. He was capable of being truly caring and unselfish. When Stelan was able to talk without too much pain, he told her how Darius had worked to free him, how he had stayed with him, talking to him until they were able to get him out. Darius had remained with him every moment until Lady Eemya arrived.

The time that they spent together in Stelan's sick room was very companionable and friendly, and Eemya found herself looking forward to Darius' language lessons. When he read aloud, the sound of his voice gave her a thrill. The only thing that held her back was the memory of his forced attentions the night they met. What would happen the next time he lost control?

By the middle of the second week, Eemya was comfortable enough with Stelan's progress to leave him and join the others in the hall for dinner. Darius made sure that she sat next to him so they would be served from the same vessels. That way, Staid tasted her food as well.

Lord Retand and his lady were both pleasant, but Darius had observed her looking at Eemya with narrowed eyes. Anytime Lord Retand spoke to Eemya, Lady Aylusia frowned. In the aftermath of Stelan's accident, Darius had forgotten about the possible peril a lady could face here. He sent messengers to Eemya's blacksmith to discover their level of progress on a cart with springs on the wheels. If they could finish it in time, it might allow them to transport Stelan in relative comfort so he and Eemya could return home earlier.

One morning, Darius excused himself to write several messages, send them out, and check on his men. Yarin had left the day before to visit Lord Paynid who wanted to consult on some legal and financial matters. Darius had talked him into going without him. He did not want to leave Eemya at Adamantine alone. He was absent from Stelan's room for a little over an hour.

On the way back, he passed an elderly maidservant with an empty pitcher, but thought nothing of it. When he entered Stelan's room, something seemed off, but he couldn't tell what. The captain was sleeping. Eemya went to a side table to pour herself a cup of wine. The decanter had not been in the room when he left.

"Wait!" cried Darius, and he grabbed the goblet from her. "Has Staid tasted this wine?"

"Oh, no. He went out to get some fresh air, and they just brought it. Sorry, I was not thinking."

Darius clicked his tongue and went into his room down the hall to call Eshan to look for Staid. A few minutes later, though it seemed like an hour, the manservant returned with the food taster. Darius held out the cup to him and Staid took it solemnly.

First he sniffed it. Then he dipped his finger in the wine and put a drop of it on his tongue. Instantly, he spit it out. "Nightshade. Quite a lot of it, and from the berry, not the leaves. The berries have a sweet flavor, and you would never suspect poison, especially in wine, if you were not familiar with the taste. Someone was definitely aiming to kill. I have developed some resistance to it, but I will go take a pinch of Calabar bean powder from my pack, just in case," and he bowed and left.

Eemya's face had gone white, and Darius' countenance was full of fury, ready to spill over. "If I had not come back in time . . ." he could not finish. Lady Aylusia must have been waiting for an opportunity to catch Eemya alone and sent a servant in with the poisoned liquid. The lady must be crazed indeed to have such unreasonable hatred toward an innocent woman.

Darius put his hand on the hilt of his sword, which he was never without, and stalked out of the room. As soon as she had recovered from the shock, Eemya asked Eshan to stay with Stelan and rushed after him. She was both curious and afraid of what he might do.

Darius reached the door of the hall, where he knew Retand was conducting business that morning, and stopped to compose himself. His anger was controlling him again. He could feel the darkness in him rising and trying to assert itself. Now that he knew what was going on inside of him, he wanted to master it. He needed Effan to keep him from spiraling out of control, but he was not there. Yarin was not there. Stelan was incapacitated. He wanted to burst into the hall, sword swinging, and slay lord, lady and maidservant alike, and he would feel justified, but that might not be the best way to handle things under the circumstances.

While he stopped to take a few deep breaths, Eemya caught up with him. She stood quietly, wondering at the cause of his delay. "What should I do?" he whispered, eyes fixed on the floor. He looked so lost. Eemya had never seen him unsure of himself like this. He had been unsure of her reactions, especially during his humble apology to her, but he had always had a clear objective in whatever he did. She didn't know what he needed or how she could help.

When she didn't answer, he continued, "In Berush, this would be a crime worthy of death, even for the attempt. I would go in there and kill them both, and it would be right. But I fear that . . . my judgment is clouded in this matter. Cyrus does not want me to alienate the islanders, and I," he looked at her, "I do not wish to alienate you."

Eemya took a deep breath and replied with some emotion, remembering her own experience with administering justice, "Sometimes . . . death is the only appropriate punishment. But, we do not have any actual proof. Proof that it was she who put the poison in the wine, or proof that she has done it before. Or that Lord Retand knows of it. That is why you include him in your wrath, is it not?"

Darius nodded, thinking. "So, we need a confession, then." He turned decisive. "Go and fetch the decanter and goblet before someone else retrieves them. We should not have left them. I am going to get a few of my men. Meet me back here."

Eemya obeyed. Eshan was still in the room, and no one had removed the decanter. She carried them slowly, being careful not to spill any. When she returned to the door of the hall, Darius was directing several men to guard the exits and not let Retand or his lady out. He took the cup and decanter from Eemya and pushed open the door. Lord Retand was speaking with several of his retainers, and his wife was hovering nearby. He took one look at Darius and dismissed his followers. "What can I do for you, Prince Darius?"

"I was just going to complement you on the interesting taste of this wine. Can you tell me the vintage? Try a sip and see if you can identify it." He held out the goblet. Lord Retand's face paled and he shrank back. His wife took a step forward, but was silent. "Do you not drink wine, my lord?" said the prince mockingly.

"No, thank you, I am not thirsty."

"Why do you refuse? Answer me or I will pour it down your throat!" yelled Darius, and moved to carry out his threat.

"No, my lord, it was me! He had nothing to do with it!" cried Lady Aylusia, throwing herself between the prince and her husband.

"You put poison in the wine?"

"Yes!"

"Why?"

"Because I am not sharing my husband with anyone!" her face became distorted with rage and jealousy. "That green-eyed witch wanted to take him away from me!" she gestured at Eemya, standing next to Darius.

Without warning, she flew at Eemya and put her hands around her throat, choking her. Automatically, Eemya used the technique Darius had taught her and released herself from the lady's hold. Darius grabbed Aylusia by the shoulders and shoved her into a chair. Subdued, she continued to glare at Eemya, but remained seated. The prince's fists clenched, but he ignored Aylusia and spoke to Retand.

"How many others has she poisoned?" Retand looked away. "You knew of this and did nothing to stop it! I am revoking your authority over these lands. Your last act as lord will be to decide on a fitting punishment for you and your wife. I will return in an hour to hear your decision." He left the decanter and goblet on a table and left the room. Eemya followed in his wake, looking over her shoulder at the stricken couple.

"No one in or out until I return," Darius ordered to the guards at the door. Then he turned to Eemya and put his hands on her shoulders. "If anything had happened to you, I could not have been answerable for my actions. Go back to Stelan. You do not need to be here for this."

"You think they will drink the poison?" she glanced at the door, shaking slightly from her struggle with Aylusia.

He nodded. "It is easier this way." He rubbed her arms and slid his hands down to hold hers. "It is not your fault," he reassured in case she was thinking this could have been avoided if she had stayed home. "She is an evil woman. Who knows how many she has killed. I will need to interview the servants to find out if any of them were complicit in this, and who exactly has died so that I can speak to their families. They will want to know that we found out what happened. We also need to find her stash of poison, but I will see to that. Go," he repeated. "I will come to you when it is over."

"I am all right," she said, "and Eshan is with Stelan. I can help with the interviews. The maidservants might not talk to you."

"If you are sure, that would be helpful."

She reiterated that she was able to continue, and Darius sent men to round up the servants. Eemya would see the women in the kitchen, with a guard within call, and Darius would see the men in Retand's study.

Before they began, Darius glanced over the women quickly to see if he recognized the servant he had seen coming down the hall that morning. "That one with the black shawl. She probably delivered it," he pointed her out to Eemya so she could question her closely. Then he went off to interview the men and search the lady's rooms.

Eemya had volunteered to help, but she wasn't really sure how to begin. There were only five female servants in the whole castle, and they all looked like they had been there for a long time. She couldn't really come out and say, 'Your mistress is a poisoner. Did you help her?' She decided to talk to them one at a time and have the others wait in the scullery. The cook was the first one she called in.

"Hello, I am Lady Eemya. Prince Darius has asked me to talk to all of the servants. He has some questions about how the castle is run," she decided that was vague enough that it was not actually deceptive. "What is your name?"

"Dru, my lady."

"How long have you worked here?"

"Oh, for forty years now, since I was a girl."

"So you were here before his lordship married?"

"Yes," she nodded.

"What do you think of your mistress?" Dru looked uncomfortable. "She will no longer be mistress after today, so you need not fear to speak your mind."

"No longer mistress? What has happened?"

"Prince Darius is removing Lord Retand from control of this holding. A new lord will be appointed."

"Oh my," she appeared worried and sat absorbed in thought for a few moments. Eemya wondered if she was afraid she would lose her own position. "Well, all I can say is she's a strange one," she said finally.

"How so?"

"All smiles one minute and then back-hands you the next. Screaming at the servants. Some of them got sick, and a couple girls died. Then no one would let their daughters work for her. I pretty much stick to my kitchen, so I saw her less than most. She mostly lets us old bats alone."

"The girls who died, do you know their names?" The cook told her and she committed them to memory. "What did they die of?" The cook said she didn't know, but the symptoms she described were similar to what Eemya knew about nightshade poisoning. "Did they eat anything unusual? Wine or berry tarts?"

"None of my cooking every made anyone sick, I can tell you that!" said the cook becoming ruffled.

"Oh, I'm sure your cooking had nothing to do with it," placated Eemya. "Could someone have put something in the food without your knowing?"

"I have nothing to do with the food once it leaves the kitchen." Eemya dismissed the cook. The next three maids provided no further information.

When she came to the last woman, who Darius had pointed out, she received some more interesting details. The woman's name was Karyn, and she had been Lady Retand's nurse from the time she was born. "Tell me about your mistress," prompted Eemya.

Karyn took on a dreamy look. "She was a beautiful child. And so passionate! Some thought her spoiled, always screaming and throwing fits to get her way, but it was just her temperament."

"And when she married?"

"She decided she would have his lordship, and have him she did. He was completely taken with her."

"But they could not have children?"

"Oh, they could." Eemya's confusion showed on her face, so Karyn continued.

"They had a lovely little boy, but my lady thought he took up to much of her husband's attention."

"So what happened to the boy?"

"My lady saved him from the misery of this world," she sniffed. Eemya was so shocked she could not speak. Obviously this woman was as delusional as her mistress. She was so blinded by her love for her lady that she believed she could do no wrong. Eemya had wanted children so badly, and Lady Aylusia had killed her own child because she was jealous of it. She could not believe it.

There was one more question she needed to ask. "You delivered the decanter of wine to me in my captain's room, did you not?"

"Yes, my lady."

"Did you know what was in it?"

"Yes, my lady," she looked at Eemya condescendingly. "You cannot come between my own sweet lady and her husband."

"Thank you, Karyn, I believe that is all I need to know."

∞∞∞

Darius found out little of value from the menservants. A couple of them mentioned the lady having trouble with the maids, but all of them agreed that Retand was a fair master, and the holding was well-run. It appeared, thought Darius, that Retand only had one weakness: his wife. In the lady's chamber had been several vials of juice of nightshade berries, powdered leaves from the plant, and several other poisons. He steeled himself to go into the hall. If they had, indeed, drunk the poison, it might take hours for it to take full effect, but he had to check. Retand might have forced his wife to take it only, and would try to blame it all on her.

Darius opened the door and walked with long, quick strides across to where Retand sat in his great chair. It was immediately obvious that they had both drunk the wine. Between them, they had emptied the entire decanter. Retand sat staring with dilated pupils, breathing quick, shallow breaths. It looked like the lady was already in a coma. She would have had to drink a lot of it since she probably built up some resistance due to repeated handling of the substance.

"Shthee thloveth me," Retand slurred with effort. Darius had to bend down to hear him. The lord's eyes pleaded with Darius to understand. "Shthee thas everthing thoo me. Withouth ther, nothingth."

Darius shook his head, but put his hand over Retand's. His eyes rolled back, and his head sagged forward as he, too, sank into a coma. Darius straightened. The man had not wanted to live without his wife, even though his wife was a jealous, insane murderer. He looked at Lady Retand.

A startling thought popped into his mind. He was not so very different from her. If it had not been for Lady Eemya's strong character, and the influence of Stelan, how far might he have gone for love? Not even love, then, but a lesser, baser desire. If Stelan had proved to be a rival, would he have killed him? He didn't know. Even the thought of his brother's displeasure might not have stopped him from making a complete mess of things. He shuddered and was thankful that he had been saved from going further down that path.

Leaving the morbid scene, he turned and walked out the door. Eemya was waiting for him. Her eyes were brimming with unshed tears, and his own were threatening to spill out. Both were emotionally raw for different reasons, but they found sympathy in each other's angst. She told him what she had learned from the nurse. "She killed her own child," Eemya said incredulously.

Darius instructed the guards to stay at the door, and scheduled others to relieve them throughout the night. They would remove the bodies in the morning. Dinner was served in the kitchen, and everyone had to line up and file through to get their food, taking it to eat in the inner ward. Fortunately, it was not raining.

Neither Eemya nor Darius could eat. He took her hand and led her back upstairs. Staid and Eshan were with Stelan, and they were all hungry for details of the day's events, but none dared ask anything after looking at the faces of their lord and lady. Darius kissed Eemya's hand and bid her goodnight, and the others followed him out. After the first night, Eemya had been given her own room, so after checking on Stelan, she departed to her own quarters where she stared numbly at the ceiling until nearly dawn.

CHAPTER THIRTEEN

Over the next week, Darius was so busy that Eemya hardly saw him other than dinner. He was occupied with overseeing Retand's estate. First there was the funeral. It was a very somber affair. Karyn cried and sobbed as if it were her own daughter in the grave. Others stood around in shock, although everyone felt that they had known something was wrong somewhere.

Eemya convinced Darius that Karyn was not mentally competent, and they retired her to a small farmhouse where a widow woman would look after her. Together they visited with the families of the servant girls Lady Aylusia had poisoned and gave them some closure. Eemya didn't know if it made things better or worse, but at least they knew what happened.

Then Darius had to learn more about the workings of the holding, delegate authority to competent workers who knew what they were doing, and think about who he could appoint lord over the holding. The other island lords were informed about what had happened, and many sent messages of shock and condolence. Most of them also suggested that it would be easy for them to take over the management of the holding for the sake of Artylia. Those with adjacent land were particularly anxious to expand their territory, and they paid visits in person. Darius told them all that he was not ready to make an appointment yet. When Yarin returned, he was shocked to find out what had passed, but he was proud of Darius for not losing control of himself.

Stelan was recovering quickly. He was already able to stand up and walk around for short amounts of time. At least part of the day, he came and spent time with Darius in his office. The prince helped him with his Berushese, and he had Stelan read aloud some of his correspondence with Cyrus for practice. The boy provided crucial moral support for the prince as he remained confined indoors with paperwork. The special cart was finished and would arrive any day. Then Stelan and Lady Eemya would return to her holding. The harvest would soon begin, and they would be needed.

Darius had come to lean on Eemya as much as he did on Yarin or Effan. Besides brightening his day whenever he saw her, she could assist him in many ways that a man could not. More servants had been needed, at least temporarily while Darius and all his men were in residence, and Eemya interviewed, hired and supervised several new maids. Now that Lady Aylusia was gone, they were more than willing to work in the castle.

Before he met Eemya, Darius had never really thought he needed a wife. Even knowing how valuable Sashia and Marthi were to Cyrus, he had felt he had everything he needed in Effan and his men. Women were just a pleasant distraction. Eemya was different. With a partner like her, a man could face the worst life had to offer, even the darkness inside himself, without being overwhelmed by it. She shone light into every corner of his life.

Lately, she had been very friendly with him, and even seemed happy to spend time with him. When he returned from Lord Retand's he had planned on speaking to her again. However, events had unfolded differently, and he had not deemed it appropriate, after Stelan's injury and the deaths of Lord Retand and his wife, to bring up the matter yet. Then, he had doubts about whether he should even pursue her. She was too good for him. Could he really ask her to share his life when so much of it was stained with blood and darkness? But he could not send her away. He needed her. He loved her, and it was tearing him up inside.

∞∞∞

Eemya was no longer in doubt of her own feelings. She loved Darius. When she had found him standing outside the hall, wrestling with himself, her last objection had been put aside. He had chosen not to give in to his anger. Even though the result was the same, he had discovered a way to find proof of Aylusia's wrongdoing and avoid shedding blood with his own hand. If he had killed them with his sword, on suspicion only, the other lords might not have approved his action. It could have negated all his efforts to establish goodwill with the island. His restraint had proved to her that he not only wanted to change, but he was capable of changing.

Now she was waiting for the right opportunity to let him know, and it had not presented itself. They had both been very busy, and when they saw each other, they were never alone. At last, she decided she would have to find the courage to create an opportunity herself.

Nearly a month after their intimate breakfast, when Darius had given her his heart, she determinedly set her feet on the path to his office. It was late afternoon, and the door was open to allow the summer breeze to flow through the open window. She could hear his voice speaking with Yarin and Stelan. Outside the door, she stood with rapidly beating heart and dry throat. Then she took a deep breath and walked into the room.

The prince looked up and saw her and rose from his seat. He was unable to read her expression, and it concerned him. "My lady, what can I do for you?"

She opened her mouth to speak, but just then, running footsteps were heard pounding up the corridor. Effan skidded through the door and put his hand on the wall to steady himself as he caught his breath. "My lord," he gasped, "Cyrus has sent news that the Cerecians have assembled a large fleet, and the Artylian navy is sailing to meet them. He asks that we prepare the island for invasion and take the two warships we brought and patrol the shores."

"When did this news arrive?" Darius barked.

"Yoused received word of it yesterday morning. He sent out riders immediately and one reached me at Lady Eemya's castle last night. I rode to Woldyn's, gave him brief instructions, switched horses and brought the news to you as swiftly as I could."

"Assuming it took a day to reach Yoused at his castle, this news is three days old." Darius spread out a map of the island on his desk. Everyone gathered around it. "I sent word two weeks ago to have one of our ships sail to Yoused's port. That way I could sail out of either one, if needed."

"Yoused took the liberty to send your ship around the island. It will anchor offshore of this holding and send longboats to fetch us," Effan informed him. "The ship should be waiting for us by the time we arrive."

Darius was surprised by the Yoused's foresight. "Excellent. That will save us days of wasted travel," he frowned at the map. "Three days." Some of his hair had escaped the tie at the back of his neck, and he absently pushed it back behind his ear. Eemya found it maddeningly distracting, and had to struggle to fix her attention back on the conversation. "A war at sea could have been won or lost by now, and we would not know," continued the prince, unaware of her thoughts.

"It is my understanding," interjected Effan, "that the fleet was first spied by fishing boats. Cyrus decided to send them south instead of the warships as they would be less remarkable. The fleet was still in Cerecia at the time. We do not know when they planned to move."

"My lord," Stelan broke in, "there has been a strong wind from the north for the past week, and the weather has been stormy. It changed just this morning, and is now blowing from the west. If their ships are powered by sail, they might have had to wait for favorable weather."

Darius' eyes lit up. "They do have some galleys that can be moved by oar, but they are slow. They would want their whole fleet. You are right, they may not have been able to leave until today. If so, we can still intercept them." He looked at Effan. "How did you leave things at Lady Eemya's holding?" he knew she would want to know.

"Byden and Jayred are preparing to withstand a siege, if necessary. Men at every holding are being instructed to keep watch on the coastline and set up defenses at possible landing points. Messengers are ready to call all your subjects to the castle," he turned to Eemya, "if they should need to take shelter there." Turning back to Darius, "I took the liberty of leaving Halem there to advise them."

"I must return at once," cried Eemya, and she made a move toward the door.

"No!" she was arrested by Darius' booming voice. "You will do no such thing! By the time you arrive, it could be already under siege. We cannot spare the men to accompany you. This castle is much more defensible, and highly fortified. You will be safer here than you would be at home."

"But-"

"I will not give you a choice in this!" he stated firmly. Then more softly, "Your people are prepared. There is nothing more you can do. I cannot leave unless I know you are safe."

Eemya looked into his eyes and felt her heart melt. How could she deny him anything, especially when he had her own interests in mind? "Very well, I will remain here."

Darius had been prepared for more argument, and he looked at her askance, not sure whether to believe her, but he turned to Stelan, "You will be in charge of this castle while I am gone. Do here the same as the other holdings." Stelan nodded his acceptance of this responsibility, though he wished he was well enough to go with Darius. "Take care of my lady," the prince added. This was the most important task he would give anyone. "Yarin will be here to advise you should you need anything."

Finally, he turned to Effan again. "Prepare the men to ride out. We leave as soon as they can be ready." Effan bowed and went to summon the men. Darius looked at Eemya. "I do not know when I will return, my lady, but there is nothing that can prevent me from coming back to you as soon as I am able," he bowed and turned to leave.

"Wait, my lord," she called, and he looked back at her. "I must speak with you," Eemya glanced at Stelan and Yarin, and they quietly exited the room.

"My lady," Darius waited expectantly. Eemya stepped closer to him until they were nearly toe-to-toe. His knees became weak with a sudden hope that she might be about to say what he had been most longing to hear. She placed her right hand over his heart, where it had rested just a few weeks before.

"Before you left my castle, you gave me your heart." With her left hand, she took his right and kissed his palm. He made a sharp intake of breath. She put his hand against her cheek and then placed it over her own heart. "I am now ready to give you mine."

Darius' face was suffused with joy. "Eemya!" he cried and put his arms around her waist. He hugged her to himself and spun her around in a circle. "Do you truly mean it?" he laughed, giddy with happiness.

"I love you," she replied simply. "I want you, more than anything," and she reached her arms up to encircle his neck as proof. "I could not let you leave without knowing," she whispered softly, as their lips met in an explosion of passion.

Darius kissed her as she had never been kissed before. She had not known she could feel this deeply about anyone, and had only dreamt of being cherished in such a way. He kissed her until she felt lightheaded, and found herself lost to all but his touch. "What made you change your mind?" Darius stopped kissing her mouth to ask the question, but his lips brushed her cheek as he spoke and then he kissed her neck.

Eemya moaned, closed her eyes, and ran her fingers through his hair, which had come completely loose. She could not concentrate enough to give more than a one word answer, "You."

A knock sounded on the door. "We are ready, my lord," came Effan's muffled voice through the heavy oak.

Darius sighed and put his forehead against Eemya's. "You have made me happier than I thought was possible," he said as he stroked her cheek, "but your timing is terrible."

"It is Cerecia's timing that is terrible," she said breathlessly. "I will be waiting for you."

He gave her one last kiss. It was the type of kiss that was all-consuming, full of love and desire, full of the triumph of requited passion and the sorrow of parting. Finally letting her go, Darius traced her lips softly with his finger, and a shiver ran through her body. "If every man had such a love to come home to, no one would ever go to war. Since I must go, I will fight all the harder, so I may return all the more swiftly." He tore himself away and left with Effan who was still waiting in the hall.

It took Eemya a few moments to recover herself. At first, she felt wobbly, and she could hardly walk. Then, she wasn't sure if she wanted to cry or laugh. Propelling her legs forward, she raced to the battlement to watch them ride out.

Not since the day Darius had first ridden through her gate had she seen him and his men in full battle armor. Most of the men only had a leather cuirass or chain mail, but Darius and Effan had fitted breastplates. All had some sort of helmet and bracers or gauntlets. She observed as Effan helped Darius quickly into his armor. They looked quite formidable. Extra men from the castle rode with them to lead back the horses as they would not be needed for a fight at sea.

Eemya felt more bereft than the day she knew she was losing Faryn to the fever. She told herself there was no greater warrior than the Berushese prince. He would prevail against any enemy. He would come back to her.

CHAPTER FOURTEEN

Darius rode out with his men and did not look back. He couldn't. He knew if he did, that he would not be able to leave. It had been difficult enough for him to leave her before, when only his own emotions were involved. But now that she loved him in return, his desire for her was overwriting every other thought.

The ride to the seashore went by in a blur. They gathered a few more men on the way, asking anyone good with a bow or sword to join them. Some of the men they met were told to report back to the castle for patrol assignments. Darius let Effan take charge of this while he tried to settle himself. He had to stay sharp. Soldiers could not afford to be distracted.

The first light of dawn was tinging the sky when they arrived at the only beach along Retand's holding where a rowboat could put in. Everywhere else, the coastline was rocky and inhospitable. The black, volcanic sand looked strange to Darius, used to the golden sand of his own country. Silhouetted against the sunrise was the waiting warship, the *Horizon*.

The longboat was already drawn up on the beach.

It took five trips to row all of Darius' men, plus the island archers who volunteered, to the ship. Yoused had sent an extra twenty of his own soldiers, so that brought the number of men aboard to nearly ninety. Since the horses no longer took up the lower deck, more men were easily accommodated.

Ninety was a good number, but not as many as would man a Cerecian galley. He was glad to see Oribus, the Berushese ship captain. Darius was inexperienced in naval warfare, and would have to rely on the captain to maneuver the ship and to advise him in tactics and strategy.

The Artylian ships were lateen rigs, with two triangular sails aligned fore-and-aft. These sails pivoted, and the design allowed the ships to tack around the island or patrol the channel in almost any type of wind. The mizzen mast was perpendicular to the deck, and the foremast leaned forward at an angle. The length of the ship was about nine horse lengths.

It would take about two days to sail to a point where they might encounter the Cerecian fleet. Darius passed the time by learning the workings of the ship and acquainting himself with the specialized weapons and stock of arrows and other projectiles. He, the captain, and the seasoned Artylian first mate also discussed the most effective methods of fighting oared ships, and the typical tactics used by the Cerecians in naval battle.

On the morning of the third day at sea, they rounded the southern tip of the island and entered the channel. Cyrus had asked them to position themselves to protect the island, so the captain sailed just far enough into the channel to keep the island's coast in view. Several Artylian ships could be seen sailing toward them. The remainder of the vessels were already lined up along the entrance to the channel. In addition to the twenty-odd heavily armed warships, many large fishing boats could be seen carrying soldiers from the island and the mainland. The captain estimated the number of ships to be nearly two hundred.

Darius' ship took a position at the eastern end of the line. If an enemy ship tried to skirt around the fleet to beach their ship somewhere other than Yoused's harbor, they would face the *Horizon*. Oribus ordered the sails to be lowered enough to maintain their position without drifting too far.

They did not have to wait long. Stelan's guess was correct, and the Cerecians had not set out until the wind changed. The bulk of the enemy fleet was in a tight formation headed straight toward the middle of the Artylian defenders. The central configuration was flanked by a small line of ships on each side. They knew from the scouting reports how many ships to expect, and since they were nearly all visible from the *Horizon*'s position, it appeared the Cerecians meant to attack the island rather than the Artylian mainland.

"They mean to break through our line, and then surround us on both sides as we attack the center," cried the captain.

"What do we do?" asked Darius.

"If the Artylian commander has any sense, our ships will form into a 'V' with the point toward the Cerecians. We must hold our position and not rush forward."

Darius watched while the Artylian ships did just as Oribus predicted, with a few ships forming a second line inside the 'V'. As the Cerecian galleys approached, the prince was able to get a better look at their construction. There were two rows of thirty oars on each side, which meant one hundred twenty rowers. The ships had a single, square sail, and so required a smaller sailing crew to manage it than the Artylian ships. The square sails were not very useful unless sailing downwind, so they had been taken in. That meant that the rowers had been rowing for three or four days, maybe lying at anchor a few hours a day to rest, and would be getting tired. The Artylian navy would need that advantage, as their ships carried less men.

About thirty galleys led the attack, with one hundred or so smaller sailing ships behind them. Each of the galleys held nearly twice the number of men as those of their opponents. The galleys were also better equipped to maneuver in tight quarters. The turning radius of an oared ship was much smaller than that of a sailing ship. The front of each galley was fitted with a ram, and plated in bronze. They would try to set fire to an enemy's sails, then either ram them in the side, or come alongside and board, overwhelming the enemy force with sheer numbers. Smaller fishing boats could be broken in half without even trying. The Artylian sailors also told Darius about some mysterious 'magic fire' employed by the Cerecian archers to disable enemy ships.

The Artylian side had advantages as well. The sailing ships' decks sat higher above the water, so they could jump over the side to board an enemy ship instead of climbing up. As long as the wind blew, they could maintain speed indefinitely and not tire. Since the wind still blew from the west, the sailing ships could tack north or south through the channel without difficulty.

The Artylian ballistae were also far superior to their Cerecian counterparts. Uriya's predecessor, when Cerecian piracy was in its heyday, oversaw the outfitting of the warships with the most advanced weaponry. Theirs were made from metal and had a much farther range than the wooden version of the opposition. These machines were similar to giant crossbows, capable of shooting either bolts or stone shot, like a catapult, but with a flatter and more accurate trajectory. Many of these had been mounted at strategic points around the castle in Letyna as well, but no one had been manning them.

As the center of the formation began to engage, the arms of the 'V' sailed forward to prevent the enemy from flanking. The galleys in the rear of the Cerecian formation were not immediately able to take a role in the battle, which was fortunate since they outnumbered the Artylian warships. Fishing vessels on both sides hung back, waiting to assist in boarding once a ship was disabled.

The *Horizon* was fast approaching a galley that looked like it was trying to sneak past the line. Darius put himself under Oribus' command and made sure his men were ready. The first pass would be their best chance. If they missed, they might not be able to catch up with the galley if they rowed at full speed. Just outside the range of the Cerecian ballistae, the expert Artylian operators prepared to shoot a volley of stone shot at the side of the galley. At the same time, archers would shoot at the exposed upper deck of rowers. A distance of one hundred fifty horse lengths was too far for accuracy for the archers, but any arrows that fell inside the ship would cause a disruption. Any that hit a target would be a bonus.

"Loose!" ordered Oribus as they drew even with the starboard side of the galley. One projectile fell short, but three others hit the side of the galley. Two broke oars, and the third penetrated the hull near the waterline. The archers achieved their aim, and the galley faltered. Missiles shot by the Cerecian ballistae splashed harmlessly in the water.

Oribus immediately directed his sailors to shift the yards to the opposite side so the ship could come about without the sails pushing against the masts. The Cerecians had shot a volley of fire arrows, and they fizzled and burned brightly. A few tore small holes in the sails, and the men worked rapidly to put out the fires with wet sacks. The 'magic fire' missiles were almost impossible to put out, and they threw most of them quickly overboard. The sails could not be allowed to catch fire, or they would become a sitting target for the galley's ram.

Darius thought briefly that he would have to look into this new incendiary threat. He had never seen anything like it before. They did not look like traditional arrows and flew somewhat erratically. A few soldiers were injured or burned by the projectiles, but there was little time to treat them as they prepared to make another pass.

Meanwhile, the galley tried to recover, but was significantly slowed by the hole in its side and was beginning to take on water. They also had to take time to replace injured rowers. The sailing ship was easily able to overtake them, this time coming in closer. Now that they were moving in the same direction, there would be time for more than one volley. The ballistae had been swiveled around, and this time the operators aimed for the enemy weapons, taking out their machines before they could fire. Then they quickly rearmed with grappling hooks.

The island archers armed themselves with their own version of fire-arrows. Patches of oil-soaked rag had been tied to arrows and were now lit. These arrows could not be shot as far as regular arrows, or at the same speed, because the air flow could extinguish them during flight. "Aim for their store of magic fire!" Nearly half of them fizzled out before reaching the galley, but one of them must have found its mark. A shower of sparks spewed from a barrel and then there was a huge explosion, and black smoke belched everywhere.

Then everything began to happen very quickly. The grappling hooks were shot, and then reeled in using large winches mounted on the side of the ship for that purpose. Archers continued to shoot arrows from both sides. For a few moments, the smoke made it nearly impossible to aim, but the wind quickly cleared it away. One of the ropes was cut, and the archers concentrated their arrows around the remaining hooks to ensure they remained in place. An arrow hit Darius in the chest, but it did not penetrate his armor. His men put up their shields, trying to protect both themselves and the archers.

Darius and his men readied to board, and an island fishing boat sailed up on the opposite side, ready to support the attack. A few of the Cerecian oarsmen tried to push the *Horizon* away, but the ballistae operators quickly took them out with bolts through the oar holes. The remaining oars splintered and cracked from the strain as the Artylian ship heaved into them. The captain turned the wheel, crashing the bow of the ship into the port side of the galley as a heavy gust of wind aided them in closing the remaining distance. The lines were pulled tight and made fast. Now it was the soldiers' turn.

"Over the side," yelled Darius, and he and Effan were the first to leap onto the enemy deck. Landing on top of the rowers, the Berushese soldiers hewed through their ranks like farmers scything wheat.

They were closely followed by Yoused's men. The oarsmen were armed merely with daggers, as swords would get in the way of their rowing, and they were no match for the fierce fighters who now faced them.

The infantry in the center of the galley were another matter. A dozen or so had been killed or wounded by the explosion, but at least a score remained. The close quarters and motion of the waves made it difficult to find footing. Darius' men were highly skilled, however, and the Cerecians could not prevail against them. The island soldiers from the fishing boat were engaged with the rowers on the other side of the galley, and as soon as they were able to overcome the infantry, Darius' men came to their aid and soon finished them off. The last few oarsmen surrendered when they saw that the ship was lost.

The islanders began throwing the Cerecian corpses overboard, and circling sharks soon turned the surrounding water red. Their own casualties would return with them for burial as they towed the listing hulk of the galley back to the harbor. No sooner had they cleared the deck, than an enemy fishing vessel drew up on the port side of the *Horizon* attempting to take advantage of the absence of its soldiers. The Artylian archers held them off, but their stock of arrows was running low.

Effan noticed their plight first and reacted swiftly. "Back!" he yelled, and the Berushese scrambled up the side of the *Horizon* and ordered the archers behind them as they fought with the soldiers climbing up from the smaller boat. There were only three dozen or so of the enemy crammed into this watercraft and Darius' and Yoused's men easily overpowered them. The Cerecian fishing vessel was tied to the back of the galley, and the island boat, with the forced labor of the captured rowers, began to head slowly back to the harbor.

Before they left, Darius had men scavenge the galley for additional arrows, bolts and anything else they could use. While this was happening, the Artylian sailors hustled to replace one of the damaged sails. It had caught fire during the second round of shooting, and was irreparable. They hurriedly attached a spare sail before they could be attacked by another enemy ship.

The *Horizon* had lost a dozen men, and nearly that many were severely wounded. The dead were taken below deck along with those too injured to fight. Then they prepared to reenter the fray. It appeared that the battle was pretty even. Wreckage of both sailing ships and galleys dotted the entrance to the channel. Some had been set alight, and others merely floated halfway below the surface. The *Horizon* would have to navigate carefully to avoid being torn apart by debris.

The Cerecian galleys still slightly outnumbered the Artylian warships, but the fishing boats were helping to even the score. In pairs, they sailed up on either side of an enemy sailboat, and vanquished them with superior numbers. Many of the soldiers in them were Berushese who had remained stationed in the Artylian capital with Cyrus.

Darius cleaned his sword with a shirt he had torn from a dead Cerecian while Oribus steered the *Horizon* to assist another ship under attack from an enemy galley. The galley had successfully incapacitated its opponent by setting the sails on fire, and its soldiers were beginning to board as the *Horizon* sailed silently into position on their exposed side. The oarsmen had left their oars to watch the fighting in the opposite direction, and noticed the approaching ship too late to react. Before a line could even be secured, the Prince and his followers bounded over the railing.

The rowers on this ship offered more resistance than on the previous galley, but their daggers could not defend against the attacking swords. Darius could stab a man through the heart before the man's smaller blade was close enough to scratch him. Two of them tried ganging up on him, but even in such a tight space, Darius could wield his blade so deftly that none could touch him. He removed the hand of one, slayed the other, and then finished the first with three swift strokes.

Effan had twisted an ankle boarding the galley, but was still able to overcome his opponents. A wave lifted the boat, and he was thrown off balance. Darius stepped in and dispatched a soldier who attempted to take advantage of the captain's momentary incapacity. He gave his friend a hand up, and Effan gave him a nod of thanks.

Caught between enemy forces on both sides, the Cerecian infantry did not last long. The sailors on the Artylian ship they rescued, the *Seagull*, had replaced the sail of the mizzen mast, but did not have a spare for the foremast. The captains conferred, and it was decided that the *Seagull* would return to the capital with the wounded, leaving most of its soldiers and extra arrows with the *Horizon*. It took some time to arrange all this, and Darius and his men took a moment to hydrate themselves and take a few breaths. Some dried meat and biscuits were handed around as well.

The galley was still in good condition, and they hailed a fishing boat to come and tow it away before the enemy could retrieve it. The *Horizon* covered the *Seagull*'s retreat until they were safely away, then Oribus set the point of sail on a beam reach back toward the opening of the channel. Soon, off the port side, they saw a burning island boat. A galley was headed toward it at ramming speed.

The *Horizon* was too far away to intervene, and they could only watch as the galley ran over the watercraft, splitting it in two. Men jumped into the water and swam away, but others were crushed beneath the prow of the ship. The galley was momentarily beached atop the wreckage.

Oribus turned the wheel so the ship ran before the wind. "Quickly, ready ballistae with stones! Archers, prepare to shoot!" Oribus shouted orders. They had a narrow window of time when the galley was vulnerable. "Loose!" The sound of splintering wood was heard as the stones tore through the side of the galley, and the men in the water cheered.

With the wind behind them, they passed by so swiftly that the galley could not react. With three large holes in her side, she wasn't going anywhere, so Oribus decided to make a wide circle and pass by again on the same side. Using 'magic fire' arrows they had confiscated from the other galleys, they bombarded the enemy deck, which was now tilted toward them, with their own weapons.

They were not true arrows, as the archers had quickly discovered. Once a waxen string at the end was lit, they propelled themselves forward out of a special launching tube. Even in the inexperienced hands of the *Horizon*'s crew, the missles were effective. The square sail was soon ablaze, and the enemy's own store of fire arrows exploded violently, blowing a hole in the deck.

Leaving the galley to burn, the *Horizon* returned to pick up the surviving islanders from the water. They were none too soon, as the sharks had already begun to circle. Archers shot toward the menacing fins trying to scare them off as they pulled the swimmers into the ship. A few survivors of the galley swam over begging to be saved. Oribus let them board and tied them up below deck. At one time, Darius would have refused them, but Oribus was in charge on this vessel, and Darius was learning how to be more temperate and merciful. Eemya, he knew, would have saved them.

There were now very few Cerecian vessels left in the channel, and as the *Horizon* caught up with the Artylian ships to re-form a line, what was left of the enemy turned tail and ran. In the remaining hours before dark, the *Horizon*, along with the rest of the Artylian navy vessels still afloat, searched for survivors and any crafts that could be salvaged.

Casualties were heavy, but the enemy losses were much worse. Out of thirty galleys, eleven were sunk, fourteen salvaged, and only five escaped. Nearly all of the enemy fishing vessels were destroyed. Ten Artylian warships circled the wreckage, and over two-thirds of their smaller boats were still afloat. At dusk, they headed back toward Youred's harbor to return the island soldiers to their home.

Even though they arrived late, the piers were lined with wives and children waiting for their husbands and fathers. The surviving fishing boats had all returned, but there were still men missing. When the *Horizon* sailed into port and they saw the number of men on the deck, the crowd cheered. The men rescued from the waves, as well as the men Yoused sent and the men from Retand's holding, disembarked to welcoming arms. There were still many men who would not be coming back.

Yoused himself met them at the docks and came aboard to hear the latest news. Darius recounted to him the results of the battle. When they were done speaking, the faint light of dawn was brightening the sky. After Lord Yoused left, Darius was so tired that he went below with his men and was asleep before his head hit the floor.

CHAPTER FIFTEEN

Darius slept most of the day. Eventually, his empty stomach woke him with its rumbling. Yoused did not have an actual castle at the port, but he had a large house with a hall, and food was served there all day for any who were hungry. Darius wanted nothing better than to ride as fast as he could back to Eemya, but he needed to find out if Cyrus had any other instructions for him. They would need to create a policy for dealing with Cerecia going forward.

The Artylian lords had only had a few weeks to begin training troops and shoring up their defenses. If the Cerecians attempted a land assault, they would not be ready. They had lost nearly one thousand men yesterday. Fortunately, the enemy casualties had to be nearly triple that. Darius didn't know the disposition of Chysh's remaining forces, and this would have to be looked into. He would have to go to Letyna to see his brother.

If he could not go to Eemya right away, he could at least write her a letter. As soon as he had eaten, he availed himself of Yoused's study to write his missive.

Eemya, my dearest love,

Our defense against the Cerecian invasion was successful, and the island is safe, as am I. My greatest wish is to return to you at once, but that it not possible. I must confer with Cyrus and await his orders.

Every moment I am away, the taste of your sweet kisses and the warmth of your embrace will sustain me. I am still in awe that such a beautiful, intelligent, talented lady has given me her affections. It is a love that I do not merit, but will try to live up to it for the rest of my life.

My love for you is so powerful that I fear my heart may rebel and tear itself from my body to fly home to you where it belongs. If you are ready to return to your own holding, I will seek you there as soon as all my duties are fulfilled. There I hope to make you my own.

Your ardent lover and humble slave,
Darius

He sent the letter by one of his own men with instructions to place it in Lady Eemya's hand wherever she might be found. As soon as the ship was ready to set sail, the *Horizon* headed across the channel into the sunset.

∞∞∞

"Brother, I am heartily glad to see you!" Cyrus exclaimed as Darius walked into the hall of the castle at Letyna three days later. Tomus was there, as well as Byrd and several other lords. Everyone was involved in heated discussion about their casualties, and many tried to cast blame on Cyrus for ousting

Uriya and creating instability.

Lord Byrd tried to inject some sense into the conversation. "Friends, King Chysh was already rallying his forces for an invasion, before Berush ever became involved. In reality, without King Cyrus' intervention, our navy may not have been prepared to counter their attack. He ensured that our ships were manned and their supplies replenished. He sent boats to spy on the Cerecians, and they gave us advance notice of the enemy's plans. Uriya would have done nothing! The Berushese have saved us, sacrificing many of their own men in the process." His logic silenced the complaints.

"There is nothing to gain by exploring what might have been," Cyrus took up the reigns. "We must decide what is to be done now."

A lively debate followed, and Darius was asked for his input. "I do not believe we need fear another attack by sea for some time. The Cerecians lost almost their entire navy. Their bellies will be empty because their fishing boats were all sunk. They might try a couple of quick raids, as they have in the past, but they cannot send another invasion force through the channel until they build more ships.

"We still have enough ships to patrol our shores for now. More should be built to replace those that were destroyed, but we won the battle, and our warships now outnumber theirs. They suffered immense casualties, so I doubt they will be ready to march across the mountains any day soon either. Compared to the Berushese mountains, the southern Artylian range is almost impassable in the best of conditions.

"We must build a reliable spying network, patrol the borders, and train soldiers so that we are ready for the next attack, whenever it comes. Our spies must focus on discovering the source or recipe for their 'magic fire.' I fear the substance may be used to develop even more dangerous weapons than we have yet seen." Darius knew 'magic' was just a term given to something you did not have the wisdom to understand, and they needed to understand it in order to protect themselves against it.

The rest of the day was spent finalizing the logistics of their plans. Tomus knew several scouts who spoke Cerecian fluently, and they discussed ways they might be able to infiltrate the enemy ranks. Darius had given his input, and he was chafing to get away. Cyrus sensed his restlessness, and at the earliest opportunity he took him aside. "How is your other endeavor progressing?"

Darius could not help grinning widely with misty eyes. "She loves me! I still cannot believe it."

"I can believe it, brother. You are a man of great value. I am happy for you!" Cyrus looked at him benevolently. "Go. Be with her. I will send for you if I need you." Darius clasped his brother's arm and turned and ran out the door.

∞∞∞

Effan's ankle was still swollen, and he was resting in bed. Darius came in to retrieve his pack and told him where he was going. Effan made a move to rise and go with him, but Darius ordered him to stay. "You have earned the rest, my friend. Bring our men with you when the warship has been refitted."

"You should not go alone, my lord," Effan remonstrated with a concerned expression.

"This is one mission for which I do not need assistance," he grinned.

Effan's eyes reflected the happiness of his prince.

The captain smiled back at him, but then turned serious again. He reached under his tunic and lifted a braided, leather rope from around his neck. At the end was a small pouch. "This is sand from my home village. Berushese sand. I carry it so that I am never away from home. Take it."

Darius was greatly moved. "I cannot take it Effan. It is yours."

"Please," Effan insisted. "We have never been separated by water since I have been under your command. Take it, my lord. I will collect it from you when I see you again."

Darius reached out and took it, and he placed it around his own neck underneath his leather cuirass. "Thank you, Effan." He squeezed his friend's shoulder. "I will see you soon."

The prince wended his way out of the city and down to the harbor with a determined, but lighthearted, step. He had to restrain himself from sprinting the entire way. When he reached the docks, they were a bustle of activity. Every damaged ship that was not in need of dry dock had been brought into the harbor for repairs. Sails were spread out everywhere as men and women busily mended them. Carpenters carried boards, sailors cleaned decks, and the sound of hammers and saws filled the air. It was a vastly different scene from the first time Darius had seen the harbor.

At the end of one pier, he saw a small, one-masted, lateen-rigged fishing vessel. A man and boy had just raised the sail and appeared to be inspecting it. Darius hailed them. "I need a ride to the island. I can pay you well if we can start immediately." Darius took out his purse and jingled it.

The man shook his head. "My lord, it will be night soon. We have had a long day and are very tired. We can take you in the morning, once we have caught up on our sleep."

"Name your price, I will pay it," Darius insisted. The man looked at his son, but still hesitated. Darius weighed his options. Threatening the man with his sword was his first instinct, and it was usually a very effective method of persuasion, but it was not one he could use in this instance. Eemya's face appeared before his eyes. He could not bear to be parted from her any longer. "Have you ever been in love, man?" The fisherman turned and looked Darius in the eye. He stood up straighter, but his look had softened. "My love is waiting for me on the island," the prince continued, his voice heavy with emotion. "I must return to her." Something in Darius' eyes must have convinced him, for he nodded and named a price. The prince paid it, and they made ready to set sail.

The man introduced himself as Davyn, and his son, a boy of thirteen, as Petyar. Davyn sent his son for provisions, and lashed Darius' pack securely in the bottom of the boat. Petyar returned with food and one more sailor, an uncle, who would take turns manning the sail and the tiller so they would be able to sleep in shifts through the night. The wind was still blowing from the west, so Davyn headed them north toward Kirdyn's harbor to avoid the wreckage still being cleared from the eastern end of the channel.

Darius asked to be let ashore directly on Eemya's lands, but Davyn explained that the shore there was rocky, and there was no safe place to put in. Even if the prince tried to swim ashore from a short distance, the waves would dash him against the rocks. Darius reluctantly gave in to Davin's superior knowledge of the island. Besides, he thought, there might not be any villages nearby where he could acquire a horse. Kirdyn would, no doubt, have several stabled in his castle at the harbor.

As darkness fell, the night turned cooler, but the breeze from Artylia was still warm. Davyn took the first shift at the tiller and told everyone else to try and sleep. If the wind held steady, he would need no help with the sail, and would call one of them if he did. The night was clear, and navigating by the stars would be easy. Darius stared up at them. He wasn't sure if he could sleep, but the gentle rolling of the waves and the peaceful night eventually lulled him into a deep slumber.

∞∞∞

In the morning, Darius was awakened by shouting. It took him a few moments to remember where he was. A wave sprayed salt brine onto his face as he sat up. The sea was rougher than it had been the night before, and the sky was filled with dark clouds. Davyn was yelling directions to the other two men, but Darius could hardly hear him over the wind.

"The wind has shifted, my lord," shouted Petyar, who was the closest to him. "There is a storm on the way, but do not worry. We have weathered many storms," he said with confidence.

"Are we still on course?"

The boy shook his head. "We are mid-channel, but the wind is blowing us south. We are reefing the sail, and will stay as close to the wind as we can to ride it out."

Darius nodded and tried to stay out of their way as they worked. He could feel the wind off the starboard side of the boat, and could not help feeling disappointed in the delay. Sailing this direction would be the safest under the circumstances, but it would not take him closer to Eemya. A gust of wind ripped through his hair, and drops of rain stung his face.

They sailed for what seemed like hours. Darius himself took a turn at holding the tiller. It was hard work steering it in a storm, and the others were beginning to show the strain. Davyn had not any time to rest, and took a moment to close his eyes. He slept for a short time, even while the storm raged, then returned to the tiller.

The wind had not let up, and a strong gust tore loose the lines that had been used to shorten the sail. Petyar sprang up to catch it, but the boat rolled and he lost his balance. Darius stood quickly to grab hold of him and threw him to safety at the bottom of the boat. As Darius pushed his arms forward to block Petyar from going overboard, the boy's momentum transferred to the prince and he plunged over the side and into the waves.

If anyone called out to him from the boat, he did not hear it. The waves pushed him under. When he finally broke the surface, coughing and gasping for air, the vessel was already a bowshot away. Another wave broke over him, and in the brief seconds he made it to the surface again, he did not see the boat. Darius wondered if Davyn would turn around and look for him, or if he would give him up and focus on taking his crew safely through the storm. Even if he did turn around, the heavy rain made it impossible to see very far, and the chances of finding one bobbing head in a vast sea were grim. Both the wind and the tide were working to take him farther away with every moment.

The temperature of the water was warm enough that he would not soon die of cold, so he concentrated on trying to stay afloat and not tire too quickly. It was lucky he wasn't wearing his metal breastplate today. He made himself into a ball to conserve heat and energy, and took as deep a breath as he could whenever he surfaced. Even this could not be kept up indefinitely. He wished he could remove his boots, but the knots were tight, and obtaining air took all of his effort.

Between waves he looked around for anything he might be able to grab hold of. Just when he was thinking he could struggle no longer, he spotted something dark out of the corner of his eye. A random piece of flotsam, probably a section of deck from a ship, floated past him. It was farther north than he would have thought it could be, but he was not going to reject it. Possibly it had come loose from a ship that had been towed to Kirdyn's harbor.

He used every ounce of remaining strength to kick as hard as he could, then he reached out and grabbed it. A jagged splinter cut a hole in his palm, but he ignored the pain and heaved himself up onto the debris. There was a short length of rope stuck between two of the planks, and he tied it tightly to the section of deck to give himself a good place to hold on. He did not tie himself to it because he would drown if it flipped over. Instead, he slipped his arms under the rope to the elbows and held tightly to the edge of the wreckage with his hands.

With an open mouth, he caught a few drops of rain, since it might be the only fresh water he would have for a while. Then he closed it as a wave crashed over him. He hoped fervently that someone would find him before too many hours passed.

∞∞∞

Eemya woke to the sound of thunder. She pulled back the curtain around her bed and saw rain streaming down her window. Darius' letter had arrived the morning before, and she already had it memorized. She had encountered the messenger on the road, having left Adamantine when the first news of the battle began to filter in with the returning men.

After counting the days it would have taken to reach her, and the time it would take him to travel to the capital and back, she had calculated that today was the earliest he might be able to set sail back to the island. Surely he would have to wait another day now, at the least. No one would want to sail through this. Except Darius. She knew from experience that he could be very single-minded.

Eemya frowned. What if her calculations were off? Could he have possibly set sail sooner? What if he had left before the storm blew up, or convinced some captain to sail into it anyway? What if he was lost at sea, or shipwrecked somewhere? She became distracted with worry, and wondered what, if anything, she could do. Then came the question unbidden: what would Darius do? That, she knew the answer to. He would take action. He would ride through rain or fire to find her. She would do the same.

Ringing for her maid, she quickly began dressing herself in a riding habit. Maygla arrived just in time to help her finish. She threw on a cloak and went to find Halem. "Ride as swiftly as you can to Kirdyn's main castle with one of my men as guide. Convince him to send men to his port with instructions to send out rescue boats. Do not take no for an answer. I fear your prince may have been at sea in the storm. Tell them to search between there and the capital."

Halem opened his mouth as she spoke as if to question her sanity, but he closed it, hearing the urgency in her voice. He nodded, and spun around to walk rapidly toward the stables.

"Jayred," Eemya turned to the steward who waited at her elbow, "Tell Byden to pick several men to ride with me and saddle my horse. And one extra," she added as an afterthought. "We will leave as soon as they are ready."

"In the rain?" he gaped.

"Yes, in the rain," she snapped and dismissed him with a wave of her hand. She went to the kitchen herself to gather provisions rather than wait for someone else to do it. By the time she had enough food readied for the journey, the horses were ready. She stowed the supplies in her saddlebags and mounted her mare. Without speaking, she set off at a trot on the road to Sonefast with her men following.

It was the worst ride she had ever taken. Even her goat-hair cloak was not keeping out the rain, and she was wet through. At least the wind was at their backs, so the rain was not driving in their faces. They stopped at Masyn's village and took a few moments to refresh themselves in the tavern. Their host served them some warm, mulled wine. It was comforting, but even while standing in front of the fire, it did little to take the chill out of their bones.

She had sent a villager to find Yoused's young scholar and bring him to her. "What do you know about the currents and tidal patterns in the channel?" she asked when he arrived.

The question took him aback, but he answered promptly, "A little, my lady." She lifted her eyebrows to prompt him to elaborate. He adjusted his crutch and took a deep breath. "Well, the currents in the channel are dependent primarily on the tides, unlike those in the open sea, and change direction accordingly."

"If you knew the time, weather conditions, and position of a ship that capsized, could you predict the best place to look for survivors during the succeeding hours?"

"Er, possibly. I would need to study some maps and charts and make some calculations."

"Very good. You will ride with us. Lord Yoused should have everything you need once we arrive." She marshalled her men and they again braved the rain. Restyn managed to climb up on the extra horse. His right leg was weak, and shorter than the other, but it had enough strength to hold him up, with the help of his crutch, until he could push up in the stirrup with his left. His crutch was secured to his saddle and they set off.

Eemya led them on, and they arrived at Sonefast just after nightfall. The rain had finally stopped, and they entered the hall as Yoused and his family were at dinner. Lord Yoused stood in surprise, and walked around the table to meet her. "My lady," he exclaimed, appraising her sodden condition, "What brings you here in such inclement weather?"

"I have come to inquire as to the normal procedure for sending out rescue boats after a storm. If you fear someone has been lost at sea, are ships normally sent out to look for them?" Eemya had been considering how best to frame the question during the journey, and this was the best she had come up with.

Yoused didn't miss much however. He raised an eyebrow. "Someone?"

"Prince Darius had planned to return to the island around this time." She tried to keep her face from giving anything away, but her eyes told him everything he needed to know.

Yoused's own eyes became just a little sadder, but his voice was nothing but encouraging. "We will do what we can," he assured her, "but before we speak any further, you must let my daughter-in-law help you into something dry before you become ill." He motioned to a young woman and gave her instructions.

Eemya wanted to protest, but she was tired and cold, and her soggy clothes were chafing her, so she allowed herself to be led away. As soon as she had dried off and changed into warm, clean clothes, she hurried back downstairs to find Yoused and Restyn already pouring over maps and charts in the study. Restyn had also changed into dry clothes, she noticed, and Yoused handed her a cup of wine and motioned to some hot food on a table. She took a slice of bread and dipped it in the wine while they explained to her what they had been discussing.

"The most plausible assumption is that the prince has not yet set out." Eemya took a breath of relief, but was not entirely convinced. Yoused continued, "But if he did, it would have been before the storm began. No captain would set out toward the island in a storm with winds blowing from the north, not with so much wreckage in the channel. They would have had to sail due east, right into the thick of it, if they expected to make any progress. So, if he set out sometime yesterday, they most likely would have sailed toward Kirdyn's harbor."

Yoused pointed to a line they had drawn on the map, and Eemya leaned in to study it. "The wind was blowing from the west yesterday, so they could have easily navigated to the middle of the channel before the storm struck." Eemya's chest tightened, and she felt with certainty that this is what he would have done. "The storm came up quickly once the wind changed, and they could have turned and run before the wind to make it to my port, except for the debris in the channel. If they decided to take that risk, they could already be in port."

"Unless they struck some wreckage," Eemya put in somberly.

"Yes." Yoused did not speak for a moment. "Their other choice would be to ride out the storm, sailing as close to the wind as possible, and try to avoid dashing themselves on the coastline or any floating hazards. If they took this option, they would still arrive at Kirdyn's port, just a little later." Yoused looked at Eemya reassuringly. "The prince is probably waiting safely in the capital for the weather to clear, but if he set out earlier, our fishermen and ship captains are all very experienced, and should be able to guide him safely into harbor."

Eemya nodded, but looked at Restyn. "And if not?"

"If they ran south and wrecked sometime between the eleventh and seventeenth hours when the tide was coming in, survivors and debris could have been swept into the eddy between these two headlands." He pointed at a point on the map. "A lot of things get caught in there. With all the movement in and out of the shipyards right now, it is likely they would be spotted."

"But they could also have been swept out to sea?"

"Actually, that is not very likely. Because of the constant change in current direction due to the tides, an object may move only a few miles north or south daily, maintaining a relatively consistent position. The tide would have turned before anyone could get that far."

"That is why all the wreckage from the battle must be towed away," interposed Yoused. "Otherwise, it will float there threatening ships for weeks, maybe longer."

"In the more plausible event that they went north, if they capsized the tidal stream would have carried them south for a way, and then back north. Depending on the time of the wreck and how far they had sailed prior to that, a survivor might still be in the middle of the channel right now," he took a breath, "or they could be heading out to sea. Especially if they sailed into the storm at a northwesterly tack. They may have made it to the mouth of the channel. Then they would be subject to the currents of the open ocean, not the tidal stream."

Restyn was refreshingly concise and unemotional. Eemya contemplated the map. Bleak were the chances of finding anyone lost at sea in a storm. Even in the middle of the channel, the space was too vast to cover. She had to hope that Yoused was right: everything was fine, and she was worrying for nothing. "What are these little circles?" She indicated a line of oblong shapes out in the ocean, ringing the entrance to the channel.

"Those are small, volcanic islands. Mostly inhospitable mounds of hardened lava formed before people ever arrived in these lands. It is not possible to land a vessel on any of them," answered Yoused.

"They are similar to the rocky shores on our island?"

"Yes. A couple of the larger ones have a few trees growing on them now." He gave a half-smile. "I did some exploring when I was younger."

"If someone was swept out to the sea north of the channel, could they take refuge on one of these islands?"

"It is highly unlikely. Even if they still had the strength to swim, they would be dashed on the rocks by the waves."

"But it is not impossible," she persisted.

"Not impossible," he conceded. Eemya felt him studying her while she studied the charts. She had no right to ask him to do anything. There was nothing she could offer him in exchange except the one thing she could never give. Her heart already belonged to Darius. It would only offend Yoused if she offered him money. He must have been able to read her thoughts, or at least her downcast expression, because he put his hand over hers and said in a fatherly tone, "My dear, I will empty the harbor and send a boat in every direction until we hear some news, even if it is that the prince is still in the capital. I will leave myself, tonight, and arrive at the port by dawn."

Eemya looked up at him with shining eyes. "I cannot repay you for this," she said softly.

"It is not necessary." He squeezed her hand, gave a slight bow, and left the room. A maidservant entered a moment later to show Eemya and Restyn to their rooms. Eemya laid down on her bed and tried unsuccessfully to sleep.

∞∞∞

Darius could not see land anywhere. He could not see anything but rain and waves. There was nothing by which he could take his bearings, but at some point he sensed that he was travelling in a different direction. The tide must have turned. The wind seemed to have lessened, and Darius took the risk of sitting up and cupping his hands to catch some rain. The waves were not as rough, and he stretched his tired, aching muscles.

For hours, he drifted around, unable to take any action to change his circumstances. Eventually, the clouds had given up all their excess moisture and the rain ceased. Slowly, the sky cleared and the sun sank behind the horizon. The stars came out, and Darius lay on his back and counted them, naming the ones he knew. He could not afford to fall asleep. He might miss the light of a ship, or roll off into the water and lose the raft. The sharks had all taken refuge in deeper waters during the storm, but they would be back. The section of plank was the only thing he had between him and them. He must stay awake.

∞∞∞

At dawn, Eemya sprang out of bed. She dressed hurriedly and rushed to find Yoused's steward. When she found him, she discovered that Yoused had indeed left by river the night before. That was good, she thought. At least he could get some sleep while someone else piloted the boat. Hopefully he would receive more rest than she had.

Eemya had spent a restless and anxious night trying to decide what she should do next. Eventually, she had decided to return home, where she could more easily find some task or other to keep herself busy. Not knowing from whence news would arrive, it was the most central location to wait. It was also the first place Darius would look for her.

She asked the steward to convey the message to her men to prepare for departure. Then she went to find Restyn to thank him for his help. She praised him highly and told him to remain behind, as he had learned everything he had been sent to learn, but he was free to return any time or write if he had any further questions. One of her men would return later with the rest of his belongings.

The steward brought her news that the men were ready to go, and after a quick breakfast, they began the journey back. Upon arriving home, Eemya went straight to bed. After two long days of riding, Eemya was exhausted and slept deeply.

∞∞∞

All day the sun beat down on Darius and his small raft. He began to wish the rain would return. Taking off his leather cuirass and tunic, he placed the latter over his head to protect his face. Though the wind had died down, and the surface of the water was calm, Darius had the sensation that he was moving faster. Did that mean he was out of the channel in the open ocean? He began to despair that anyone would ever find him. Then he shook himself. He had been in dire situations before. There was no reason to give up hope. On the contrary, there was every reason to hope. Eemya was waiting for him.

Hours passed, and Darius scanned the seas regularly, but he did not spy a single ship. After fighting for so long to stay awake, with the calm sea and his head shaded from the sun, Darius succumbed to weariness and slept. But not for long. Just before sunset, the raft bumped into something hard, jarring Darius awake.

Ever since his capture by that renegade tribe, he had a fear of being restrained while sleeping, and the rope around his arms produced sudden panic when he awoke. He sat up quickly, struggling with the lines, and the motion unsettled the raft, dumping him into the water. The cool, wet reality of the sea brought him back to his senses. One arm was still caught in the rope, so he didn't lose the raft, but his knees scraped against something hard, and Darius realized he had run into a small island.

A wave crashed over him and knocked him onto the rocks. He scraped his hands breaking his fall, and the raft smacked him in the shoulder. He decided he needed to get out of this dangerous position quickly, and looked for the best route up the rocks. The island was only the width of two warships, and the length of maybe three, but it was steep and slippery.

Slowly and painfully, he climbed up the side of the mound, dragging the battered section of deck with him. At the top, he rejoiced to see a small stand of coconut palms. Leaning the raft against one of the trees, he picked up a fresh, ripe coconut that had fallen and wedged itself in a crack in the rock beneath its parent. Gratefully he took his dagger from its sheath where it had been safely kept from falling to the bed of the channel. His sword, he hoped, was still inside the boat where he had left it. Would Davyn present it to Cyrus with the news that he had gone overboard? He couldn't think about that.

Patiently he set to work removing the husk. Since these trees also grew in Berush, it was a fruit he was familiar with. A dagger was not the best tool to use, but he made it work. Then he used the tip of the dagger to bore through one of the holes in the shell and drank the milk thirstily. Lastly, he found a large rock with a sharp edge and bashed the shell against it at just the right angle to crack it open. Using his dagger again, he gouged out pieces of the meat to eat.

By now, it was fully dark, with only starlight shining on the water. Darius finally removed his boots and set them out to dry. Then he dragged his raft to a sheltered spot under the trees, laid it across the rough surface of the rocks, and lay down to return to sleep and dream of his love.

CHAPTER SIXTEEN

Eemya spent her day fretting and pacing, unable to focus on anything. Her ladies fussed around her in the solar, so she left them. She tried to work in her office, but the words on the papers swirled and swam before her eyes. Jayred tried to get her to eat something, but all she could do was nibble at some bread.

There were a couple of patients in the infirmary to see to, but Yula said her restlessness was making them nervous and shooed her away. It would have been nice to talk to Stelan, but he and Yarin were still at Adamantine. She reread Darius' letter several times and burst into tears, then felt herself so silly that she got up and paced again. Eventually, she ended up helping a maid beat the rugs. It felt good to hit something.

By evening, her nerves were so raw, that she could not face dinner in the hall, and had it served in the study. But all that she could think about was the last meal she and Darius had taken together there. Love had more extreme emotions, on both ends of the spectrum, than she had anticipated. Eemya folded her arms on her desk and rested her forehead on them, trying to talk herself into being rational. Footsteps came pounding down the corridor, and she sat up quickly.

"My lady," burst in Jayred without knocking, but she would forgive him this time. He took a moment to catch his breath. "A messenger from Kirdyn."

"Well, show him in!" she exclaimed impatiently. The man stepped in past Jayred, who left and closed the door. The messenger was Halem. He looked harried and drawn, with circles under his eyes.

"Lady Eemya," he bowed, "I do not bring good news." His voice faltered.

"Tell me." Eemya's hands tightened their grip on the arms of her chair, and she steeled herself to hear whatever he had to say.

"I managed to convince Kirdyn to ride with me to his port. He made all kind of sympathetic remarks, but I could tell he did not want to bother himself over a woman's fears, if you will pardon me, my lady." Eemya nodded impatiently. She could very well imagine Kirdyn's reaction, and motioned for Halem to continue. "However, I insisted he accompany me, as you urged. We left the next morning and rode at his slow, tedious pace, and arrived at the port that evening." Halem paused and shifted his weight, and it took all of Eemya's control not to scream at him.

"The harbor master met us at the gate and said he was just about to send Lord Kirdyn a message. A fishing boat had arrived that morning with urgent news. The master had been otherwise engaged," Halem said this with sarcasm, "and had only just gotten around to receiving them. The fisherman told the master that Prince Darius had employed him to sail him to the island. They had been caught in the storm, and were riding it out when the sail started to come loose. The man's son went to tie it back, but lost his balance. Darius saved the boy from falling overboard, but . . . he . . . fell into the sea himself." Halem's eyes were sorrowful and full of sympathy.

Eemya would not let herself feel anything until she had heard every detail. "Did they search for him?"

"I heard the man's story myself, and questioned him thoroughly. He said they turned around and searched for several hours, but in the driving rain, they could not see very far and found no sign of him."

"So that means Yoused was right, and they must have gone northwest." Eemya thought aloud. The fact that she had been right as well, and Darius had left before the storm, was not something she stopped to dwell on. She stood and began to pace. Darius could not have drowned. He simply could not. The Berushese prince was not someone who just died, she told herself, irrational as that seemed. He was strong and resourceful. He could have survived. "Was he wearing his armor?"

"Uh, no, he was not. His sword and pack were still in the boat. The fisherman was going to take them to Cyrus, but I told him to wait until the search ships return."

"Kirdyn sent out his ships?" Eemya was so relieved to hear that Darius had not been wearing his armor, that news of Kirdyn's search party nearly made her jump for joy.

"Yes," Halem did not attempt to conceal his disdain for the northern lord, "he was ready to consign the prince to the deep, but I told him Darius was Berushese, and you could not count him out so easily. I did not have the authority to do so, but I told him that King Cyrus would not be pleased if he did not put forth the greatest effort possible to find his brother. I may have intimated that Cyrus would remove him from his post if he did not initiate a thorough search."

Eemya smiled. "I am glad you did. Thank you for all you have done." She rose. "I suggest you eat and get some rest. Tomorrow, you may do as you think best. You have fulfilled your obligations to me."

"Thank you, my lady. In the morning I will return to the port to await news from the search. I will be there to hand the prince his sword when they bring him back." He bowed and departed.

Halem's determined optimism had bolstered Eemya's spirits. Her emotional tension temporarily released and left her jittery and shaking. She forced herself to eat something, and then went to bed with her lover's letter clutched against her heart.

∞∞∞

Darius awoke with the dawn. The rays of the sun shone directly onto his face. He rose and found another coconut. This time, he wedged it between some rocks and dropped a heavy rock on top of it, twice on each end, and it cracked the husk enough that he could peel it off without using his dagger. This method proved more efficient, and he ate half of the coconut, saving the rest of it for his dinner.

Next he set out to explore his small domain. Even though they were still wet, he pulled his boots back on. It would do no good to get his feet all cut up. The main goal was to find means of starting a fire. If he did sight a ship, he would need to be able to signal them. The coconut husks and the planks from the deck could be used as fuel, but he had nothing with which to spark it. His flint was lying uselessly in his pack on the boat.

Aside from the five mature palm trees in the center, there were several smaller palms and scrubby bushes growing in crevices around the island. Taking his dagger, he cut off the longest branches from the bushes and set them in a pile to dry. He ventured closer to the water to see if anything else might have washed up. There were some edible varieties of seaweed that had been left by the waves, and he chewed on some of it. Artylians were fond of all types of seafood, and the bitter, then tangy taste was one he had experienced several times.

Scurrying over the rocks, feeding on the seaweed, was an even better find: rock crabs! He skewered one with his dagger. It would have been preferable to eat it cooked, but at least he could cut the meat out with his knife and clean it. He and Effan had eaten raw scorpions once before during a tribal initiation ritual. It couldn't be much worse than that. After cleaning it, he cut it into small pieces and swallowed them without chewing. His constitution was strong, and he hoped the meat would not disagree with him. A diet of raw coconut alone was enough to keep anyone's system moving.

In a sheltered depression in the rocks, Darius found a small puddle of water. He dipped his finger in it and tasted a drop to see if by chance some rainwater had collected there. It was sweet! He threw himself on the ground and sucked it up. Restricting himself to only half of it, he saved the rest of it for later. It would not last long, even though it would be shaded most of the day. The rising temperature would cause it to evaporate. The black lava absorbed the heat of the sun very rapidly.

When the sun rose higher in the sky, Darius retreated to the shade of the trees, laying his boots out to continue drying. He propped the raft against two of the palms and sat cross-legged on the south side of it where he could watch for boats. The sun would travel in a slightly northern arc, so he should remain protected from its rays.

As he sat, he felt the weight of the pouch around his neck. He fingered the leather braid and pulled it out from under his shirt to look at it. Effan's charm had been kept safe from the waves by the tightness of his cuirass. Darius had never known his captain to be either sentimental or prescient, but he would certainly never discount anything he said in the future.

Meditation had never been one of Darius' strengths, and his thoughts and emotions wandered all over the place. Sitting doing nothing but scan the horizon for hours was the most tedious occupation he had ever had. To keep from giving in to depression, he amused himself by imagining what Eemya would do if she were in his situation, or Stelan. He wondered if Stelan had ever gone hunting, or had to kill his own food. Surely his father had taken him fishing when he was young.

Darius remembered his own father teaching him to fish and swim in the lake by their palace. They even had a special pool for bathing in one of the palace courtyards. Someday he wanted to take Eemya there. Then the prospect of never seeing her again loomed before him, and he had to get up and move. He had begun to feel rather smug about his survival skills, but he realized that if just one factor had been different, he would be dead. Luck had been his friend. Hopefully it would continue to be.

It was early evening, and he explored the edge of the island again now that the tide was low. Finding nothing remarkable, he went and ate the other half of the morning's coconut. Both coconuts and crabs would need to be rationed. The fruit grew year-round in this climate, but it would not grow as fast as he would eat them. He collected a little more seaweed and chewed on it. By the time the sun sank and the stars were out, he was ready to sleep if only to avoid being awake.

The next morning passed very much like the first. The prince's stomach was only mildly disturbed, so he ate another round of the same and drank the rest of the fresh water. His pile of sticks was dry enough to attempt a fire. On patrol in the mountains, he had often had to make do in less than ideal circumstances, and he was an expert at feeding a fire once he had a spark.

He had never had to start a fire without his tinder box, but theoretically he knew it was possible. Friction would create the heat, and air would fuel it. Too much air would blow it out, so he took his tools behind his little shelter to work since the breeze was still coming from the north. First he separated the fibers from the coconut husks to use as tinder. He stripped the dry leaves off of the palms for added fuel. Then he took the largest stick, which was about the diameter of his thumb, and split it in half. He trimmed one of the halves into a blade-like tip, and split the other half again, but this time only to the center, and then carved out a grove.

Next, he rubbed the whittled stick against the split one. It took him a few trials to get the hang of it, but before long, he was rewarded with a wisp of smoke, and the stick began to turn black. He stuck some fibers in the crack in the stick, and kept going until the fibers started to smoke, then he removed them and placed them in the center of a pile of tinder and blew the fire gently to life.

Unfortunately, there was not enough fuel to keep

it going for long. If he took apart his raft, he would have little shelter and nothing to float on if he tried to leave. He decided that he could not continue to feed the fire, but at least he knew he could start one. The coconut husks created an inordinate amount of smoke, and he watched it billow into the sky until it dissipated.

His gaze wandered back out to the ocean, and he jumped up, not certain of what he saw. There was a speck on the horizon. Heart pounding, he grabbed the fibers and leaves he had set aside and threw them on the fire, coaxing it back to life. He piled the rest of the sticks on top of it, and soon the flames were licking them ravenously. Then he wrenched a plank free from the raft and added it to the blaze. Once it was burning, he added another. The speck was definitely a boat, and it was headed his way.

Darius was incredulous. He had counted the days before Cyrus could possibly hear the news and send out search ships. It had barely been four days since he had been lost overboard. Even if Davyn had sailed straight back to the capital and informed the king, there was no way someone could have reached him already unless they knew exactly where to look. Was it just a coincidence?

As the boat drew closer, Darius recognized it as Lord Yoused's pleasure yacht, and he laughed aloud. Was this how Yoused usually vacationed? He waved and hailed the boat joyfully. The yacht could not come too close without being in danger from rocks just below the surface, but it sailed to the leeward side of the island where the waves were calmer. The tide was just about to turn, and the water was as smooth as it was going to get.

Yoused cupped his hands around his mouth and called to him, "Can you swim it?"

"Yes!" Darius left his boots, cuirass, tunic and shirt, and he tied Effan's sand securely around his belt next to his dagger and entered the water wearing only his trousers. It was only a bowshot away, and the current was not strong there, but he didn't want anything extra weighing him down. He picked his way through the rocks to the water's edge and waded out to where it became deep enough to swim.

With powerful, swift strokes, he swam straight toward Yoused's craft. The water was clear, and he saw several fish and small sharks, but nothing that would bother him. In moments he felt several strong hands reaching down to pull him into the boat. Panting, he lay on the deck for a moment to catch his breath. He looked up at Yoused. "Just out for a pleasure cruise?"

"Evidently, I am proving that the impossible is possible," he grinned and gave Darius a hand up.

"So you were looking for me? How did you know I was even lost? The news cannot possibly have travelled that fast. Not that I am not excessively pleased to see you!" He placed his hand on Yoused's shoulder.

Yoused's expression was inscrutable. "The day of the storm, Lady Eemya arrived at my castle with news that you were expected back at the island. She was afraid you may have been out in the storm and I offered to go and look for you."

Darius was speechless. He should have known Eemya's mind was behind it. He was sorry to have caused her worry. The reason Yoused was so easily persuaded to help, he could only guess at. Only a few weeks ago, the thought might have caused him intense feelings of jealousy, but now he was just grateful to Yoused for his willingness to come to his aid, whatever his motivation. He knew where

Eemya's feelings lay and did not doubt her.

Still, it amazed him that Yoused found him so quickly. "How did you know where to look? You must have come directly here."

Yoused explained how Eemya had brought Restyn, and they had studied the tidal charts and ocean currents to predict the most likely places to find the prince. Darius shook his head in disbelief. The lord then insisted that Darius go below and refresh himself. He sent a man to doctor his scrapes and cuts and anoint his sunburned hands with lotion.

Darius put on clean clothes borrowed from one of the men as he was taller and broader than Yoused was. He washed his face and took a long, luxurious drink of fresh water. Then he devoured the meal Yoused placed before him. After a glass of wine, Yoused gave Darius his own berth, and he slept comfortably for the first time in days.

Yoused assumed that he would want to take the shortest route to Freosyd, so he headed to Kirdyn's harbor. They hailed every ship they passed to give them the news that the prince was found. There was quite a parade of boats following them into the port when they reached it, including the *Horizon*, which had set sail with Effan and the rest of Darius' men as soon as it was ready.

It was a rather emotional reunion on the pier. Halem was the first to greet him, and he knelt to return his sword. Davyn also was there to offer profuse apologies as well as thanks for saving his son. Kirdyn made a big fuss and fanfare that Darius didn't even listen to. When Effan heard what had happened and caught up to the prince, Darius gave him back his sand and clasped his arm. "Thank you for this, my friend. I hope you are ready for a long ride, because I'm not leaving you behind again!"

Lord Yoused attempted to sneak away quietly, but Darius sought him out before he could get underway and gave him his sincere thanks. "Let me know if there is anything I can ever do for you."

"There is only one thing," he looked at Darius with an earnest intensity. "Take care of her."

Darius nodded and replied with equal solemnity, "I will." He gave Yoused a salute and rejoined the crowd.

There was only one face that he looked for and did not see. He had not expected her to be at Kirdyn's, but he could not help wishing she was. Halem noticed him looking around and spoke in his ear, "The Lady Eemya is awaiting you at her castle."

Darius wanted to mount a horse immediately and ride to her, but he looked at himself in his sailor's clothes, felt his beard, and decided to take time to look his best. He repaired to Kirdyn's Aerie to change into his own clothes and get a shave. So that she would not worry, he sent Halem ahead to notify her to expect him shortly. When he had stopped at Yoused's port after the battle, Darius had sent orders for Stelan to send some of his horses to Yoused's and some to Kirdyn's so he could ride from either port. That meant that half of his men could ride with him, and half of them would stay with the ship for now.

The river that fed into Kirdyn's harbor was rocky, with numerous falls in it, and Darius was glad sailing up it was not an option. Having a horse under him again felt much more comfortable than a boat. They set off at a gallop, leaving Kirdyn to wonder at the propensity of the Berushese to wear out their equines.

∞∞∞

After she had received confirmation from Halem that Darius had indeed sailed northwest, Eemya had considered riding to Kirdyn's port to await news. She soon rejected this plan, however. Not that she cared what Kirdyn thought about anything, but she did not want him to see her grief if the news was bad. If the news was good, she wanted to be able to receive Darius in her own home, in her own bed. She blushed at the thought. He had won after all. She was happy to admit it. Happy that his feelings had grown into real love, and that she was able to return it.

Now Halem had brought her news that Darius had been found, and he was on his way! She was still fidgety and restless, but now in anticipation, not anxiety. Her ladies fixed her hair and dressed her in her best dress. She was sure he would follow soon after his messenger. It was, in fact, only a few hours later that the watchman announced his approach. On the steps she waited, wringing her hands.

When he rode into the courtyard her heart soared with joy. He rode all the way to the steps and she flew down to meet him. He caught her in his embrace as soon as he dismounted and held her tightly. The noise of the other horsemen riding in receded, and she heard and felt only him.

"Beloved," he whispered, "I have been so longing to see you."

"And I you."

"How did you know I was lost?"

"I did not know, but I know you. You and your single-mindedness. I knew you would come to me the instant you were able, and that put you at sea in a storm. I was so afraid, my lord!"

"Darius," he corrected gently.

"*Darius,*" she smiled through tears of joy.

"Do not cry, my darling Eemya," he wiped away a

tear. "You have saved me. You have saved me more than once." He bent and put an arm under her knees and the other under her shoulders and smoothly picked her up. "You will notice that this is not a position I have taught you how to escape from." His eyes twinkled as he carried her up the steps.

She put her arms around his neck and leaned her head on his shoulder. "I have no wish to escape. I love you."

"You are no longer afraid of me?"

"No."

"I am so sorry you ever were."

"I know," she kissed his cheek.

When they arrived at the door to her room, Darius set her down, but did not let go of her. "Though all the conditions of our original agreement have been met," he said rakishly, "I would like to request an amendment."

"Is that so?" Eemya raised one eyebrow.

"Yes," his voice became husky with emotion, "I want you for more than one night, Eemya."

"I do not believe the number of nights was specified," she murmured coyly.

"I want to specify it now. I want you for every night, Eemya, every night for the rest of our lives. I want you to be my wife. Will you marry me?"

"Marry you?"

"Yes, marry me. Say you will," he pleaded.

"Where will we live?"

"I will live wherever you are my darling. Are you trying to torture me? Say you will marry me."

"Of course I will marry you!" She smiled widely, and he cupped her face with his hands and kissed her. Stepping back, he reached into his tunic and took out a folded sheet of parchment wrapped in oilskin.

"I have been carrying this close to my heart every

moment since I received it except for the journey across the channel. Thankfully, I had stowed it safely inside my pack, and it was not lost."

"What is it?"

He unfolded it and handed it to her. "I am unfamiliar with the marriage customs of the island, but in Berush all that is required is the consent of the couple's parents or immediate superiors. As acting governor of the island, I am yours, and Cyrus is mine, so that was easy," he grinned. "As a member of the royal family, my marriage requires a formal document. All that remains for it to be legal is your signature."

Eemya read over the document, which was written in both Artylian and Berushese, and then screwed her face into an expression of disbelief and pursed her lips. "Darius, this is dated nearly a month ago! Well before I made my declaration!"

Darius' face took on a sheepish expression. "I had hope. When I returned from Sonefast to ask you to forgive me, I had already decided I wanted to marry you if you could ever be persuaded to return my feelings. I could not take advantage of someone I loved. With you, everything has to be right." Eemya was still silent. "You are not angry, are you?"

Eemya rolled her eyes. "I should be furious at you," she laughed, "but I just cannot manage it." Only then did she spy the small table placed in the passage with a pen and inkwell set on top of it. "How did you . . . oh, Halem." She picked up the pen and looked at it and then at the prince. "What would you have done if I said 'no'?"

He shuddered. "I would not give up, but I might have had to go away for a while."

Putting the paper and pen down, she squeezed his hand and put her other hand on his cheek. At that moment, she felt more love for him than she could have imagined possible. What an honorable man he had turned out to be. "I love you so much." Her arms went around his neck and their lips met. He pressed her tightly against his body and kissed her frantically. There was one more thing she had to know, and she pulled back. "What if I bear you no children?" Her eyes showed a hint of worry.

"Oh Eemya, you have made me happier than I have ever been in my life. I want *you*, children or no children," and he kissed her again to prove it. He kissed her ardently, again and again until she thought she would faint.

"Let me sign that paper!" she managed to say. Darius moved to stand behind her with his arms around her waist. He kissed her neck and nibbled at her ear. She elbowed him. "Stop! You are going to make me write all wobbly." She tried to sound stern but couldn't help giggling. With a flourish, she finished her signature and set down the pen.

"My wife," crowed Darius happily.

"Come with me, husband," she smirked. Then she took his hand and led him through the door to her bedroom, and he closed the door behind them.

∞∞∞

The light of the moon poured through the window illuminating Eemya's soft, white skin through the open curtain of the bed as she slept. Her red hair radiated from her head like rays of the sun spreading across her pillow. Darius listened to her even breathing and traced her curves with his eyes. She was so beautiful. Making love to her was more wonderful than he had ever dreamed of. He still could not believe she was his.

Carefully he eased his arm out from under her head slowly, without disturbing her. With one more look at her, drinking her in, he grabbed his pillow and made a bed for himself on the floor.

CHAPTER SEVENTEEN

Sunrise at Eemya's castle was blocked by the mountain, so dawn appeared to progress more gradually there. Used to sleeping outdoors while on patrol, Darius sensed the smallest change in the light. He climbed back into the bed hoping Eemya had not missed him. He felt a little guilty about sneaking around like that, but he did not know how to talk to her about his fears. They would have to have a discussion about it soon. But not yet.

Eemya sensed his warmth in her sleep and turned to snuggle closer to him. He lay there, barely breathing, until she finally awoke. In an almost feline manner, she stretched her arms and arched her back, then laid her arm across his chest. "Mmm. Good morning," she purred. He replied with a kiss.

∞∞∞

Later that day, when they became hungry and finally had to call the maid to bring them something to eat, Eemya brought up the subject of a marriage feast. "Generally, the feast is the same day that the groom takes the bride into his house," she spoke reprovingly, but her eyes were teasing.

"Our traditions are the same," confirmed Darius.

"We will have to schedule ours at least a week out to give Stelan and Yarin time to arrive."

They agreed on a date, and Eemya delegated the task of drafting and sending out invitations to Jayred so she could dedicate all her attention to her husband. Darius wrote one brief letter to Tomus, but wouldn't let her see it. "It is a surprise," was all he told her.

The prince managed to extricate himself from his wife's embrace without her noticing for the next two nights. After that, the island received another downpour of rain, and the weather turned briefly colder. The castle became damp and chilly. Eemya shivered in the night, and turned to her husband for warmth, but he was not there. Worried, she sat up and looked around. Seeing a shape on the floor, she rolled over to the other side of the bed to get a better look.

"Darius." He sat up quickly and looked around. His hand grasped his sword which was lying next to him. Eemya noticed the action. "Everything is fine, it is all right, but whatever are you doing on the floor?"

Darius sighed, ran his fingers through his hair, and came and sat in front of her on the floor while she looked at him over the edge of the bed. He covered her hands with his and took a deep breath. "I dare not fall asleep next to you, my love."

In the dark, he could not read her expression, which was maybe just as well. Turning his gaze to the floor, he tried to gather the courage to explain. She kissed his hands. "Tell me. I can bear it."

"I do not wish for you to bear it."

"We are married. I will bear it whether you tell me of it or not. Sometimes bearing a grief you know nothing of is worse than knowing."

He was not sure if she was right, but he had to tell her something. Nodding his head, he took the plunge. "I have dreams . . . not every night, but often. Dreams of terrible things I have seen, have suffered, and have done to others." He tried to convey the essence of the problem without burdening her with specifics. "Frequently I wake in a state of uncertainty, ready to fight, not knowing what is real and what is not." He hesitated, desiring not to relate the episode from which his worst fear stemmed. "The last woman I fell asleep next to . . . I almost killed her when I woke because I thought she was an enemy."

Eemya kept very still. She could tell it was painful for him to share these things with her. If she was not careful with her words, she might cause him to retreat back into himself. Resting her cheek against his hands, she contemplated her potential responses. "If you feel this is the only possible solution, I will accept it, but I do not like it."

"Thank you, my darling." Darius kissed her on the forehead. "I do not like it either. Perhaps the two of us will be able to come up with another answer together, but it will not be easy."

"I never presumed that living with you would be easy, my lord," teased Eemya.

"Take me seriously, Eemya. If I ever hurt you, I could not live with myself."

She quickly became sober, her voice breaking. "And I would rather risk dying by your hand than to be without you, but I will respect your wishes." They sat in silence for a while, both choked by emotion. "Can you at least come warm me up? The night has grown cold."

Darius rose and scooted in next to her as she made room for him. She put her head on his shoulder and they held each other tightly. A hot tear escaped her eye and he felt it on his chest. It was so unfair that she had to suffer because of his experiences, he thought. If only he was strong enough to overcome it, but he wasn't. His anger was becoming manageable, with help from his friends, but the dreams were something else.

"There is a face I see in my dreams sometimes," Eemya broke into his thoughts as if she could hear them. "It is a horrible, nasty face. It happens less often now, but when I see it, I always wake with my heart beating like the hooves of a galloping horse. I know it is nothing like what you see, but perhaps it can help me understand a little."

"Yes, it is a little like that. Do you thrash around and try to push it away?"

"I try to, but I usually feel frozen. I try to scream, but I cannot. Once, I did manage to fall out of bed."

"I am sorry that you see that," Darius stroked her head. "For most people, the body does not respond to the mind's commands during a dream. A few can walk in their sleep and wake in another room. I could fight an army in my sleep and find that I have just shredded my bedsheets."

"Hmm." Eemya knew nothing that could help with this. If they had to live this way, then that is what they would do. She would have to try and learn more about it, but not tonight. "Tell me a story to help me sleep. Tell me something about your mother."

Darius told her story after story, and he sang the lullabies his mother had sung to him as a child. He did not stop until he felt that Eemya was breathing softly and evenly. Then he held her and kept her warm the rest of the night with his eyes wide open.

∞∞∞

When she absolutely could not avoid leaving her room, Eemya got up to help with preparations for the feast. Extra servants were hired from the nearby towns, beer and wine were ordered and sent to every village in the holding so that everyone could partake in the celebration, and the best musicians and entertainers on the island were summoned. Jayred had done an excellent job, but everyone still wanted her opinion on everything, and everyone wanted to offer her congratulations. Her people were delighted about her marriage and glad for her happiness.

Later in the day, Eemya took refuge in the stables for the dual purpose of avoiding all the activity elsewhere and looking for Darius. She came upon Effan who was grooming a horse. The thought came to her that if anyone knew how to help Darius with his dreams, it would be Effan, but it did not seem her place to bring it up.

"Good afternoon, my lady," Effan greeted her as she approached. "A farmer came to request assistance rounding up some stray cattle, and Prince Darius rode out with a few men to help."

"Ah, thank you." Eemya was surprised and pleased that Darius was taking a personal interest in the affairs of her holding. She smiled. Perhaps he was also trying to escape the celebration preparations. She turned and began to walk away, then became curious. "How long have you been riding with Darius?"

"Fifteen years, my lady."

"That is a long time." Effan stopped brushing the horse's mane and looked at Eemya expectantly, waiting for her to continue. "Do horses have dreams?" she blurted out.

The captain blinked uncertainly and looked at the horse. "I do not know." He looked a little uncomfortable, and started brushing the horse's back absently. "This horse—this horse has been through many battles. He is well trained and has never flinched or bolted. On the boat crossing the channel, however, he became crazed and kicked his stall and struggled in his sling."

"What did you do?" Eemya held her breath waiting for the answer.

"I could not get near him with his hooves flailing, but I spoke to him calmly. I repeated his name soothingly and explained that he was safe." The gelding turned his head and nuzzled Effan's shoulder. "Then I talked to him about where we were going and why. Once he understood what was happening he stopped fighting it."

"How do you think he will behave on a second trip?"

"He will be nervous, but I will talk to him. We may be able to set up a sling on the deck, instead of down below, and that will be better for him. Horses hate dark, confined spaces."

Eemya considered this for a few moments. She patted the gelding's nose. "He is lucky to have you. Thank you, Effan." He bowed his head as she left.

Darius rode through the gate as she exited the stables, dismounted, and sauntered over to her jauntily. He caught her in his arms and kissed her. "Darius, everyone can see," she hissed at him, only slightly embarrassed.

"Let them, or better yet, let's go somewhere where they cannot." He took her hand and pulled her along with him. Eemya followed happily.

"Did chasing after cattle put you in this good

mood?"

"I prefer to chase after my wife," he teased, "but I was also working on your surprise."

"Ooh. When do I get to know what it is?"

"You will see it at the feast."

"I missed you this afternoon," Eemya whispered as they entered their marital retreat.

He kissed her as he closed the door. "And I missed you."

∞∞∞

On the afternoon of the feast, servants moved busily like ants in an anthill, the castle was overflowing with guests, and Eemya's ladies were finishing sewing her special gown. Maygla had insisted that she have an extra fancy dress, and she and the other ladies had been working on it unceasingly. It was two shades of green, with gold trim, and was lined with red. When Eemya lifted her arm, the red lining could be seen inside the drop-sleeve. The green brought out the color of her eyes and helped to set off the red and gold trim and the red of her hair.

"Cousin, you look absolutely gorgeous!" Lydima's head of honey-colored curls popped through the door.

"Lydima," Eemya embraced her. "Thank you for coming."

"I notice you do not say 'how lovely to see you,' but I am the only family you have, so you will have to be content!"

"I am glad to see you."

"Liar," Lydima grinned and flopped down on the bed. She arched her brows and looked at Eemya slyly while smoothing the covers. "So, have you—? Ooh, you have! I can tell by your face. And before the feast, too!" Lydima pretended to be shocked.

Eemya's cheeks had flushed red as raspberries. "Technically, we are already legally married. The celebration is just a formality."

"You do not have to justify yourself to me cousin, but you must allow me to gloat a little bit. I flatter myself that I had some small effect on the outcome of this relationship."

Eemya crossed the room to sit next to her cousin, put her arm around her and kissed her cheek. "You did. You convinced me to forgive him, and that was the hardest step. You were right, about everything."

"Well . . ." Lydima swung her legs, mollified, and smiled.

"How is your campaign for Lord Woldyn progressing?"

Lydima made a face. "Not well. I must not be the marrying kind."

"You are more than welcome to stay here if you ever need to."

"And be constantly subjected to you and your husband's starry-eyed mooning? No, thank you."

Maygla motioned Eemya into a chair so the ladies could finish her hair. When she was deemed ready, Eemya made a move to go, but Lydima blocked her exit. "Oh no, I have been given strict instructions not to let you leave until someone comes to tell us all it is time." Eemya made a feeble protest, but gave in.

They did not have to wait long before there was a knock on the door. Lydima opened it to find Stelan on the other side with a grin that filled the doorway. He looked as handsome as ever and seemed to be back to full health except for the left arm, which was still in a sling. "My lady, all is in readiness." He offered her his good arm, but Eemya hugged him, not too tightly in case his ribs were still sensitive.

"Stelan, I am so glad to see you. You are well?" He assured her that he was, and they proceeded down the stairs to the hall. Lovely music floated down the passage, and when they entered the door of the hall, a loud cheer went up. Most of the lords and ladies of the island were present, along with elders from each of Eemya's villages, and all the members of her own household.

Tears were already pricking at her eyes when she saw the tables. Sparkling bowls and vases of blown glass were filled to overflowing with gorgeous red-tipped lilies with white and green striped centers. Darius came to meet her. He was dressed in a rich brown tunic with gold trim that matched her own. "Do you like the flowers?"

"They are beautiful! I love them."

"Tomus brought the Berushese glass, and I had every lily that could be found brought in from the forest. The first time I rode through the mountains and saw them they reminded me of you."

Gazing into each other's eyes, he led her to their places at the high table. The rest of the evening passed in a blur. After a long and delicious dinner, the prince and his lady walked around and greeted all their guests. Darius introduced her to Tomus. Onia was unable to make the journey as she was expecting their first child and her stomach was sensitive enough without the rocking motion of a ship. Cyrus had already departed for Berush when the invitation arrived. Lord Yoused was not in attendance, but he had sent a cask of wine with his eldest son as a wedding gift. He had already given them the best gift possible by restoring Darius to her, Eemya thought.

Representatives from every village in the holding presented them with gifts, poems and musical tributes. It was very late before things began to wind down and their guests became drowsy. Darius and Eemya were exhausted by the time they retired, and Darius fell asleep in the bed with Eemya in his arms.

∞∞∞

Something was restraining him. Darius struggled to free himself from whatever was holding him down. He tried to sit up, but couldn't. He rolled out of the bed and looked for his sword, feeling something heavy slide off of him as he did so. Eemya, who had been lying with her arm across Darius' chest, was flipped onto her back as he rolled out from under her. It took her a moment to fully wake and register the fact that her husband was up and wandering around the room.

"Darius," she called, keeping her voice even. "Darius, did you have a dream? Everything is fine. We are safe. We are safe, Darius," she repeated, remembering what Effan had said and not going near him. He had found his sword and unsheathed it and was looking wildly around the room. Eemya kept talking to him, and he lowered his sword and took some deep breaths. Her words had penetrated his subconscious and he came to himself.

Slumping into a chair, he put his head in his hands. "I am sorry."

"You have nothing to be sorry for."

"I might have hurt you. I did not hurt you, did I," he rushed to her side concernedly. She shook her head.

"I am fine."

"But you might not be next time. I need to think," he threw on a shirt and trousers and moved toward the door.

"Wait!" Eemya commanded. Her tone arrested his movement. She walked over and stood in front of him and spoke in an earnest and assertive voice, "I will give you time to think alone if you need it. I will suffer you to sleep on the floor if you think it best, but I cannot be married to a partner who is absent, either emotionally or physically. I have already done that once. We can figure this out if we work together, but not if you shut me out or begin to feel sorry for yourself. Come back when you are ready to talk to me, or do not come back at all."

Darius felt himself becoming angry at her harsh words. How dare she give him an ultimatum when he was only thinking of her well-being? He stalked out of the door before he could say anything he might regret, but as soon as he closed it, he felt remorseful. She was right that their relationship could not continue like this. He had thought that he wanted her help facing the darkness inside of him, but the reality of doing so was excruciatingly painful. It was like a complicated type of surgery that was as dangerous to the surgeon as the patient.

He wished he had someone to talk to, but his brother was a week's travel away, Yarin and Stelan did not have the battle experience he had, and Effan was not married. Distraught, Darius wandered aimlessly around the castle, finally pausing on top of the western watch tower, and leaned against the battlement gazing unseeingly at the setting moon. He sighed and ran his fingers through his hair and tried to think of what to do.

Byden was on duty, and observing the prince, came over to offer assistance. "Is there anything I can do for you, my lord?"

"I do not think so." Darius could not help sighing again.

"If you need anything at all, you only have to ask."

"Thank you." After a few silent moments, Darius felt he needed to talk to someone, or he would go mad. "Are you married, Byden?"

"I was married, for thirty years, but my wife has passed on."

"I am sorry." More silence as Darius mulled over how to frame his questions. "You fought off Cerecian raids in your younger days? Is that correct?"

"Yes, my lord."

"Tell me about them."

"Well," Byden hesitated as he considered where to begin. "Their ships would sneak up on the harbors at night. Their large, oared galleys were far superior to anything we had on Lyliana and carried many men. They would burn our boats, ransack the towns, often killing the men and raping the women.

"The island was not as heavily populated in those days, and we did not have an army to fend them off. As many of us as could be mustered were sent to guard the ports and easy landing places and sometimes we were able to fend them off, but the next time, they would return in greater numbers. They would come whenever our harvest was in and steal the sacks of grain from the storehouses.

"One spring, when I was stationed at Yoused's port, an especially brutal gang of pirates came ashore. We had nothing for them to take, and it seemed they came purely for pleasure. My wife . . ." his voice broke, and he could not continue for some moments. "I tried to stop them, but they overpowered me. They made me watch and tortured me for the fun of it. I have the scars to prove it," and he pointed to several visible on his arms.

Darius was shocked. "Byden, I had no idea. You have suffered much. I am sorry I asked you to speak of it."

Byden shook his head. "I tell you because I can speak of it now. There was a long time when I could not. It was a long time before my wife could speak of it. But we survived, and we overcame it, and lived for many years in peace."

Darius gaped at him. "How did you overcome it?"

Byden gave a cynical laugh. "We had no other choice. For weeks after, I could hardly look at her because I felt I had failed her. I was unable to protect her, and I felt guilty. She felt sullied and would not let me touch her. Fortunately, the island procured the protection of Artylia, and we had no further trouble from Cerecia.

"We returned to our little farm, and in our small, one-bedroom house, we had no escape from each other. We went through stages of silence, yelling and screaming, and eventually talking with each other. Through the talking, we came to understand each other's feelings, and we were able to finally help each other move on."

"Did . . . either of you have nightmares—after?"

"Yes, my wife especially. She would wake screaming and push me away. After we were able to talk about it, they happened less and less frequently. It was many months before she would let me love her again. I would have given my life to have saved her from that experience."

"But you were able to find happiness with each other again?"

"We were. Many years. And we had a son. He is captain of the *Seagull*."

"Ah! I have met him! A good man."

"He owes his life to you and the men of the Horizon, I hear. I thank you."

Darius shook his head. "I am more than repaid by

your honesty with me this evening. It means more than you know." He put out his hand, and they clasped arms, and Darius' thoughts turned to his wife and his feet hastened to follow.

When he opened the door to their room, Eemya rushed to his arms. "I am so sorry, my love," she sobbed. "I had no right to speak to you that way! I want you to return no matter what! Can you forgive me?"

"There is nothing to forgive," he kissed the top of her head and stroked her hair. "You have every right. You are my wife, and I have been shutting you out. Come, I have things I want to share with you."

CHAPTER EIGHTEEN

Well into the next morning, the newlyweds talked and shared and laughed and cried. Darius repeated Byden's story to her, and then he told her about the time he was held hostage. He explained how the experience had made him wary and how he could not sleep if he felt restrained. He told her about his worst battle experiences and how they haunted him.

Eemya told him more about her first marriage, how empty it was, and how much she longed for intimacy, both physical and emotional. She told him how much she appreciated the things he did that made her feel loved and cherished. They took their knowledge and regard for each other to new heights, and it increased their mutual passion.

Darius decided that in order to sleep peacefully in the same room with Eemya, he needed to give up his sword for the night. Even though he had known Effan for many years, it was still difficult to confide something this personal to him, but he did, and he asked Effan to stand on guard outside their room and keep his sword while they slept. If Eemya needed help to calm Darius after a dream, she could call him, or if there was a real emergency, he would have the prince's sword at the ready as well as his own. Just knowing he was there, helped Darius to relax, and he was not as worried that he would harm Eemya while in the throes of one of his night terrors.

One morning, after Eemya had persuaded him to try sleeping next to her again, he opened his eyes after a dreamless night to find his arms around her, and his heart felt ready to burst. He recalled how enthralled he had been the first time he saw her, and recognized that his love for her increased each day as he grew to know her more.

He longed to introduce her to his family so they could love her as well. When she woke, he broached the subject with her. She was hesitant to leave her holding, but excited to see her husband's homeland. Darius had appointed Stelan as the new lord over Adamantine, with Eemya's blessing, so someone had to be left in charge of Eemya's domain. Yarin had returned with Tomus to be his advisor in Letyna. Halem would be remaining on the island with half of Darius' men and one of the warships. He would be responsible for giving training to the soldiers in various holdings, though, and would be based in Yoused's harbor.

"I think I would like to leave Lydima in charge," Eemya surprised Darius by saying.

"Lydima? Er . . ." he was at a loss to discover the benefit of this appointment.

"She is finally getting to a place where she is tiring of her lifestyle, and the responsibility might be good for her."

"Hmm."

"Stelan and Yoused would be willing to advise her if needed, and Halem will be within call should any unrest occur, which I really cannot imagine. Jayred and Byden could really carry on alone anyway. Lydima will just be a figurehead."

"If you really think it is advisable. The farmers are now beginning to harvest their crops, are they not?"

"Yes, but my people are experienced, and there are many hands to help. What is the worst that could happen?"

Darius could think of a lot of things, but felt it wiser not to say. "Jayred will not be offended if you do not leave him in charge?"

"I will ask him to teach Lydima everything about running the castle as a favor to me."

Darius shrugged and let Eemya do as she liked with her own holding. He had no reason to doubt her decision-making ability. Yoused agreed to serve as interim governor until they returned. Darius was considering serving permanently as governor so he and Eemya could live full-time at Freosyd when they returned from their visit to Sherish.

As they packed and made decisions for the trip, Eemya remembered something she had heard about her husband's family. "Does not your brother have two wives?"

"Yes, he does. But do not worry, you are more than enough for me!" Eemya narrowed her eyes at him. "In Berush a man cannot take a second wife unless his first agrees," he continued hastily, "and Sashia actually initiated the transaction. You will love both her and Marthi, really."

"It seems very strange to me."

"I do not pretend to understand it either, but it works for them. You will just have to see."

"I would never want to share you with anyone that way."

"Nor I you. I tend too much toward jealousy as it

is."

When the time came for them to depart, Eemya was both excited and apprehensive. Her stomach seemed unsettled, and she clutched Darius' arm nervously as they boarded the *Horizon* in Kirdyn's port. "I have never been off of the island," she confessed anxiously. "I have never even been in a boat, silly as that seems for someone living on an island."

"You will be fine. I am with you every step of the way. Or every wave," he teased. "I have a lot of experience with the ocean now."

"None of which we want to repeat!" Eemya had no need to worry, however. Aside from some queasiness the first day out, she quickly found her sea legs and enjoyed the way the ship sped through the water. The vastness of the ocean amazed her. She had seen the sea, of course, but only from the land. Standing in the bow, the waves sprayed salty water in her face and she laughed, enjoying the sense of freedom as the north wind propelled the ship swiftly westward. Even with a hat, she was getting a little sunburned, so she had to wear a veil over her face as well, to help keep off the sun.

They only brought two horses with them this time, Darius and Effan's Berushese horses, and they made room for them on the deck. Effan's gelding was much happier this trip.

They arrived four days later, and Darius gave Eemya a choice of riding to the capital or taking a barge upriver. She was quite enjoying travelling on the water, and since the late summer weather in Berush was very warm, she chose the barge. Darius approved since it would afford the most stunning view of the palace to approach from the lake. Effan would travel separately with the horses. Darius had been having less trouble with his dreams after taking Byden's advice to speak of them with Eemya more fully and felt he could make do without the captain for a short time.

The trip upriver took two days with the wind at their backs. Eemya and Darius stood on the deck, and he put his arms around her and whispered stories about his homeland and his childhood into her ear. Eemya listened intently and studied everything with wide eyes. Everything she saw was exotic and new. When the barge entered the vast lake, and they approached the palace with its gleaming, gilded turrets reflecting in the shimmering water, she nearly cried. "Oh, Darius, it is so beautiful it hurts. You must have missed it so!"

"A little, but I have not spent that much time here the last few years. When I am with you, I am not homesick at all, for you are my home now."

In awe of the palace's majesty, Eemya began to feel timorous. "Do you think they will like me?"

He turned her to face him. "They love you already, because I love you. They will love you even more once they know you. Who could not? Everyone who has ever known you has loved you. They have told me so." She hugged him tightly, only partially reassured.

They drew up to a pier close to the castle, and Tarin, who had not yet returned to the port after Cyrus' absence, was there to meet them with a litter for Eemya. "Greetings, Lady Eemya, and welcome to Sherish! The rest of my family is anxiously awaiting your arrival! I have been waiting here the better part of the day to escape their constant pestering as to the time we could expect you."

Eemya had never ridden in a chair before, and she allowed Tarin to hand her into it with an amused look. The four men bearing the litter lifted her smoothly, keeping the chair level the entire time. There was a canopy over the top of it that kept her shaded from the sun. Her new nephew led the way to the palace entrance while Darius walked beside her.

Once they were inside the gate and past the guards, they were met by a tall, stately man whom Eemya could only presume was Cyrus, eight children of various ages and levels of exuberance, and two lovely women, one of whom held a baby. Darius handed Eemya out of her chair, and everyone surged forward. Cyrus took her hand in both of his. "My dear Eemya, we are so pleased to finally meet you. You have made my brother very happy. You are now a princess of Berush, so please consider this palace your own home while you are here."

Then followed a lengthy list of introductions. Darius had already recited all their names to her, so now she only had to match them with their smiling faces. Eemya was glad she had learned some conversational Berushese so she could greet her new relatives in their own language. The children wanted to drag her off right away to see the pool and the gardens and all their pets, but their mothers reined them in with promises that there would be plenty of time for that later. They had planned on a lengthy visit, and Darius' sister was on her way to meet them as well.

Sashia put her arm around Eemya. "Come with me, and I will show you your rooms so you can take a breath. Then we will have a pleasant dinner and we will soon know everything about each other."

Sashia's confiding smile invited Eemya to return it warmly, and she walked through a doorway arm in arm with her sister-in-law. Darius started to follow, but Sashia shooed him back. She took Eemya to the rooms that had been prepared for her and Darius, and Eemya exclaimed delightedly over them. The bedroom had an open balcony that looked out over the lake. Sheer curtains were drawn across the opening, and accordion shutters were folded behind them in readiness to protect against rain or colder weather. The view was breathtaking.

Sashia surprised her by giving her a huge hug. "I am so glad you are here!" She stepped back and took her by the hands. "We have been worried about Darius, but no longer. When I looked in his eyes today I saw peace and joy. It has eased Cyrus' mind greatly to know that his brother has you. Thank you for that."

Eemya's eyes teared up, and she did not know what to say. Sashia did not seem to expect an answer, but squeezed her hands. "And you will soon have a new joy of your own. That is so exciting!"

"What do you mean?"

"You are expecting your first child, are you not?"

Eemya's jaw dropped. "What? How can you tell? It is not possible. I am not even late yet!"

"I can hear your body humming, creating a new life," Sashia declared indisputably.

"Really?"

"Absolutely." Her eyes twinkled merrily. "I have a gift about these things." Eemya went and sat down on the bed while she absorbed this new information. "Shall I send Darius to you? I will not say anything to him, but your face will give everything away as soon as he sees you. You will want to tell him privately, before everyone else."

Eemya nodded, still in a daze. Sashia skipped away to fetch him as excitedly as a young girl. Darius came into the room searching for her with concern on his face. "Sashia said you needed me. What is it?"

Eemya stretched her arms out to him and he came and sat next to her. "She says I am pregnant!"

"You are? Darling!" Darius grabbed her and kissed her.

"Is she usually right? It is too soon to know."

"Always. She always knows." Darius' voice conveyed no doubt. "We should stay here until you deliver. Sashia is the best midwife in all of Berush, probably the world. You should not travel any more in your condition."

"That will be nine months! More than a year before we could travel with a baby."

"I could not risk either one of you. My mind would be much easier if we stayed here."

"Alright."

"A baby, Eemya! Think of it! Are you not happy?"

"I have wanted a baby so badly, Darius. It does not seem real to me yet. It will not seem real until I hold him in my arms."

"You think it will be a he?"

"I am still trying to believe that it will be at all."

"If Sashia says it will be, it will be. Let yourself be happy, my love."

"Are you happy?"

"Every day I am with you, I am expanding the capacity of the human heart for happiness."

Eemya laughed. "You should have been a poet."

"Maybe I will put up my sword for the pen. I have no shortage of inspiration." He kissed her again. "I would seek more inspiration right now, but we are expected for dinner. Are you up to it?" Eemya nodded and took his hand, smiling with joy.

∞∞∞

Nine months later, Darius waited anxiously outside of the birthing room. Cyrus waited with him, as he had waited many times himself. When Sashia came to tell him he could enter, Darius bounded to Eemya's side. She was tired, and dripping with sweat, but her face was radiant. "We have a son!"

Darius looked at the small bundle by her side with wonder on his face. He had not thought it was possible to be happier than he was already, but he took one look at his son and was filled with a new kind of love and tenderness for the small life in front of him. As the warmth and happiness washed over him, he could not find words to express his feelings. He brushed the small head with its fuzzy hair, kissed it, and wept.

The End

AUTHOR'S NOTE

Post-traumatic stress is a diagnosable condition that can develop after a person is exposed to a traumatic event. Symptoms can include disturbing thoughts, feelings, or dreams related to the events, mental or physical distress, difficulty sleeping, and changes in how a person thinks and feels. If you or a loved one is suffering from PTS, there are many resources available to help you including:

https://www.ptsd.va.gov/public/where-to-get-help.asp

WWP Resource Center: 888.WWP.ALUM (997.2586) or 904.405.1213

https://www.woundedwarriorproject.org

Sexual harassment is illegal and should not be tolerated. Harassment can include unwelcome sexual advances, requests for sexual favors, and other verbal or physical harassment of a sexual nature. If you experience harassment, it should be reported to your employer or other appropriate authority. For a more detailed definition, facts and laws pertaining to harassment visit:

https://www.eeoc.gov/laws/types/sexual_harassment.cfm

THEOLOGICAL AND PHILOSOPHICAL MUSINGS

If you don't enjoy abstract discussions of gray areas and hypothetical situations, then you don't want to read this section. What follows is a description of my thoughts on reconciling Christianity and the possibility of multiple universes and an explanation of the setting for this book. This essay does not address the issue of the truth or validity of Christianity in general. That is an entirely different discussion.

When I started writing this novel, I wanted to have a completely fictional setting in order to have the freedom to take the story wherever I wanted it to go without regard to our history's order of scientific discovery or word etymology. However, I needed to have a world very similar to ours where the laws of physics still apply. Creating a story with compelling characters was much more important to me than having a completely unique setting.

Introducing a second moon, for example, would drastically alter the way the planet worked and would necessarily drive the narrative in a different direction. It would make the story much more about the planet than about its inhabitants. Therefore, the natural laws and requirements needed to support life in the world in this story are the same as ours. The history is different.

Many Christian authors of fiction (as distinct from authors of Christian fiction) have dealt with the subject of multiple or alternate universes. Two of my favorites are C. S. Lewis and John White. The most difficult dilemma for a Christian in writing this type of fiction is where to fit God into the picture.

God does not change, so His nature and character must be consistent across all of His creation(s). For eternal beings to be in the presence of God, they must be without sin. If God wants all of the humans He created on this planet to be with Him, then one could assume that he would want the same for any beings created in His image, no matter what universe. All have sinned, so a sacrifice is necessary for eternal salvation.

In order to have conflict, there has to be evil, or sin, or it would be a very boring book. My imaginary world has sin, so there is a need to be redeemed from the consequence of it just like there is in ours. Other authors have dealt with this by having Christ sacrifice Himself in a different body under a different name multiple times. The Bible is very clear that Christ died once for all. It doesn't seem plausible to stretch that to mean once per universe.

When I read of Christ's anguish in the Garden, I don't get the impression that it was something He had done before. When it was over with, I don't think He would say, "Yeah, I'm totally up for doing that all over again somewhere else, maybe this time as a lion."

You could propose that He died spiritually once (whether He died spiritually is another debate), but simultaneously died in multiple bodies at the same moment in multiple universes. However, can you be fully God and fully man when inhabiting several bodies at once? Mathematically, that doesn't work out, but I can still enjoy the stories based on these ideas.

I came up with three other options. One, that the people on my imaginary planet, or universe, had a body, mind, spirit, and soul, but their souls were not eternal. They would have a conscience to help govern their decisions, but they would have no need of eternal salvation if the soul ceased to exist when the body died. No sacrifice would be necessary. This version of mankind seems disposable and therefore not loved as much, but it is the simplest solution.

The second option would give them eternal souls, but they would be judged only on their response to their limited knowledge of God from the evidence of creation and their own consciences. Is the faith that there is a Creator enough for salvation? Could God send angels to them as missionaries to tell them about the sacrifice of a Savior on another planet or in another universe? I did not set out to write a "Christian" book, and this would just make it seem preachy. I am also not doing a universe-jumping thing. That, again, would take the story away from the characters and into a bigger picture.

As a third option, I could also have an afterlife that is not directly in God's presence, something like Valinor in Tolkein's works. A person would either have to be good enough to qualify, or everyone is let in regardless of their actions. I don't really like this idea because Christ's sacrifice and the idea of salvation through faith by grace is so revolutionary compared to other religions that I feel like anything else would just be wrong to write. Besides, how do you determine how good is good enough?

Why does any of this matter? Isn't it just fiction? The problem is that humans like to have explanations for everything, including their origins and the origins and history of their planet, and my characters would have the same thoughts and questions that we do. What do I tell my characters when they want to know where they came from?

Because all of the above scenarios are problematic in some way or other, I have decided not to tell them anything. They are a figment of my imagination, so I am their creator. I will not be able to give them, or you, an explanation of how they are or are not connected to our universe or reality. If I can't come up with something that makes sense to me, and I really like things to make sense, then I'm not going to address it directly in the story. I also hate leaving questions unanswered, so I will continue to ponder the origin dilemma.

If there is no higher being to impart a moral code, the characters must learn from natural consequences and rules put in place out of necessity to maintain social order. Without bringing God into it, it is hard to come up with rationales for many moral choices, but I have done my best to make the characters' choices seem reasonable. This novel was written solely for entertainment purposes. However, I want the morals and decisions of at least some of the protagonists to align with my own. Otherwise, it would not be a story I would want to read, much less write.

If you read and enjoy this book, you may superimpose whatever theological, philosophical or atheistic construct you chose. Or don't even think about it if it doesn't interest you. If you can come up with any other Biblically sound options for inserting God and an afterlife into the story, I would be interested to hear about it.

References:

Lewis, C. S., *The Lion, the Witch and the Wardrobe*, The Chronicles of Narnia, (New York: HarperCollins publishers, 1994)

The Bible, any version: James 1:17, Revelation 21:27, John 3:3, Romans 1:18, 2 Peter 3:9, Romans 3:23, 1 Peter 3:18, Luke 22:39-44, Colossians 2:9

Tolkein, J. R. R., *The Silmarillion*, Second Edition, (New York: The Ballantine Publishing Group, 2001)

White, John, *Gaal the Conqueror*, The Archives of Anthropos, (Illinois: InterVarsity Press, 1989)

DISCUSSION QUESTIONS

1. Describe the relationships Darius has with his captain, Effan, and his brother, Cyrus. How are these relationships important to him? Are they helpful or not helpful? Give examples.

2. Darius' initial behavior toward Eemya was an example of what type of harassment? How would you deal with that type of behavior? How did he arrive at a place where he allowed himself to act that way?

3. When do you think it is appropriate to forgive someone? What does forgiveness mean?

4. What advice did Lydima give that was good (if any)? What advice was bad? Explain.

5. What symptoms of PTSD did Darius show? What symptoms did Eemya show? How did they deal with it?

6. Why do you think Lord Retand tolerated his wife's behavior so long? Compare and contrast that with how Cyrus dealt with Darius' behavior.

7. Which character in this story exhibited the most moral strength and why?

ABOUT THE AUTHOR

Ever since I was a little girl, I have loved to read. One of the first books I remember reading was a Wonder Book version of *Cinderella*. It was in the reading station in my kindergarten class, and I loved the illustrations. I would pick that book out every time, so my teacher finally removed it from the shelf to force me to expand my horizons. Now I have my own copy.

Another book that influenced me very early on was Richard Scarry's *Busy, Busy World*. It told a story of two creative painters who painted a mural of a large sun inside someone's house. I thought the idea was genius, so I drew a large sunshine on my wall with crayon. It was scrubbed off, but I continued to have a desire to express myself artistically.

In middle school, I enjoyed writing, and my English teacher told me I would write a book someday. I still loved to read, sometimes reading late into the night. When I was not reading, I was making up stories in my head for my own amusement, but I never wrote them down. I was more interested in drawing and painting than writing. I have since painted numerous works of art, including some very large outdoor murals.

Over the years, I have had a lot of trouble with insomnia. I had heard that if you write down your ideas, it will help you to be able to go to sleep. That didn't help, but I did end up writing some complete novels. Finally, I was diagnosed with narcolepsy, and understanding my sleep patterns, along with scheduling at least one nap during the day, has greatly improved my quality of life.

The line between dreaming and wakefulness for me is sometimes blurred, and some of my ideas come straight from my dreams. Others are worked out while I'm lying in bed unable to sleep. It was fun to type them out, and I am planning to continue writing. I hope you enjoy my stories and characters as much as I do.

Visit me online at www.facebook.com/paintbyamber

51368253R00186

Made in the USA
Columbia, SC
16 February 2019